D0935881

THE CROSS BEARER

Six hundred years after the suppression of the Knights Templar the whereabouts of their fabled treasure has become a matter of myth and legend. At an exhibition Arnold Landon, of the Department of Museums and Antiquities, meets a man who claims to have the clue to the flight of the Templars and the location of their treasure. Arnold agrees to help Sinclair in his search, but soon finds himself involved in allegations of political corruption.

When the body of a prominent businessman is found floating in the Tyne, Arnold is plunged into a dangerous vortex of murder, Masonic intimidation, council corruption and police pressure, climaxing in a threat to his own life in the suffocating darkness of the Templar tomb of the Cross Bearer.

BY THE SAME AUTHOR

Arnold Landon novels

BLOODEAGLE
A SECRET DYING
A WISP OF SMOKE
THE DEVIL IS DEAD
MEN OF SUBTLE CRAFT
A TROUT IN THE MILK
MOST CUNNING WORKMEN

Eric Ward novels

A KIND OF TRANSACTION
A NECESSARY DEALING
THE SALAMANDER CHILL
PREMIUM ON DEATH
A BLURRED REALITY

ONCE DYING, TWICE DEAD
A LIMITED VISION
DWELL IN DANGER
A CERTAIN BLINDNESS
SEEK FOR JUSTICE
A RELATIVE DISTANCE
A VIOLENT DEATH
AN INEVITABLE FATALITY
AN UNCERTAIN SOUND
NOTHING BUT FOXES
A DISTANT BANNER
etc.

THE CROSS BEARER

Roy Lewis

HarperCollins*Publishers*

Collins Crime
An imprint of HarperCollins*Publishers*
77–85 Fulham Palace Road, London W6 8JB

First published in Great Britain
in 1994 by Collins Crime

1 3 5 7 9 10 8 6 4 2

A catalogue record for this book is
available from the British Library

ISBN 0 00 232508 X

Set in Meridien and Bodoni

Photoset by Rowland Phototypesetting Ltd
Bury St Edmunds, Suffolk
Printed and bound in Great Britain by
HarperCollinsManufacturing Glasgow

Fye upon the churle quhat solde
Haly erthe for heavie golde;
Bot the Tempel felt na loss,
Quhan David Setoune bare the Crosse.

Satirical poem *c.*1560

Prologue

1310

He hated the north.

Accustomed to warmer, southern climes, Simon de Goncourt shivered in the dark chill of the early morning as slow wisps of mist rose from the cold surface of the lake. His gaunt, dissatisfied features were twisted in a grimace of distaste, his ascetic mouth thin lipped as he shrugged deeper into the warmth of his woollen cloak, but there was still a gleam of cold fanaticism in his eyes as he stared fixedly out over the dark, mist-shrouded waters.

Behind him, men shuffled in the darkness: there was the jingling of a bit, the clink of iron, and a horse snorted, jangling its harness as it tossed its head impatiently. A pale edge of light touched the dark cloud high above the encircling hills, the first hint of dawn, and something vague and indistinct moved on the surface of the shrouded waters.

The tall, black-bearded man at de Goncourt's shoulder stood quietly, impassively; still confident in his cool independence and de Goncourt hated him for his arrogance, almost as much as he hated the north.

'Where in God's teeth are these boats?' de Goncourt rasped angrily in a low voice.

The tall man, Sir Robert Moray, representative of Bishop Lamberton of St Andrews and openly hostile to the will and intentions of his companion, nodded coldly. 'They're coming. Have patience.'

Patience! Simon de Goncourt's mouth twisted angrily.

It was now all of two years since the first arrests had been completed in France – a swift, striking campaign carried out in utter secrecy and with an efficiency for which he himself had taken credit and for which he had received due reward from Philippe the Fair. Throughout the country, in the early morning hours, men at arms had broken into the chapels and the chantries, the houses, the treasuries and the churches and carried out the arrests.

Two years since the first arrests . . . and more than three months since the English king had at last cast aside his infuriating, dilatory, prevaricating, vacillating tendencies and issued his own decree, after pressure from Philippe the Fair and the Holy Father in Avignon. But only now had the first moves been made in Scotland – only now were they near to striking at the viper's nest in the north.

He glowered, conscious of the powerful presence of the man at his shoulder, aware of the restraining influence that Moray hoped to bear; angry, and determined that he would not be baulked at this last hurdle. Philippe and the Holy Father had given de Goncourt his commission and no backyard bishop would rise out of his Scottish midden to prevent the assault on the blasphemers.

Then, as he stood there with teeth clenched and the sour bile of frustration in his throat, the movements on the water began to take shape: ethereal at first, shivering through the mist, then more solid and real as the boats began to emerge, dark wraiths slipping out of the drifting, smoky vapour of the lake. There were three of them, their oars dipping almost silently, leaving a soft trail of phosphorescence in the water, a ghostly silver sheen marking their passage. As the boats approached the shore, de Goncourt turned his head, snapped an order to the men at arms behind him and Moray stepped to one side as de Goncourt gestured the armed men towards the boats.

'What is it you hope to find out there?' Moray asked quietly, in his cool, distant tones. 'The Master has been taken, the Preceptor has gone beyond the seas –'

Stung by the contempt in Moray's voice, de Goncourt

swung around angrily. 'More than we achieved in that God-blighted place across the Irish Sea! I don't understand you people! When his Holiness himself has issued an edict, when Robert Bruce has been excommunicated, when your own English king has ordered the arrest of all those heretics still at large, you still display no enthusiasm for God's work!'

'God?' Moray was silent for a few moments, one hand touching his thick beard as his eyes flickered over the men scrambling into the boats on the shore. His tones were still level when he replied. 'I am not alone when I see the hand of Man rather than of God in these enterprises. It is not salvation of lost souls that are at stake in these great events, but the lining of a king's coffers.'

'You speak treason!'

'I speak truth,' Moray replied calmly. 'But I will do my duty, to my king and to my bishop.'

He moved smoothly past de Goncourt, drawing his cloak across him as he stepped into the first boat. He seated himself at the stern, huddled in his cloak as de Goncourt scrambled aboard, thrusting the scabbard at his side across the gunwales.

Quietly, the three boats moved out into the mist.

The lake was over twenty-five miles in length, varying in width from half a mile to a mile. There were some two dozen islands scattered along its surface, some connected to the mainland by ancient causeways, built before measured time began. As they had come north to the lake, de Goncourt had heard some muttering about the monster that was said to haunt its depths: the Beathach Mor, a serpent-like creature with the head of a monstrous horse and twelve scale-sheathed legs that could smash a boat into matchwood. He shivered at the thought, then gritted his teeth: these mist-shrouded, barren, godforsaken hills could strike chills into a man's soul, but he was on God's work and the buckler of prayer lay between him and the devil's minions.

The boats moved almost silently down the eastern edge of the lake, the muffled oars trailing slivers of silver as the air began to lighten, the pale edge of dawn broadening, a thin golden sheen appearing above the fir-covered hills above them. They passed a small island on their right, and de Goncourt glanced inquiringly at Moray as he saw the solid, dark walls of the castle.

'Innis Chonnell,' Moray said quietly. 'Clan Campbell's primary seat. Sir Neil Campbell is not there just now. He's across at Edinburgh, well away from this sorry madness. And we have . . . about a mile to go.' He smiled grimly at de Goncourt, aware of the man's tension. 'Assuming the Beathach Mor allows us passage.'

They rowed on in silence, Moray keeping further thoughts to himself, de Goncourt scowling ahead into the wispy fog. In a little while they saw the craggy outline looming ahead of them: this second island was smaller, fringed with lean, emaciated, yet strangely menacing trees. They moved closer, the oars whispering in the water, until they reached the jetty that stretched out from the stony shore.

The men needed no orders now: they knew what they had to do, and they knew that silence – and surprise – was essential if unnecessary blood was not to be shed. They pulled in gently near the jetty, avoiding the two small boats that lay tied up there, and quietly clambered up on to the crude planking.

They were eight in number, well armed, experienced, hand picked and committed. Simon de Goncourt had every confidence in them. More than he had in Sir Robert Moray. As though Moray realized his name was in de Goncourt's mind, he said gratingly, 'Remember, my friend – anyone we take here on the island falls under the jurisdiction of the Bishop of St Andrews.'

'His Holiness's edict –'

'Will be followed by the bishop. Not by his hireling.'

The word stung. Gritting his teeth in anger, de Goncourt swung himself up on to the jetty. The armed retainers had fanned out in front of him, swords in hand, and they moved quietly through the scattered trees, treading the turfed edge of the stone path, making their way towards the dark mass of the walls of the building that loomed up ahead of them.

The golden cast of the sky was now fading and a greyish light spread above the horizon of the hills; under the trees it was still dim, however, and lank, wet grass soaked the lower part of their cloaks and leggings.

The men slowed, hesitant now, and de Goncourt stepped forwards, peering at the fortified house ahead of them. There were no rushlights in the embrasures of Kilclogan, and no armed guard in the small courtyard in front of the tower. They were confident, these vermin, de Goncourt thought viciously; secure in their belief that a protective hand lay over them – the kind of protection that had served them well in Ireland. There, for all de Goncourt's impassioned urgings, only thirty had been taken, and no burnings nor executions had taken place. Here, in the ungodly hills of Scotland, he vowed it would be different. Once he had the miscreants in his hands, the bishop could look out for himself: de Goncourt had the edict of the Pope to advance his cause.

The men were at their stations: de Goncourt waved an arm. They advanced across the courtyard towards the great door of the house. As they grew near there was a murmur of muttered surprise, quickly stifled. The great studded door gaped open, defenceless.

Something cold moved in de Goncourt's stomach. He pushed forwards, shouldering a man aside in his eagerness and stepped into the doorway. His iron heels rang loudly on the stone of the flagged floor; above his head he heard the rush of wings as a nocturnal bird of prey was flushed from its perch. The room opened out in front of him – dark, cold and empty.

He stared around him in the empty room, as the first grey light of dawn filtered dimly through the apertures high above his head. He shouted to his sergeant, and three men ran clattering up the twisting stairway into the tower while the others fanned out, moving swiftly into the ground floor chambers, breaking open doors, shouting, cursing. The echoes of their voices and of the clang of steel against stone from the rooms about him told their own story, and de

Goncourt stood in the great hall, simmering with fury.

They returned to the great hall and silently dropped a scattering of implements at his feet. He glared at the weapons as they lay on the stone-flagged floor before him; he made out a broken iron helm, a few arrows, a rusting dagger and a short stabbing sword. He wheeled around on his heel, slowly, staring around the hall: in the corner of the room, against the foot of the stairs, he saw a single lance.

The last of his men who had been climbing the stairs, searching the rooms above, came clattering noisily down. They were empty handed. There was no point in asking the question: de Goncourt knew it was too late. In a great wave of frustration, de Goncourt threw back his head and howled like an animal, the frustration of a hungry wolf denied his quarry, his blood lust unslaked.

Behind him, Sir Robert Moray moved into the house of Kilclogan and looked around sardonically. He stood there silently for a little while, until the echoes of de Goncourt's anger had faded and died. He grunted. 'Well, de Goncourt, it seems the Holy Father will be doomed to disappointment. And the Bishop of St Andrews is to be saved the necessity of a trial.'

He chuckled, grimly and derisively, jeering as de Goncourt turned on him in fury. The man had been defeated, after all.

'It would appear, my lord, that the soldiers of Christ have flown.'

1

1

It had been a bright sunny morning when Arnold drove to work in Morpeth.

The first day of spring had lived up to its promise: the daffodils were blooming in the formal gardens – a splash of yellow and white against the freshening green of the sward – and crocuses shone blue and yellow and white under the trees. He had heard the curlews on the moors at the weekend when he had walked for almost ten miles: their plaintive cries as they swept above the heathland, preparing for another nesting season, had lifted his heart. The morning sunshine had been warm and pleasant and he had managed to get a parking space in Morpeth without any difficulty. It felt good to be alive, and there was the prospect in the offing of a visit to the newly-discovered Romano-British site at Barn Scar, where the sectioning of a bank and ditch had exposed what promised to be chambered tombs of a kind not previously noted in the area.

He had been reading the file the previous Friday and was looking forward to visiting the site. Now, the note on his desk that suggested he should proceed at once to the office of the director of the Department of Museums and Antiquities, blighted the morning and cast a gloom of foreboding over him.

A summons from the DDMA, Mr Brent-Ellis, rarely caused joy for the recipient.

The basic problem was that Brent-Ellis, tall, flamboyantly-suited, walrus-moustached, and remarkably insensitive to atmosphere, had been appointed largely because his wife held considerable influence as a local councillor. He himself had little or no interest in his job. He enjoyed the salary and the directorial power, but took advantage of both by playing as much golf as he could. Arnold suspected Mrs Brent-Ellis felt it kept her husband out of mischief.

Not that he would have got up to mischief with his Teutonically-presenced secretary, who had been chosen for him by his wife. Mrs Brent-Ellis clearly felt her husband needed a *gauleiter* in his professional life, or else she wanted to encourage him to spend as little time in the office as possible. The secretary glowered at Arnold, as she always did when he arrived within her purview: her beetling, Germanic brows expressed contemptuous displeasure at the thought he would be disturbing the Great Man, and her thin lips sneered the warning that it would bode ill with him if he were to keep Mr Brent-Ellis busy for too long.

'It's *he* wants to see *me,*' Arnold protested half-heartedly.

That was clearly no excuse in her eyes. If she could have frog-marched him to the door she would have done so: instead, she contented herself with a quick march, a sharp rap on the glass door, and the clipped announcement of his presence. The sniff that followed, as she closed the door behind Arnold, was an underlining of her views.

Arnold stood in front of the director's desk.

Brent-Ellis did not ask him to sit down. Indeed, he barely glanced at Arnold. He had in front of him a computerized personal organizer which was clearly furrowing his brow. He pored over it, poking at it with a tentative finger and chewing at his cigar-stained moustache, pretending to be intelligent. 'Tuesday,' he said sagely.

'Sir?'

'It's Tuesday,' Brent-Ellis repeated in vague irritation, looking up at Arnold as though daring him to deny it.

Arnold hesitated. 'Er . . . actually, it's Monday.'

Brent-Ellis frowned and glared at the personal organizer.

'Hmm. Bloody Japanese . . .' He snapped the organizer shut with an angry gesture and pushed it across the front of his desk. 'Well, anyway, what can I do for you . . . er . . . Landon?'

Arnold sighed as he watched Brent-Ellis's glance stray towards the window, his thoughts already moving to distant golf courses and golf shots he wished he had once played. 'You wanted to see me.'

'I did?' Brent-Ellis appeared nonplussed for a moment, reached for the personal organizer, opened it, pressed a few keys and stared at it, then snapped it shut again. He picked up a leatherbound desk diary with a somewhat shamefaced frown and opened it. There was a short silence.

'That's right,' Brent-Ellis said suddenly. 'The *sudarium*.'

'Sir?'

'That piece of cloth you found. How's it going?'

'How's what going, sir?'

'The exhibition, of course!'

Arnold, with a feeling of relief, understood. After the discovery of the *sudarium* in Northumberland* there had been protracted discussions with the British Museum, in which Arnold had taken part. The *sudarium* was not, of course, the real cloth that had been used to bind the face of Christ in death, but merely a medieval forgery, used to attract funds and worshippers to the medieval church. Nevertheless, its discovery at Brunskill Castle had aroused a great deal of interest locally – the British Museum had wished to look into its provenance more closely and there had been a certain reluctance on the part of the department to release it once it was realized that it might bring visitors to Morpeth and Northumberland. Accordingly, a deal had been struck: an exhibition, in which the *sudarium* would be prominently displayed, would be established, remain open for seven months and thereafter the cloth would be removed to London for safe keeping and further investigation in Bloomsbury.

'The exhibition opens today, sir.'

* *A Secret Dying*

'You've not looked in?'

'It's only nine-thirty. Doors open at twelve.'

'Hmmm.' Brent-Ellis looked almost longingly at the computerized personal organizer. 'Well, I think you should get down there today, just check everything's all right. And then there's the matter of Mr Bannock –'

'Bannock?'

Brent-Ellis nodded. 'The opening talk. It's to be done by Colin Bannock.'

Arnold's mouth was suddenly dry. *He* had been asked to talk on the opening evening about the discovery of the *sudarium;* he had not welcomed the invitation because he was not a practised speaker, but he had gone over it all; Jane Wilson had helped him smooth the rough edges off the speech, and he felt he now had a talk that would go down well. It had been a honour he had not looked for, but now that he had worked it up . . . 'I'm afraid I don't understand.'

A less insensitive man would have looked uncomfortable. Brent-Ellis managed to appear quite cheerful. 'Oh, you know how it is, Landon! We workers of the world never get a fair crack of the whip, hey? I was talking to Ted Flint the other day, and it seemed to us both after a couple of gins that it wasn't really on to have an officer . . . an employee giving such an important talk at the opening of the exhibition, when the Lord Lieutenant will be there, and the new High Sheriff and so on. No, make a better show if someone from the council stepped in, one of our political masters, you know. Still, the good news is that you won't have to give the speaker your speech to use. He's got one of his own. Quite well up on *sudariums*, it seems, Colin Bannock.' Brent-Ellis furrowed his brow. 'Or *sudaria*? Anyway, Bannock's doing the job, and you're chairing him.'

'I'll be chairman for the evening?'

'Well, of course! You did find the bloody thing, after all! I know the exhibition is about a lot more than that damned bit of cloth – history of Northumberland, the Venerable Bede, the Church in the North, the pillaging of the Vikings, all stirring stuff, but the *sudarium* is a sort of centrepiece, or springboard, or whatever you want to call it. So it's right you should chair. As my wife mentioned – you'll be there to field any awkward questions.'

'That Mr Bannock can't answer,' Arnold replied sourly.

'That's the idea! Got it in one! Knew you'd see things in a sensible light.' Brent-Ellis grinned broadly, rose from behind his desk and stood in front of the window, gripping his hands together and going through the motions of a slow, exaggerated golf swing. 'Then, talking of Ted Flint, there's the other thing.'

Arnold waited. He felt angry but it was a cold anger. He had put in a lot of work on that talk, and Jane Wilson would be turning up to hear him deliver it. Now he was to chair a politician who hadn't been involved and deal with any difficult issues that might arise. Dogsbody.

'Ted Flint is chairing that committee looking into the dig at Ogle: I believe you already knew that.'

'Yes.'

'It meets on Wednesday. I told him you'd be able to appear as a witness at the committee hearing. Get it into your diary, hey?'

'I've already made arrangements to go up to Barn Scar, sir. That new discovery – the chambered tombs –'

'Oh, I'm afraid that'll have to wait, dear chap,' Brent-Ellis interrupted airily. 'When the politicians crack the whip we all have to jump, don't we? No, better cancel that Barn Scar jaunt so you can make yourself available for the Ogle committee. I gather there's some trouble brewing up there.'

Which is why the director himself would not be attending the meeting, Arnold concluded as he walked back disconsolately to his office. He sat down at his desk and stared at the papers piled up there.

Somehow the spring pleasure of the morning had been dissipated.

He worked at the papers on his desk for the rest of the morning, and made a few phone calls to set aside the arrangements already concluded about his visit to Barn Scar. At one-thirty he left his office and walked around the corner to the small café where he knew he could get a sandwich and a cup of coffee without being disturbed by many of his colleagues, who tended to eat – more cheaply – in the office canteen.

At two o'clock he thought he'd better do what the DDMA had suggested and take a look at the display in the main hall. The official opening, with the speech by Colin Bannock, chaired by Arnold Landon, would be at six, but it would do no harm to check on arrangements now.

He entered the hall, nodding to the young woman in the blue dress who was on duty in the foyer, surrounded by county brochures and pamphlets. She barely looked up from the operation of buffing her nails to acknowledge his presence and he wandered past to inspect the glass cases, the exhibition posters and the exhibits themselves.

It was quite a good display. There were only half a dozen adults and about six children wandering around but the information at hand was well set out and amply illustrated. There were six thousand-year-old elk bones that had been excavated by a tractor driver from Hexham, and an iron arrowhead dug out of a decayed tree at Bolam. Various Romano-British artefacts were on display and a large wall chart demonstrated the march of the centuries in Northumberland. There were papers relating to the Danelaw when the Vikings held sway in the north and there was a section devoted to castles, the Normans, and the thirteenth century. It was here that the *sudarium* was on display.

The scruffy, meagre piece of cloth had been placed in a glass case, roped off from the public, with an explanatory notice, and guarded by a sleepy-looking man in a dark blue uniform. He had a security flash on his shoulder and he seemed bored. Arnold walked past him to the room on the right where the talk was to be held. It had already been set out for the lecture he would have given: there were about fifty seats there, with a raised dais for the great and the good. On this occasion it would include him, albeit in the role of functional chairman. He stood there for a little while, thinking of how it would have been, feeling a wriggle of chagrin that a little hour of fame had been torn from him, and then he smiled to himself. He had never sought fame, so why was it important now?

Because he had found the *sudarium*. Because he and Jane had worked at the speech. It would have been his night – even if only ten people had turned up. He went back to his office, still in a somewhat disgruntled frame of mind, to continue with his papers until five-thirty, when he would return to welcome Colin Bannock, the Lord Lieutenant and the High Sheriff – if Brent-Ellis let him near them before the talk itself commenced.

In the event it was not Brent-Ellis who interposed: the chief executive, Mr Powell Frinton himself, turned up with the Lord Lieutenant and the High Sheriff in tow. They both seemed a little too sparkling around the eyes, and Arnold guessed they had been entertained in Powell Frinton's office before facing the ordeal of the exhibition. And just behind them came Colin Bannock.

During the afternoon session at his desk Arnold had felt somewhat miffed about Colin Bannock, but gradually he had overcome his annoyance and rationalized that his demotion was not Bannock's fault – it had been a put-up job between Councillor Flint, who was chairman of the Museums Committee, and Brent-Ellis. So Arnold was determined to be pleasant to Bannock and hide his disappointment that the lecture opportunity had been taken away from him. Accordingly, when Bannock entered the room a little way behind the platform party Arnold went forward and extended his hand.

'Mr Bannock, we have met before, perhaps not formally, but in committee meetings. I'm Arnold Landon.'

'Ah. The discoverer of the *sudarium*. And my chairman this evening.'

'That's right.' Arnold was aware he was being looked over, critically, and he returned Bannock's gaze. Colin Bannock was about forty-five years of age. His hair was dark, greying at the temples and cut fashionably long around the ears. He had light grey eyes that held a piercing, somewhat disconcerting light, and the kind of glance that could make a man feel uncomfortable. A solicitor by background, he had a successful practice in Morpeth, and hawkish features that were well known around the magistrates courts. His thin, pinched nostrils seemed to quiver slightly, as though sniffing the wind for danger or scandal, and his long-fingered, almost womanish hands caressed the leather file case he carried. Smartly dark-suited, smooth in speech and manner, there was nevertheless something about him that reminded Arnold of a snake – quiescent, somnolent, and yet ready to strike in a flash. But Arnold himself was being dismissed as an opponent or likely prey: Bannock was already turning aside to greet the Lord Lieutenant as an old friend.

Bannock's practice would have brought him into contact with many of the Northumberland notables, Arnold was sure. His practice, and his seat on the council. Oddly enough, for a man of his intellect, presence and experience, Bannock seemed to have made no great impact on the council: he seemed content to take a back seat, although Arnold had heard the odd rumour in the office that Bannock was not all that he seemed: he pulled more strings than many realized and in some way was a puppet master *extraordinaire*. But rumours were always rife in the office, and Arnold discounted them.

The room was gradually filling up. They took their seats on the dais, Arnold a little to one side in spite of being chairman for the evening, Bannock, the Lord Lieutenant and the High Sheriff being fussed over by Powell Frinton, who gave Arnold barely a glance. Powell Frinton had strong views about Arnold: he had already moved him from one department to another in the hope that he would be forever lost to sight.

At six o'clock precisely Powell Frinton, a man of precision, rose to his feet, welcomed the dignitaries and asked the Lord Lieutenant to say a few words. While Powell Frinton was speaking, Arnold saw Jane slip into the back of the room and take a seat. He managed a smile in her direction and she nodded.

The Lord Lieutenant had acceded to Powell Frinton's request. He told two hoary jokes and sat down. The High Sheriff contributed another anecdote, the point of which he himself missed and then in his turn sat down. Powell Frinton raised his aristocratic nose to Arnold and the evening's chairman stood up to introduce Colin Bannock.

It was quickly done, with no jokes, no undue servility and with a brevity that perhaps reflected Arnold's feelings, if he were honest with himself. Bannock did not seem to mind. He rose and began his talk. As he did so, Arnold caught sight of Jane's face: she seemed puzzled, and she frowned at him.

Bannock had been well briefed, well prepared. In spite of his subdued annoyance, Arnold was forced to admit that Bannock spoke well, and was in control of his subject. He spoke of the Crusades and the intervention of European kings in the affairs of the East. He dwelt upon some of the iniquities of the time and drew attention to the criticisms of the early Church. He moved on to describe the activities of the Knights Templar, the soldier monks of Christ, and their work in Jerusalem. And he turned to their destruction in the fourteenth century, by a king who was jealous of their power and who lusted after their wealth.

'Philippe IV of France had grand designs for his country and little compunction about crushing those who stood in his way. He engineered the kidnapping of one Pope and probably orchestrated the death of another by poison. He hijacked the papacy, relocated it at Avignon and with the Holy Father in his pocket moved against the Temple.'

Arnold glanced around the audience. They were held by Bannock's easy speaking style, even though the subject was a little esoteric for some of them. He listened as Bannock continued.

'His motives? He had – insultingly – been refused entry to the Order, even though Richard I had received it previously. And he needed money: the wealth of the Templars made him salivate. And then there was the threat to the stability of his rule: when the Holy Land fell to the Saracens the Knights Templar – perhaps the best trained, best equipped, most professional force in Western Europe – were left without a *raison d'être,* and without a home. They were dangerous. So Philippe prepared a catalogue of crimes and in a raid worthy of a modern secret police ordered the seizure of all Templars in France at dawn on 13 October, 1307. Their goods and wealth were seized. The Order was driven underground. And the Templars who did escape took their relics and their religious treasures with them in their flight . . .'

Arnold listened while Bannock reconstructed the story of the shroud and the *sudarium* in Templar legend; their concealment in Jerusalem; their mystical reappearance in Europe; and the quest that had led to the discovery of the treasure of the de Bohuns at Brunskill Castle. He was vaguely amused by the fact that virtually no mention was made of his own part in that discovery, although the department was mentioned several times. Jane was clearly not amused: when he glanced at her she appeared furious. His own thoughts drifted then, to the death of Ben Gibson, and the dark, claustrophobic horror of entombment in the walls of Brunskill.

He was brought back to the present with a jerk, as he realized Colin Bannock was sitting down. His talk was over, and polite applause was beginning to wash around the room. It was Arnold's turn to rise, and suggest that questions could now be directed to the speaker. As he did so, his glance swept around the room and with a sense of shock he recognized another familiar face: John Culpeper, the Detective Chief Inspector who had been involved with Arnold in the Brunskill affair. Arnold faltered, wondering what Culpeper was doing there, and then bit his lip, concentrating on the task in hand. Questions.

There weren't many, and most of them were banal, demonstrating that fluent though Bannock might have been, some of his audience could hardly have been listening. Culpeper himself left the room before the session was over, with a vague smile in Arnold's direction. There were certainly no questions that Bannock himself was not easily able to deal with and the awkward questions that had been the reason for Arnold's presence on the dais never emerged.

'Congratulations, Mr Bannock,' Powell Frinton intoned after Arnold had wound up with a few words of thanks to the speaker, and the crowd began to filter out of the room. 'I think that went very well: a suitable way in which to launch the exhibition. And you certainly gave an interesting account of the discovery of the cloth. However . . . can I suggest we might now adjourn? I've arranged a small dinner party for yourself, the Lord Lieutenant and the High Sheriff back at the King's Arms, a private room, and I'm sure we could all do with a little gin and tonic before we start.'

Colin Bannock's back was towards Arnold; he had the grace to turn his head and nod, but his eyes were cold and it was a mere gesture, lacking in warmth or appreciation. The platform party filed away, moving through the straggle of individuals who remained in the room. Arnold hesitated, then stepped down from the dais.

Jane was waiting near the door.

'How *dared* they!' she expostulated.

'Now, Jane, it's not important,' Arnold replied uncomfortably.

'But you worked so hard at your talk. And it was far better than Bannock's! God! *Politics!*'

'I'm only sorry that the work you put in – helping me – went to waste.'

'Oh, to hell with that. I'm just annoyed for you.' She frowned, wrinkling her snub nose. 'You should have complained.'

'I'm an employee. He's a politician. Besides, it wasn't important.'

She grimaced. 'I'm angry for you . . . but I suppose I would also have been angry if you'd thought it was important. You don't need idiots like that guy Powell Frinton, Arnold.'

'I need a cup of tea.'

'Ha! I'm sorry I can't join you but I've got to dash. I'm going up to meet some old school friends – sort of hen party – in Alnwick, but you and I hadn't arranged anything, had we?'

'No.'

'OK, I've got to make a run for it. We'll talk more about all this, though. Dinner Friday evening?'

'That would be good.'

He watched her as she hurried away, smiling briefly at him, and then he moved out into the hall.

He was not surprised by what had happened. A mere employee could not expect to join the platform party at their private dinner – and he had no desire to be of their number. Nevertheless, it would have been nice to be asked and he felt somewhat put out. Powell Frinton had barely acknowledged his presence, and the evening itself had completely played down his part in the discovery of the *sudarium*. He smiled involuntarily; his own talk, had it been given, would have made no mention at all of his part in the discovery, so what did he really have to complain about?

'Got it wrong,' said the man standing by the display board as Arnold made his way through the main hall of the exhibition.

'I beg your pardon?'

'You're Landon, aren't you?'

'That's right.'

'I'm surprised you didn't speak. Surprised you didn't contradict the speaker . . . though I got the impression at one stage you'd sort of drifted off, weren't listening too closely. Anyway, he got it wrong.'

'Got what wrong?'

'What he said about the wealth of the Templars. How Philippe the Fair got his hands on it.'

'He didn't?'

'He didn't. The fact was, his surprise dawn raid wasn't as secret as many think. The Templars got advance warning. The Grand Master, Jacques de Molay, burned a lot of the books and documents relating to the secrets of the Order. There's evidence of an organized flight. And of the ones who fled, they all seemed to be under the orders of the treasurer. No, the legendary wealth of the Order wasn't captured by Philippe.'

'That's interesting.' Arnold glanced around him, seeking

escape. He could do without amateur enthusiasts who thought they knew better than platform speakers.

'It was spirited away.'

'Yes?' Arnold replied vaguely.

'And I know how.'

There was a quiet confidence in the man's tones. Arnold stared at the speaker. 'I didn't catch your name.'

'Sinclair.'

'You are an authority ... you're interested in the Templars?'

'And others. Like the order Bannock belongs to. He's a bit of an amateur occultist, did you know that? Dabbler, though. He's into secret societies but hasn't done the basic research – just goes along with the mystical nonsense. It came through in his account tonight. But you . . . you had a sceptical look when I said I know how the fabulous treasure of the Order was spirited away.'

'I don't really mean –'

'They took fifty horses and left Paris. The treasure was packed up and smuggled out of the preceptory there. They put to sea. They used eighteen galleys. Then they vanished utterly, along with what they were carrying. Or so it's said.'

'But you know otherwise?'

'Maybe ... Are you interested? You ought to be – you found the *sudarium*, even if that wasn't mentioned tonight. I've got some maps which explain it all. Maybe you'd like to join me this evening, and talk about it.'

Arnold had not been invited to the dinner at the King's Arms, and Jane had gone to Alnwick. He had nothing else to do.

2

Sinclair lived a short distance from the exhibition hall, at the top end of the town, in a small house set back from the main road. The cul-de-sac was quiet, the garden neatly trimmed with rose bushes precisely set alongside the path, and inside the house the furniture was elderly, but the room itself tidied with a precision that would reflect the man.

'You won't have eaten, I imagine,' Sinclair said, 'and I don't go for heavy meals in the evening. Lie on the stomach, you know. But I can rustle up a snack, so we can chew while we talk, and a cup of tea would go down well, wouldn't it?'

Arnold was still not sure why he was here. The disappointment and annoyance of the evening was one reason; the surprising comments of his host were another. He was also a little intrigued by Sinclair himself: his direct mode of speech, his sharp summing up of Bannock, and his clear confidence about the history of the Templars interested Arnold. He watched as Sinclair played the host, fussing about in the small kitchen that led off the sitting-room, making a pot of tea.

Somewhat above middle height, Sinclair was lean, a trimly-built man with a gangling walk and narrow wrists that seemed in danger of disconnection from his arms. In spite of his confident approach at the exhibition hall, he projected an expression of latent doubt in eyes that were of a startling sapphire-blue. Their vagueness sheltered beneath beetling eyebrows that seemed to serve as a protective overhang to the insecurities of his face: a large, projecting nose and high, irregular cheekbones.

There were flashes of penetrating intelligence in his glance, nevertheless, and above his brow his short, iron-grey hair was brushed straight back. It bristled in stiff protestation, perhaps a relic of his time as an officer in the Scots Guards if the photograph on the mantelpiece was anything to go by.

He brought the tea in and set it down on a small table in front of Arnold, chatting all the while: he seemed in no hurry to return to the subject that had brought Arnold to his house and as he talked, an ironic, almost impish sense of humour allowed occasional fleeting smiles to cross his features, rays breaking through dark clouds. He was a chain smoker, his fingers deeply stained from the habit and his voice coarsened by the growling cough that regularly racked his chest. An innate consideration made him refrain from smoking in front of his guest, though he did excuse himself for a few minutes in order, Arnold suspected, to step outside for a quick cigarette.

Conservatively dressed in a brown double-breasted suit, Sinclair had an old world air with his white shirt, dark tie and highly polished shoes. He sipped his tea with gusto and was clearly very fond of biscuits, for they emerged from innumerable caches he seemed to have in the room. He dredged in drawers in the sideboard and rolltop desk: oatmeal biscuits here, chocolate covered fingers there. As he did so he expatiated on the amazing open boat journey of Captain Bligh after the famous mutiny: he felt Bligh had received a bad modern press. But that topic was not what had brought Arnold to Sinclair's house.

'I see you were in the army,' Arnold remarked, nodding towards the photograph on the mantelpiece.

Sinclair nodded. 'Scots Guards. I enjoyed the experience. The formality of the army is something I've clung to all my life. Over-familiar behaviour can be destructive. Names, for instance.'

'Names?'

'First names are the seats of the soul. It is unwise to allow others to use them. I recall that it was in an unguarded moment of passion that my wife – my ex-wife, that is – used my first name. It signified the beginning of the end of our relationship.'

Arnold stared at him. He could not be certain the man was serious, but was disinclined to test the matter. 'Was it in the army that you became interested in the Templars – the soldier-monks?'

'In a way. The Scots Guards have always had a strong Templar tradition . . . did you know that?'

Arnold shook his head. 'I'm aware that the armed forces, as well as the police, have Masonic connections –'

'Ah, even stronger in the Scots Guards. When Charles VII of France created his army in 1445, pride of place was held by the *Compagnie des Gendarmes Écossais* – the Scottish Company. It held an even more élite group – thirty-three men who were in constant attendance upon the king. They were the Scots Guard and they were in fact a neo-Templar organization with a military, political and diplomatic *raison d'être*. For more than a hundred years they held a unique place in French affairs even though they drew their officers from the Scottish aristocracy – and they established their own Order of the Temple.'

'Like many men they would have sought out the mysteries.'

Sinclair poured himself another cup of tea, and nodded. 'Even before their dissolution by Philippe the Fair, the Knights Templar were shrouded in extravagant myth and legend. These were cloaked in dark rumours, surrounded by suspicions and superstitions.'

'A mystique which intensified as the centuries passed,' Arnold suggested.

'Exactly that. The genuine mysteries became ever more swathed in a spurious mystification.'

'And that led to Freemasonry.'

'Ah, well, in the eighteenth and nineteenth centuries certain rites of Freemasonry sought, with some assiduity, to establish their pedigree, relate back to the Knights Templar, if only to give themselves a spurious historical status. A conduit for them was provided, in fact, by the Scots Guards – who regarded themselves as the heirs to the Templar traditions. But they weren't alone in that, of course: other, neo-Templar organizations began to appear about the same time, claiming a similar pedigree from the original warrior-monks.' Sinclair eyed Arnold carefully for a few moments. 'Your friend Bannock, for instance.'

'The speaker tonight? Not a friend – an acquaintance only.'

'Hmm. You should talk to him sometime about his affiliations.'

'Of what kind?'

'Ask him. The fact is, in modern times there have been at least five organizations claiming descent directly from the white-mantled Templars of the Middle Ages,' Sinclair continued. 'And cynical or sceptical as the modern world may be there is still, for outsiders, something fascinating, romantic, magical about the soldier-mystics of seven hundred years ago, with their black and white banner and the distinctive splayed red cross. They have passed into our heritage; they appeal to the imagination, not just as crusaders but as something far more enigmatic and evocative.'

'My impression is that they were also high level power brokers and intriguers,' Arnold offered.

Sinclair smiled. 'As well as being sorcerers, arcane initiates, custodians of secret knowledge. And guardians of a fabulous treasure. Time has served them better than they could have anticipated at their ordeal under the hands of Philippe the Fair.'

'But apart from the . . . er . . . exotic veil of romance,' Arnold said carefully, 'there's the matter of finance. Were they really as wealthy as has been claimed?'

Sinclair sighed. 'When men fought, whored, robbed and pillaged, they had to seek a final salvation when they lay close to death: the answer was to make gifts to the Temple. Yes, the Order was very, very wealthy.' Sinclair paused thoughtfully. 'But that wasn't the whole story, of course. Their financial influence has been underestimated, you know.'

'In what way?'

'I would argue that the role of Jewish moneylenders in the Middle Ages was minor compared to that of the Temple. It's worth noting that the Temple predated the Italian financial houses and indeed established the machinery and procedures which those houses later emulated and adopted when they came to finance the ambitions of English kings. I would even say that the origins of modern banking can be attributed to the Order of the Temple.'

'Isn't that going a little too far?' Arnold demurred.

'I think not. At the peak of their power, the Templars handled most of the available capital in Western Europe; they pioneered the concept of credit facilities, and the allocation of credit for commercial development and expansion.

They were in fact, if not in name, a hugely successful merchant bank.'

'I had read,' Arnold admitted, 'that King John borrowed extensively from the Order.'

'King John was chronically in debt to the Temple; Edward I owed the Order more than £28,000 – a vast sum in those days; Henry III pawned the Crown Jewels to the Templars – it was Queen Eleanor herself who took them to the Paris preceptory of the Templars.'

'But how do you justify the argument that they created a system of credit facilities?'

'One of their most important functions was to arrange payments at a distance without the actual transfer of funds. Travel was uncertain and dangerous, and men were reluctant to carry valuables because plunder was an ever present risk from outlaws. So the Temple devised letters of credit. You could deposit a sum of money in the London Temple and receive a chit in exchange. You could travel to Paris, Rome, even the Holy Land and present that chit, to obtain cash in the local currency in return.'

'But what if the chit was stolen?'

'An elaborate system of codes, to which the Templars only were privy, precluded the robber from gaining by his theft.'

'I see.'

'The Templars also organized safe deposit arrangements through their network of preceptories – in France, the Paris Temple was the most important royal treasury, housing the wealth of State and Order, before dissolution of the Templars.'

'What about England?'

'Not quite so important – though the Crown Jewels in John's reign were kept at the London Temple. On the other hand, the Templars in England certainly acted as tax collectors. They collected papal taxes, tithes and donations but in addition they collected royal taxes and revenues. It was they who organized in 1294 the conversion of old to new money and they frequently acted as trustees of funds and property placed in their custody. They were brokers and debt collectors, and they mediated in ransom disputes, dowries, pensions and a multitude of other transactions.'

'And were they trustworthy?'

Sinclair shrugged and smiled wickedly. 'They were human. A frequently used simile in medieval England was "He drinks like a Templar". Similarly, though they took a vow of chastity they seemed to have wenched as zealously as they drank. But their reputation for accuracy, honesty and integrity in financial matters was undoubted and when one of their number fell from that standard, they could be vicious in their treatment of him. The Prior of the Temple in Ireland was found guilty of embezzlement – he was held in a penitential cell in the London Temple, a cell too small even to lie down in. He starved to death there.' Sinclair paused, and regarded Arnold owlishly. 'It took eight weeks, apparently.'

'So in your view the most lasting achievement of the Knights Templar was –'

'Economic.'

'And they did much to help the rise of modern capitalism.'

'I would say that. The problem was, the very wealth they managed and accumulated so effectively would inevitably make them an irresistible lure to a king whose temerity was equal to his greed.'

'Philippe IV of France?'

'Exactly.'

Arnold hesitated, thinking. 'And if the Templars had advance warning of Philippe's strike –'

'They would have taken steps to preserve their treasures. And they *did*.' Sinclair hoisted his rangy frame out of his chair and walked across the room to the rolltop desk in the corner. He unlocked it and extracted some documents. He came back and placed them in front of Arnold. 'I told you I had some documents. Have a look at these.'

They consisted of a series of maps, with sectional enlargements, and marked sea routes from France, around the east coast of Ireland and between Islay and the Mull of Kintyre into mainland Scotland. Arnold pored over them for a little while and then looked at Sinclair, puzzled. 'What's the significance of these routes?'

Sinclair spread his hands wide and smiled. 'By the mid-thirteenth century the Temple's fleet had become a major asset. They carried six thousand pilgrims a year to Palestine from their ports in Spain, France and Italy. They had extensive trading concessions: they used escorts of galleys. Now, when Philippe struck, the Paris Templars would have found the roads controlled by the king's men – but the Templars had ships on the Seine. And in the period before the attack they had every opportunity to transfer their wealth to the coast, into larger ships at La Rochelle. But the question is, where would they go from there?'

'Spain, Portugal?'

'They might have been welcomed there,' Sinclair admitted. 'But no records survive to show they did land in these territories. They could have gone to the Islamic world – but again, there are no records. Scandinavia? Possible, but they had no preceptories there. But Scotland . . . ah, that was a different case.'

'Why?'

'They had maintained cordial relations there. Its king – Robert Bruce – had been excommunicated and needed experienced soldiers in his struggle against the English king, Edward I. And at the famous battle of Bannockburn in 1314 there was a decisive intervention. When all seemed lost for Bruce, a fresh force suddenly erupted from the rear – a reserve of mounted men in a Scottish army consisting mainly of foot soldiers. It has never been satisfactorily explained where these men came from – heavily armoured cavalry. The English collapsed in the face of the charge . . . but who *were* these knights?'

'You're not suggesting –'

'Look at the maps,' Sinclair suggested. 'Think of the Templars fleeing with their treasure. They would find Edward's fleet blocking the Channel and England's east coast, but the route from the north coast of Ireland to Bruce's lands in Argyll was open. The Templars certainly had holdings right down through Donegal and Tyrone, where they could rest and revictual, pick up arms and men. I think that Templar ships, Templar arms and *matériel*, and Templar fighting men were transported to Scotland to fight in Bruce's cause. At Bannockburn. And they took with them the Templar treasure.'

Arnold felt the glow of the man's enthusiasm, and was affected by it. He stared at the maps, concentrating: he could see the logic of Sinclair's argument. But was there anything in the records to support it? He shook his head. 'It's all a long way from the *sudarium*.'

'Which you discovered here in the north of England,' Sinclair replied, nodding. 'But I haven't finished the story. Without doubt, the *sudarium* was part of the Templars' treasure . . . not so much wealth, as a religious icon which nevertheless was extremely valuable to them. But have you ever heard of Simon de Goncourt?'

'I can't say that I have.'

Sinclair smiled. 'Right. I will now make us some more tea and a bacon sandwich each, before I tell you about the scourge of the Templars.'

3

John Culpeper had gone to the exhibition in Morpeth out of curiosity: he was not normally interested in historical matters and he was not an attender of public lectures. But he had heard that Arnold Landon would be speaking on this occasion, and since Culpeper himself had been involved, in a peripheral sort of way, with the discovery of the *sudarium*, he had slipped out of the office at the end of the day and made his way to the exhibition hall.

The surprise he had felt when it was Bannock who had risen to speak matched what Culpeper saw when he glanced across to Jane Wilson's face. It caused him to observe Landon carefully: it was soon clear to Culpeper from the stiffness of Landon's mouth that the situation was unexpected, and it did not take Culpeper long to realize what had happened.

The local politicians had shouldered their way into the limelight.

Not that Bannock wasn't interesting or well informed in his talk – and his delivery was probably better than Landon's would have been; it was just that Culpeper felt some sympathy for Landon's position. One could never be certain what was going on behind the scenes: political pressure could be used for all sorts of purposes. And as the thought crossed his mind, Culpeper was suddenly certain that it was political pressure that had led to the deputy chief constable's visit to Culpeper's office that morning.

Culpeper didn't like Baistow: he didn't like his Midlands accent, his easy arrogance, or his youth. The two men were utterly unlike each other: John Culpeper broad and thick-waisted, a product of a hard slog from beat patrol in the Durham pit villages to detective chief inspector in his late forties; Baistow a tall, elegantly handsome, high-flying police college graduate who was clearly destined to run his own force.

Andy Baistow had spent his early post graduate days in the Metropolitan Police – he had worked in the Fraud Squad, managed to avoid some of the scandals that had rocked the Met and risen swiftly, before transferring back to his home roots in the Midlands, and then north as deputy chief. It was obvious to everyone that he would stay in the north for as short a period as possible, because he was hungry for promotion, for the chance to run his own force and get his knighthood as the youngest chief ever.

Ambition shone out of his cold, dark eyes and arrogance twisted his mouth when he spoke to subordinates. With his superiors he could be all straight-backed efficiency, but with Culpeper he was dismissive.

He had walked into Culpeper's office that morning and tossed a manila file on the older man's desk with a contemptuous twist of the wrist. Culpeper had stared at it for a moment and then, as Baistow strolled across to the window and calmly lit himself a cigarette, Culpeper glanced towards the other man in the room and gestured that he should leave.

Detective-Sergeant Sid Waters nodded, eyes wide, then gathered up the papers on his knee and slipped quietly out of the room.

Culpeper felt anger lie like a hot stone in his chest. 'I didn't hear you knock. Sir.'

A faint wisp of smoke curled over Baistow's shoulder as he stood with his back to Culpeper. 'I wasn't told you were busy, Culpeper.'

'Maybe I should put a notice on the door next time,' Culpeper suggested sarcastically.

Baistow turned, taking no offence at Culpeper's tone. He eyed the detective chief inspector coldly for a moment, a sardonic lift to his mouth, and then he walked forwards, dragged up a chair close to Culpeper's desk and coolly seated himself. 'I don't imagine I interrupted anything important, did I?'

The anger stirred, but was controlled. It wasn't wise to allow oneself to be provoked. 'Nothing I can't deal with later, sir, if you've something important on your mind.'

Baistow humphed and squinted thoughtfully at Culpeper. 'Do you always do your homework so badly?'

'Homework?'

Baistow nodded towards the folder he had tossed on to Culpeper's desk. Reluctantly, Culpeper picked up the file and opened it, glanced at the first sheet inside and felt a slow stain of annoyance mottle his face. 'How did you come by this?'

Baistow drew on his cigarette. Calmly, he replied, 'That's not important.'

'It is to me! This file was confidential, and it hasn't even been to the chief –'

'Nor will it go to him,' Baistow interrupted. He jabbed the air with his cigarette, aggressively. 'No matter how it fell into my hands. Just be thankful it did.'

'Why?'

'Because it's a sloppy piece of work. Because it's a mess of guesswork. Because there isn't a single piece of real, hard evidence in that dossier which would stand up in court. And because if those papers had gone to the Crown Prosecution Service they'd have thrown them straight back in your teeth.'

The room was silent. Culpeper stared angrily at the man in front of him, furious, and yet shaken by the deputy chief constable's words.

Baistow shrugged, almost indifferently. 'You should be thankful, Culpeper, because I've saved you – and us – from great embarrassment.'

'This case –'

'You've blown it,' Baistow interrupted. He drew on his cigarette thoughtfully. 'How did you first get into this inquiry?'

Culpeper hesitated, staring at the man's cold eyes, thinking hard. He'd got into this inquiry, as Baistow put it, a long time ago, longer than he cared to think about. But that was something he couldn't explain to Baistow, even if he could explain it to himself. He moistened his dry lips and held Baistow's glance. 'I know this man, sir. And I think I can prove all the statements in that file. He's a bad lot, is Frank Manley, and he's had a finger in as many rackets in the Newcastle area as most people on Tyneside have had hot dinners. Where petty crime is concerned he's as greedy as a pig for potatoes –'

'Colourful imagery,' Baistow sneered. 'But for Manley, no previous convictions.'

'He's got away with it until now –'

'And you've been unlucky?'

Culpeper reddened. 'What's that supposed to mean?'

Baistow leaned back in his chair, confidently. 'Oh, come on, Culpeper. There's always plenty of gossip around headquarters. No one needs to be sharp of hearing to pick up juicy titbits about senior officers. And what I've heard is that you've been running a vendetta against Manley for as long as anyone can remember. Even hauled him up a couple of times. But no convictions. It doesn't do a force much good, Culpeper, harbouring a grudge – unless you can put a villain away at the end of it. And that is something you've signally failed to do with this Manley character!'

'But this time –'

'This time you've got nothing! You've got sheets of supposition, statements from some of the shadier characters in Morpeth and Amble, a bit of hearsay from the West End of Newcastle: but what does it all add up to? Not a lot, let me tell you!'

Culpeper took a deep breath. He calmed the anger in his veins, slowed himself down. 'I don't think you quite see the whole picture, sir. I agree I've had my eye on Manley for a long time –'

Baistow snorted derisively.

'And while I took a chance a few times some years back and pulled him in . . . the charges didn't stick. But that doesn't get away from the fact the guy's a villain. And this time he's fallen into the net. We know there's a car thieving ring operating here in the north. The network extends throughout the county, and runs down into Newcastle, Shields and Gateshead. The first link in the chain is the kids, the fourteen-year-old young tearaways who get the whisper that a particular kind of vehicle is required. High performance, popular models like the Sierra, or the Cosworth. They get out on the streets, nick the car required, and hand it over to their controller for maybe fifty quid. Thereafter the profit margins are high. The car gets moved on up the line, plates changed, resprayed, shipped across from Middlesbrough or Hull to Zeebrugge often as not –'

'You're telling me nothing new, Culpeper,' Baistow interrupted.

'The ramraiders use some of these cars, sir! If we don't break the links in the ring –'

'Manley, you mean?' Baistow drew on his cigarette, waved it towards Culpeper contemptuously. 'The man may well be involved in the system, as a second or third stage buyer, but you're not going to try to tell me he's an important link. Or is he your mythical Mr Big?'

'I didn't suggest that, sir. But Manley makes a living out of this operation – I'm sure of it. All the street information I get –'

'Street information! That just about sums up your case – that's all you've got! The statements in that file wouldn't stand up in court because the CPS itself would impeach them from the start. You've got petty crooks in that grubby list of witnesses who'd sell their grandmothers for nine pence. God knows what you've promised them to come up with their little stories, but that's all they are – fairy stories. They'd crack and crumble apart as soon as they were shown the light of day. All you've got in that file is a hopeless farrago of rumour, Culpeper, and how the hell a man of your experience can be fooled into believing you can pin Manley with a leaking sieve of a case like this, I can't imagine.' Baistow paused, eyes narrowed against the cigarette smoke drifting up to his face. 'Unless there's something personal in all this.'

He was fishing, of course. No one knew about the way it had been, all those years ago. No one was going to know. Culpeper's jaw hardened. 'I've spent two months gathering this information, sir.'

'Two ill spent months, my friend.'

'I can't just let this thing drop now –'

'Oh, yes, you can, Chief Inspector. In fact, that's exactly what you are going to do.'

'Sir?'

'There's been more than enough time wasted on this. I understand you've had two constables running the streets for you, pushing and probing, checking . . . well, it's over. If this is all you can come up with,' Baistow said, gesturing towards the file, 'I doubt your judgement. So it ends here.'

'You're taking the investigation away from me?'

Baistow smiled thinly, but there was no humour in his smile. He shook his head. 'You don't seem to listen too well, Culpeper. I'm not taking you off this case.'

'But you said –'

'I'm closing the file itself. I don't quite know why you've got your knife into this Manley character, and maybe it doesn't matter anyway. I do know that whatever is bugging you about him has affected your judgement, and you've pursued him up a dead end. You've trapped yourself in a blind alley, Culpeper, and I'm doing the helpful thing by pulling you out of it. If I hand this file over to anyone else, your incompetence will be revealed to all and sundry. So I'm doing you a favour – to save us all embarrassment. I'm closing the Manley file.'

'You can't do that, sir!'

Baistow rose, and stubbed out his cigarette in the saucer of the empty coffee cup in front of Culpeper. He leaned forwards, knuckles on the desk, looming over the chief inspector. His eyes were vaguely amused, and he smelled of a sharp, pungent aftershave. 'Can't I, Culpeper? You're quite wrong there. On an issue like this I can do what I bloody well like. Or do you want to take it up with the Old Man?'

Not that a discussion with the chief constable would have done any good, Culpeper reflected sourly. He would have taken Baistow's line, supported his deputy. But for the rest of the day Culpeper had been furious. The file on Manley had been meticulously researched and even if the material he had uncovered had been supported by doubtful witnesses, that didn't mean to say they weren't telling the truth. In an undercover operation like this, they had to rely on the street, and the information Culpeper had obtained fitted, established the chain, named names. Manley was up to his eyeballs in the car theft business and Culpeper knew it. But the investigation was now effectively killed.

Yet it wasn't until he had watched Arnold Landon on the dais in the exhibition hall that Culpeper's mind began to clear. As his fury subsided and puzzlement took its place, Culpeper had wondered about Baistow's action. The deputy chief constable was no friend of Culpeper's – indeed, he was known to be a loner, a bachelor who kept very much to himself, no family life, committed to his career, ambitious, hungry for success. But he had chosen to suggest he was saving Culpeper, and the force, from embarrassment by closing down the investigation. He'd used the Crown Prosecution Service as a reason, arguing they'd throw out the evidence as unacceptable in court.

But why take that decision without testing it? Why close the file completely? And there was something hollow, something that didn't ring quite true in Baistow's tone and attitude in the way he'd spoken to Culpeper.

While Culpeper sat in the exhibition hall, the possible reason fluttered into his mind as he watched Arnold Landon listen to a lecture Landon himself should have given.

Pressure: it could all be about pressure.

At the end of Bannock's talk about the history of Northumberland, Culpeper caught Arnold Landon's glance. He nodded, smiled slightly and left the exhibition hall. He was not exhilarated, but his mood was lighter as he walked out into the street. There had been the unspoken anxiety in his mind that maybe Baistow had been right, and the investigation had been sloppy and ill constructed. But realizing that Landon had been sidelined for reasons of political vanity gave him something new to chew on in his own situation.

Pressure.

But what kind of pressure, and why?

He needed a drink before he made his way home. The house was empty at the moment since his wife had gone down to Guisborough to stay with their son for a few days – not that she'd see much of him since he was with the Cleveland Police, but she would be able to spend some time with their granddaughter. Culpeper wrinkled his nose: a grandfather, already, and sleeping with a grandmother! He needed a drink badly.

He hesitated outside the King's Head then slowly, deliberately, turned away and walked across the road, down the ginnel that led to the rather smaller Duck and Partridge. He stepped inside the doors, and made his way to the bar. He ordered a pint of Newcastle Brown Ale, and with his back to the bar surveyed the room.

The pub was fairly busy: a rowdy group of darts players were involved in a club match and the beer was flowing freely. There was a considerable amount of banter and ribaldry among the group but it was all pretty harmless. There was no one there Culpeper recognized. He took his beer and worked his way towards the snug: behind the old-fashioned panelled screen there were some imitation leather seats where, Culpeper recalled, the old soaks used to while away their declining years and one old granny used to knit while she worked her way through a solitary Guinness: one every night, essential for her health, she claimed.

The snug was empty. Culpeper sat down and sipped his beer. He waited, thinking. When he had finished the beer he rose and went back into the bar, ordered himself a large whisky. When the barman returned with the glass, he asked casually, 'Frank Manley been in tonight?'

The barman eyed him warily. 'Came in a few minutes ago, Mr Culpeper. He's in the lounge.'

'Alone?'

The barman picked up a glass and began to polish it, avoiding Culpeper's glance. 'No, he's got company. A lass.'

'Girlfriend, hey?'

The barman shrugged. 'They been coming in here together for some months now. Looks steady, like.'

'Anyone I know?'

There was a short silence. 'I couldn't say about that, Mr Culpeper. I gather she's called Edda Anstey. Comes from Berwick way. That's all I know about her.'

Culpeper sniffed. 'Ah well, when Manley gets back to the bar, just tell him I'm in.'

The barman's wariness changed to anxiety. He looked at Culpeper with panicked eyes. 'I don't want any trouble here, Mr Culpeper.'

'When did a copper ever give you any trouble?' Culpeper smiled thinly. 'Just tell him I'm in tonight, that's all.'

The barman nodded, and Culpeper returned to the snug.

It was twenty minutes before Frank Manley stood beside the partition and looked down on Culpeper. He was silent for a little while, staring; Culpeper looked up at him, waiting, controlling the slow pain in his chest, the familiar pain that came whenever he saw, or thought about Frank Manley.

'It's been a while,' Manley said slowly.

'Too long, maybe.'

Manley was thirty-eight now: broad-shouldered, slim-waisted, with the upper body development of a weightlifter. His skin was dark, his almost feminine eyes quick and black, darting as though they sought escape routes against the threat of danger. He was dressed in a thin black sweater that emphasized his muscular development, and he held a glass of whisky in his hand. He slid it on to the table in front of Culpeper and there was a cold smile on his sensuous lips.

Culpeper stared at him, noting the sprinkling of grey at the man's temples, a light dusting in the thick, curly black hair. He'd often wondered whether there was a touch of Spanish blood in Manley; certainly, the man tried to give the impression of devil-may-care adventure in his attitudes, a modern swashbuckler, a swaggering cavalier. Culpeper knew more of the grubby reality behind the façade. He touched the whisky glass with his finger. 'What's this for?'

'Commiserations.'

'What about?'

'Your disappointment.'

Culpeper leaned back against the wall, keeping the sudden concern out of his eyes. Casually, he asked, 'My whole life's been a disappointment so far, since you're still walking the streets.'

Manley grinned: his teeth were white and even, well looked after. 'And nothing's changing, it seems. You're still doomed to disappointment.'

'Don't be too sure about that.'

Manley laughed and with an arrogant confidence slid into the seat beside Culpeper. He pushed the whisky glass closer towards him. 'Go on, have a drink on me. I feel sorry for you. I can guess what it must be like, to keep pushing for something and never getting what you want. Guess is all I can do, of course . . . because I've always got what I wanted.'

Culpeper avoided the clear challenge in the man's tone. 'I don't mind waiting, Manley. Not when I know I'll get what I want, in the end.'

'Never in the world, my friend. Take the drink – it's all you'll get from me.' A harsher note crept into his tone. 'I know you've been pushing lately; I know you been talking to people on the street. But for what? You can't touch me, Culpeper. You've nothing on me.'

'You're very confident.'

'And you're lost at sea.' Frank Manley's glance suddenly hardened. 'What is it with you, Culpeper? I stay out of your way. I don't tread on your patch. I try to mind my own business, go my own way, but you're always there, always pushing, always waiting to get a grip on my throat.'

'It's a vulnerable throat, Frank.'

'No, that's where you're wrong. You've got nothing on me.'

'So you've nothing to worry about, have you?'

'Not now the rug's been pulled from under you,' Manley snapped.

There was a short silence. Culpeper did not look at Manley but picked up the whisky he had been given and drew an ashtray towards him. Slowly, drop by drop, he began to pour the whisky into the ashtray. He was conscious of Manley's harsh breathing beside him. Quietly, he asked, 'Exactly what rug are you talking about, Frank?'

Manley made no reply for a few moments. At last, he said, 'It's been a long time, Culpeper. It was over a long time ago.'

'Not for me.'

'I was just a kid.'

'You were twenty-three, Manley . . . not a kid.'

'I wasn't to blame for what happened, and you must be all twisted up inside if you can't forget about it and stay away from me.' His voice had taken on a harsh rasp as he went on. 'I've had enough of this and of you, Culpeper. I don't have to take this needling from you and I'm warning you, I can be pushed too far.'

'I haven't even started yet,' Culpeper replied. The ashtray overflowed and the whisky began to spread a slow stain across the table top. 'But you didn't tell me . . . exactly what rug has been pulled from under me?'

He looked up and Manley's face had changed: the man was angry, and the rawness of his anger had drawn back his lips in a vicious grimace. He leaned forwards and his eyes were wild. He raised a hand, flicked up a warning finger, and was about to speak when a shadow fell across them. Culpeper looked up.

There was a woman standing at the partition.

She was tall, slim, with long black hair and a pale complexion. She was in her mid-thirties, Culpeper guessed, but there was an uncertainty in her face which made her appear vulnerable. Her eyes were shadowed and there was a gauntness about her features that made Culpeper feel she might have been ill recently. She was dressed in sweater and jeans and she would have been beautiful a few years ago: now an odd desperate resignation had seeped away much of her former attractiveness.

'Frank?'

The edge of anxiety in her voice made Manley pause, draw back from what he had been about to say to Culpeper. He turned his head, looked at her, and said, 'What do you want?'

'I . . . I wondered . . . The barman . . .'

Manley glanced back at Culpeper and grinned, suddenly in control again. 'That's right. The barman. He told me there was an old friend back here – an old copper friend.' He stood up abruptly. 'Don't worry, Edda. There's no problem. I just thought Detective Chief Inspector Culpeper would like a drink on me, to drown his sorrows.'

'Frank –'

'But it seems he doesn't like whisky. At least, not if I buy it.' Manley laughed, raggedly. 'So what? It was just for old times' sake, hey? I'll see you around, Culpeper – but not if I can help it.'

He stepped away from the table, took the woman by the elbow and steered her back towards the lounge bar. Culpeper stayed where he was, his mouth tight, staring at the spreading stain of whisky on the table. The woman had interrupted Manley at the wrong moment as far as Culpeper was concerned. He wondered what Manley had been about to say, edgy in his anger.

And he wondered what might have been the reason for

the anxiety in the woman's voice when she had come to rescue Frank Manley from the consequences of a possible indiscretion.

Culpeper finished his own drink and left the snug. Outside the pub, the night air was cool. He looked up to the dark sky and thought about Frank Manley: as the man had said, what had happened between them had been a long time ago.

But there were times when, for John Culpeper, it could still be as though it were just yesterday.

2

1

The committee room was small and stuffy. It had recently been painted, and the fresh smell of the paint still lingered in the air, but it was an odour heavily masked by the thick atmosphere – there had already been two meetings held in the room during the day and the building sub-committee that now assembled was reinforced by two officers, armed with files, called in to help face the dozen or so objectors who had appeared for the first agenda item.

That first item held no interest for Arnold: it did not affect his department since it concerned the closing of a disused railway track and the planning application for the erection of permanent mobile homes – whatever that meant. Maybe he should have known, he thought vaguely, having spent some time in the Planning Department before his move to Museums and Antiquities, but if so he had forgotten. The relevant regulations had made no great impact on him. And he was inclined to put his experiences in that department to the back of his mind, anyway.

He found the discussion less than riveting and his attention wandered. Mention of the disused railway cast his mind back to his childhood and the long walks he had taken in the Yorkshire dales with his father. Though not a railway enthusiast, his father had taken him on the old Settle to Carlisle route and pointed out the scenic splendour of the Ribblehead viaduct, commenting on its Victorian construction, before taking him deeper into the dales to show him the broken down walls of ancient deer parks, the silent Georgian lime kilns high on the fells, the faint tracks of Roman roads slicing relentlessly across crags and moors, striking north and east, crossing burns and gills, leaving a thousand-year-old mark on the landscape.

The building sub-committee would no doubt also leave its mark on the landscape, but Arnold guessed it would be somewhat more ephemeral. He dragged his thoughts back to the present and watched as Ted Flint attempted to control the meeting.

Arnold came across Flint regularly, since the councillor chaired the museums committee as well as the building sub-committee. He was about forty years of age, grey-suited, stockily built, with sandy hair thinning and greying at the temples. His features were heavily mobile, fleshy with the first hint of jowls, and his eyes were quick and darting. Arnold had noted that when Flint was under pressure those eyes could hold a hint of desperation and there was a certain weakness about the man's mouth that perhaps summarized his character. For all that, Flint was a successful enough businessman, owning a string of retail men's outfitters in Morpeth, Alnwick and Newcastle; somewhat old-fashioned, but still holding their own against the competition of the big companies, in spite of the recession. A family chain, it had been built up by Flint's grandfather and changed but little in the subsequent years. Arnold had the impression that Flint spent as little time in the business as possible, preferring to concentrate upon a political career.

At which he showed some success. A pliable, popular man on the council, it seemed; one who made few enemies among the opposition, and had strong support in his own party. He avoided controversy, worked for compromise, and eschewed difficult decisions. But he was edgy enough now, attempting to overrule from the chair the objections being raised by an elderly opponent of the mobile homes scheme. His tone was hectoring, a bully taking advantage of his strength, but there was an underlying shakiness that suggested he was uncertain of his position.

As he was speaking, the door at the back of the committee room opened quietly. Arnold glanced back and saw Colin Bannock making an unobtrusive entrance. He caught Arnold's glance and after a moment smiled faintly in recognition, then took a seat at the back of the room.

When Arnold looked back to Flint, the man's eyes were on Bannock. There seemed to be an element of relief in his glance, and his manner and tone grew more hectoring, increased in confidence as he argued with the objector. Even so, he seemed further relieved when the matter was finally resolved and they were able to move on to the next business.

The young man from Planning, seated next to Arnold, grunted wearily. 'Thank God that's over,' he muttered in a grumbling undertone. 'I can slide out of here now – I think the next one's yours. And the best of luck.'

Councillor Flint was referring the committee to the sheaf of papers relating to the Ogle excavation. He looked vaguely around him. His glance fastened upon Arnold and he smiled. 'Ah, I see Mr Landon has managed to be with us.' He bobbed his head in Arnold's direction. 'I understand you will be able to enlighten us upon the issues involved in this matter.' Brent-Ellis had clearly briefed him to that extent at least, Arnold thought sourly. 'Please remain where you are while you address the committee, Mr Landon, but it would be useful if you were to stand.'

Arnold shuffled the papers in front of him and rose reluctantly to his feet. He had read the papers carefully once Brent-Ellis had sent them down to his office and he was now fully conversant with the project that had been running for some years at Ogle. He was not certain about the force of the objections, however. He had the feeling that he was going to be the centre of a storm here, though he was not clear from which direction the winds would blow.

'I suppose, Chairman, I ought to sketch in the background to these papers, by way of summary for all those present today.' Arnold paused, but when no one made any suggestion to the contrary, he went on: 'I imagine most people here will be aware that about a mile to the north east of Ogle there is an old church: St Mary's. It is a typical building in its chequered history over the centuries: some Saxon traces, a later, sturdy, medieval tower which was itself partly demolished and then renovated in the Victorian period. The church has attracted no great attention during the seventeenth century, and fell into disuse in the early years of this century. It held nothing of great interest and was recently subject to a demolition agreement.'

Someone cleared his throat noisily at the back of the room. Arnold glanced up and noticed a thick set, florid-faced man staring intently at him. His eyes were hard, glittering with suppressed anger; his mouth set firm in a thin, cold line. Arnold began to think he could guess where the storm winds would come from.

'The church itself stands on a low sandy mound, but two miles to the west there are the remains of an old pit head and the Victorian records show that St Mary's actually lies on top of an extensively mined coalfield. The situation would appear to be that a column of coal was left to prop up the church, but at some stage it had been decided to underpin the church and dismantle the tower. Suitable foundations were provided but, with waning attendances and other demographic factors intruding, the church was finally closed.'

Arnold glanced at the florid-faced man: he was still listening hard, chewing now on his lower lip, hands clenched against the back of the seat in front of him.

'The opportunity was taken some fifty years ago to undertake archaeological excavations within and around the church – the University of York masterminded the project. When the church was finally closed, a few years back, the University of Durham obtained funds from . . . ah . . . British Coal, to reopen the investigations. There was some surprise when they discovered that prior to the Saxon building of the church there had been a small cemetery on the site.'

Arnold paused. It would have been no surprise to him, because churches were often built on ancient sites of pagan origin: to the primitive mind, such locations held great

significance and to rebuild on the site only increased the power of the organization that worshipped there. It would have been a powerful incentive for a young, struggling church in essentially pagan times.

'The cemetery included one north–south orientated burial, described as a probably prehistoric burial; other bones discovered were dated to the tenth and eleventh centuries. Some interments had been undertaken with stones placed around the heads, others had been buried with quartz pebbles, or on charred planks. The significance of these rituals has not been determined.' He began to warm to his task. 'The actual building of the church is quite an interesting feature. An eleventh-century construction in the main, it was naturally made of timber, but elaborate arrangements were made for the foundations. Existing pagan burials were exhumed from a rectangular area which was then filled in, a platform of pitched magnesium limestone was laid and the timber erection thrown up. The first stone church was to replace it in about 1130, a two-cell structure with the nave enclosing the timber church –'

'Mr Landon.'

'Sir?'

The chairman was staring at him with a furrowed brow. He pursed his lips, and scratched warily at his cheek. 'I don't think it's really necessary to go through a history of the excavations at Ogle. We're concerned here with rather more . . . practical situations. While the results of the investigations over the last fifty years make, I've no doubt, fascinating reading, I don't think you should let your enthusiasm run away with you. There are those among us who have other business to attend to.'

Arnold reddened. 'I'm sorry, Chairman, but I thought the committee could usefully be apprised of the archaeological importance of the site since –'

'Quite so,' Flint interrupted with a hint of impatience, 'but keep it short, if you don't mind. So we can get down to things that concern this committee – the heart of the matter.'

He was tense, that much was clear to Arnold. Brent-Ellis

had said the Ogle situation could give rise to problems: Flint was probably anticipating them. Hurriedly, Arnold went on, 'In brief, then, the church holds a carved Romanesque lintel on the west door, some high status burials within the church, a finely carved slab of magnesium limestone bearing a foliated cross and a sword, and a probably unique oak coffin mirroring the interior shape of a stone sarcophagus. It is the discovery of this particular coffin which increased the archaeological activity prior to the deconsecration and the agreement to demolish –'

'Which brings us to the point at issue,' Ted Flint growled, and glanced with an assumed belligerence around the listening room, as though seeking to challenge an unknown enemy.

'Yes, sir. An extensive survey has been carried out, a stone by stone recording, an internal and external photogrammetric survey and the identification of major and minor phases of ancient reconstruction by the taking of mortar samples. What is clear is that the site is one of major archaeological interest – on the basis of the university's findings it is now possible to begin a detailed structural history of the church, but more important, future research could give an analysis of the population on the basis of the burials, while a great deal of information can be gleaned by the sequence of burial rites from the tenth to the nineteenth centuries. It is for this reason that the university –'

'Chairman! How much longer do we have to listen to this crap?'

The rasping voice silenced Arnold. He looked up: the florid-faced man was standing now, glaring at the chairman. Arnold waited, glanced towards Flint. The man had paled and his mouth was slack: his eyes suggested he had been expecting this interruption, but with some trepidation. He licked his lips. 'Mr Coulter, you'll have the opportunity to make your contribution –'

'Contribution be damned! One hundred and eighty thousand quid is enough contribution! And it's getting bigger all the time! I paid over cash to the church authorities after the deconsecration and I was assured that there would be no problems thereafter. I've been listening to this kind of rubbish – the sort tossed out by your clerk there –' Arnold bridled somewhat at the description '– for well over a year! It's time the talking stopped, and we saw some bloody action.'

'Your language, Mr Coulter –'

'Plain speaking never hurt anyone, Mr Chairman,' Coulter sneered. 'And I'm known for it. I take it I've got the floor?'

Nervously, Flint glanced at Arnold, who sat down with a shrug when he saw the panic in Flint's eyes.

'All right,' Coulter said, knuckling his fists against the back of the chair, 'let's cut out all the crap and get the issues on the table. Your minion there has given us a bit of history – let me give you some more recent history.' His voice was bitter with resentment.

'I persuaded the powers that be to deconsecrate the church and I then paid a hell of a lot of money to the Church authorities for that property. An agreement was drawn up to enable me to demolish the building – it was falling apart anyway.' He glared around briefly at his audience, as though daring someone to challenge his view. 'I was approached by the university for an extension of time to allow them to complete their archaeological investigations, and I agreed it – I'm no fool: I know the kind of pressure pussyfooting academics and weak-kneed environmentalists can put on councils . . .'

Flint squirmed slightly in his chair as though he felt this was a personal attack upon his own integrity. Arnold frowned, watching the man as Coulter continued.

'I've been a patient man. I've given the university the time they asked for, and now they say they want more time still. It's not me. I've paid good money for the property; I've got plans to build there, and all I'm waiting for is a decision from the council to complete the building application approvals. And what do I get? The runaround! Delays. Excuses. Long drawn out inspections. Questionnaires. When's it all going to end? I ask myself. Then this meeting is called. Is this the end? It had better be, Mr Chairman – it had better be!'

'The proper procedures . . .' Flint mumbled in a low voice,

then caught himself, dragged on his cloak of authority rather more tightly. 'We have to go through the proper procedures, Mr Coulter. Your application involves the building of several small estates on the site and the neighbouring land previously owned by the church. This had implications for the area –'

'For your friends, you mean,' Coulter snarled.

There was a short silence: Flint's mouth had whitened at the edges as he stared at his antagonist. 'I will ignore that comment and observe –'

'Why ignore it?' Coulter challenged angrily. 'Why sweep it under the carpet? I've made a statement. Why not regard it as a challenge? Or is it that you can hardly deny there's some sort of fiddle going on here!'

'I have no intention of being drawn –'

'Because you're afraid of what's likely to come out?' Coulter sneered. 'Come on, Flint, don't be so stupidly naïve. I'm a member of the business community, I have friends; we know what's going on. Are you going to tell me you don't know anything about a bid from Quinton's hypermarket chain for a site on the west end of the village? Are you going to deny they want to strike out in an entirely different direction for that outfit, and set up a theme park and leisure centre which they think will attract people up from the Newcastle area? And are you seriously going to argue that it's more important that they should set up a leisure centre than that I should build executive housing on the church site?'

'Without wishing to comment at all upon matters that lie outside the agenda for this meeting,' Flint spluttered angrily, 'I would nevertheless stress that there is absolutely no connection between the application you mention and the restrictions we are considering with regard to the St Mary's church site. Your application has been held up –'

'Damned right it's been held up! And don't give me that crap about no connection. You must think I'm a fool. I know the Ogle area. It's a quiet, laid back sort of place, easy commuting distance from Newcastle and Morpeth, ideal site for executive housing – in spite of objections that say it'll spoil the rural character of the village. But wouldn't a theme park do the same? Yet I hear no objections about that! Maybe that's because of the sweeteners the Quinton people have been putting into the area. The park concessions in Morpeth for instance, and the new bridge at Alnwick. Generous donations to the council trusts – come on, man, I'm in business! I know how these things work!'

'Mr Coulter,' Flint said firmly, but Arnold noted the slight shake in his voice. 'You're out of order in raising these scurrilous matters, and I refuse to take note of them in this arena. The issue on the table is merely one relating to the petition from the university which asks for a delay to be established to allow them to complete the excavations, prior to the builders moving in and the site being completely cleared. There is no suggestion that there will be a withdrawal of existing approvals –'

Coulter drew himself up in contemptuous dismissal. 'Yet. You forgot to add the word *yet*! Let me ask you this, Mr Chairman . . . The application from the university is signed by Professor Santana?'

'Of the university Archaeological Department, yes,' Flint replied testily. 'But I see no –'

'This Santana character is an architect by profession.'

'I believe so, but –'

'As such he undertakes various consultancy roles, in addition to his university duties.'

'I am really in no position –'

'Well, I can tell you exactly the position, Flint. Professor Santana is retained as an architectural consultant by the Midnorth Consultancy Group, based in Newcastle. That company in itself undertakes various assignments throughout the north, and I am reliably informed that it is on a retainer by Quinton's, the hypermarket chain I mentioned earlier. Now this all seems to me to be highly suspicious –'

'I see nothing suspicious at all!' Flint snapped. 'The council are in no position to vet such situations and the allegations –'

'I haven't yet finished, Mr Chairman,' Coulter interrupted imperiously. 'And I haven't yet made any allegations –

though I'm getting to that. Professor Santana works as a consultant for a company which is retained by the chain. The chain has an application in to develop a theme park in the Ogle area. The professor meanwhile submits a delaying application upon my own development on the St Mary's site. Does this not all seem slightly suspicious?'

'I see no reason –'

'And what about your *own* position, Mr Chairman?' Coulter interrupted aggressively.

Flint sat back in his chair, eyes widening. 'I don't know what you mean, Coulter.'

'Let me put it like this. You're chairman of this committee, which vets applications. You're also a member of council, which will make the final decision. What about your own business interests, Mr Flint?'

Flint licked his lips. 'My business interests are of no consequence in this hearing –'

'Are you prepared to state that categorically, as a matter of record?' Coulter persisted.

'My dear man –'

'Are you employed as a consultant by the hypermarket chain?'

'Certainly not!'

'Have you any business connection with the Midnorth company?'

'I know nothing about Midnorth, and have no connection with them! This is outrageous –'

'You have no business connections which have any bearing upon the theme park, or upon my own St Mary's application?'

Flint sat back, gasping angrily, but there was a panicked look in his eyes: he was not a man who responded well to pressure, Arnold concluded.

'There's no truth in your allegations!' Flint almost shouted.

'You're a bloody liar,' Coulter replied in a tone thick with contempt. But someone was rising at the back of the room. 'Mr Chairman – may I have a word here?'

It was Colin Bannock. He stood there, dark-suited, at ease,

in control of his emotions and his speech. His tone was quiet, and reasonable, and his words were cool in the tense, heightened atmosphere of the committee room. 'I have no status in this committee, as you are well aware, Mr Chairman – and I only stopped by to while away a few minutes. You'll all be aware,' he added with a wry smile, 'that we councillors have plenty of time on our hands.'

There was a small ripple of laughter around the room; relief at the snapping of the tension. Coulter turned, glaring at Bannock as the man continued, having already successfully reduced the rising temperature of argument in the room.

'It seems to me that if Mr Coulter has statements to make, he should make them. But in the right forum. So far he has asked questions of you, as chairman, to which you have given answers. Unfortunately, the nature of the questions may, well, leave . . . suggestive thoughts in the mind of the listeners. While I'm sure it hasn't been Mr Coulter's own intention, we all know that it's an old ploy among the mischievous – throw mud and some of it will stick. As a fellow councillor, and as a lawyer, I would like to say that it can be extremely dangerous for people to make statements which can cause others to take, shall we say, a jaundiced view of the position of a councillor. This meeting is not a privileged occasion – words spoken here can be regarded as slanderous, and Mr Coulter would be well advised to moderate the thrust of his comments and adopt rather more parliamentary language – whatever point he wishes to make. I say that in the friendliest of fashions.'

Arnold saw him flash a smile in Coulter's direction: it held an edge to it nevertheless.

'I don't think this is the appropriate situation to raise issues such as those mentioned by Mr Coulter. I am quite certain, Mr Chairman, that you would never have put yourself into any situation which would bring about a conflict of interest between your public position and your private or business life. If Mr Coulter does indeed have any information which bothers him – or questions that he would like answered – I think it would be most appropriate if he were to ask them in private, and receive the relevant assurances, rather than expose them in a public manner in a place such as this. I offer this advice as a public servant myself: there really is no need for this kind of debate.' He paused. 'Nor, indeed, is it relevant to the agenda, if I may say so . . .' He began to sit down again, murmuring deprecatingly, 'I merely make these points in an attempt to further the committee's work . . .'

Flint was clearly grateful for the intervention. It had given him time to regain his self control. There were beads of perspiration on his brow: he flicked them away with a finger, before he said, 'Thank you, Mr Bannock. Your comments are well made, as usual. Mr Coulter . . .' He paused, eyeing his antagonist carefully, in control again. 'I can give you my categorical assurance that I am in no way connected with . . . business interests in the manner you suggest. The matter that lies before us, raised by Professor Santana, is a simple one, and I have no reason to believe that the professor is in any way influenced in the manner you allude to. I intend ignoring your comments therefore, and unless you have any pertinent matters to raise with this committee, we shall be moving to deliberation – after, of course, we've heard from any other individuals who wish to make submissions before we reach our decisions in camera.'

Coulter stood rigid for several seconds. He glared at the chairman, then turned and looked at Colin Bannock, imperturbable at the back of the room. 'This is a stitch-up,' he snarled. 'You can't convince me otherwise. Be careful, Flint. If the committee agrees this delay, it won't be the end of the matter. And as for you, Mr Bannock – you'd be well advised to keep your nose out of things that don't concern you. And I'll be taking a look at just what you're up to as well now, after your . . . intervention.'

He stalked out of the room, overturning a chair as he did so. When the door banged behind him there was an audible sigh in the room; Arnold was not sure whether it was collective, or emanated from the chairman of the committee himself.

The meeting ground on.

Arnold was recalled to answer further questions about the archaeological importance of the site, and when he gave his evidence he was oddly conscious of Colin Bannock at the back of the room, listening carefully. When he finally sat down, Flint called for members of the public to leave, and the decision was taken. Arnold was not surprised at the final decision. It was one of which he personally approved whatever Coulter might think. Professor Santana's application for an extension of time was agreed, and the final approval of Coulter's housing applications was put back.

Arnold was surprised to see Bannock waiting in the doorway as the committee members filed out. He smiled at Arnold. 'Things got a bit heated in there at one point, Mr Landon.'

Arnold shrugged. 'It was perhaps just as well you were there. Your comments pulled the rug from under Mr Coulter.'

'Hmmm.' Bannock's eyes were hooded for a moment, as if in reflection. 'I always think it's rather unwise for people to . . . lose control over their language in public. It can cause embarrassment. Talking of public words, Landon, I was very interested to hear your contribution today. You clearly know a great deal about the Ogle excavation.'

'Not really. I was speaking to a brief.'

'You spoke with authority – and my guess is that some of what you said wasn't in your brief.' He eyed Arnold carefully for a moment. 'I trust you weren't . . . upset about the other evening.'

'Upset?'

'About my taking over from you at the exhibition.'

'You spoke very well, and knowledgeably,' Arnold replied quietly.

'But not as authoritatively as you, I'm sure,' Bannock murmured. 'I was given some notes you'd compiled, of course, but afterwards, over dinner with Powell Frinton, I heard a little more about you. I hadn't realized you have been so . . . immersed in the past. Timber, stone, medieval buildings . . .

I understand your knowledge can almost be described as encyclopedic.'

'I would hardly say that,' Arnold demurred.

'Others say it.' There was a short pause. 'And your discovery of the *sudarium* was no . . . lucky chance. You must have done a significant amount of research into the background . . . the Templars, the de Bohuns . . . Does that kind of research interest you, Landon?'

Arnold shrugged. 'To a certain extent. I can't say that I'm interested in esoteric cults for their own sake, but many of these organizations – including the Church itself – have left their mark, physically I mean, upon the landscape. So when one attempts to interpret that landscape, determine the age of a building, the masonry techniques used, the timber joints that appear, it's useful to know a certain amount about the background historically. And that often means learning about the lives of masons and architects . . . who were frequently members of strictly controlled guilds –'

'And secret societies.'

'You could call them that.'

Bannock's eyes were calculating as he stared fixedly at Arnold. 'Have you ever heard of the Ancient Order of Sangréal, Mr Landon?'

Arnold shook his head. 'I can't say that I have.'

Bannock half turned towards the door, thoughtfully. 'I wonder . . . perhaps later this week I could give you a ring, and arrange for us to have a drink together. Then I could tell you a little about the Order. Would that interest you, do you think?'

Arnold saw no reason why it should not.

2

Arnold had arranged to meet Jane for dinner on the Friday evening and he turned up as arranged at her bungalow in Framwellgate Moor. She had offered to cook a meal for him, but he insisted that they go out to eat. They drove along to the Royal County Hotel in Durham, parked in the area behind the hotel and went into the restaurant where Arnold had already booked a table.

'Is this by way of some sort of celebration?' Jane asked him. She was wearing a patterned blouse and dark skirt, and her hair had been cut that day. She made no claims to beauty, and was firmly of the opinion that she was plain, but there were occasions when Arnold thought she looked extremely attractive: this was one of them, with her eyes bright and her smile relaxed.

'Not really a celebration,' he replied, wondering vaguely why he never complimented her on her appearance. 'It's by way of a thank you for the work you did, helping me prepare that speech for the *sudarium* exhibition.'

'The speech that never got given,' she said severely. 'Did you say anything about that later, Arnold, to your political masters – or even to Brent-Ellis?'

'What was there to say?'

'If it had been me,' she replied fiercely, 'I'd have left a piece of my mind in certain quarters.'

Arnold laughed. 'Pieces of your mind have been left in all sorts of places, I believe.'

She grinned in response. 'I suppose so. But it really was reprehensible of the councillors.'

'Let's not spoil our meal by talking about them. Though in his own way, Colin Bannock at least tried to make some sort of amends.'

'How?'

'Dinner first. I'll tell you later.'

They were silent for a little while, devoting their attention to the menu and the glasses of gin and tonic Arnold had ordered for them. When Jane had finally decided upon whitebait and guinea fowl and he had settled for garlic mushrooms and Chicken Kiev, he finished his gin and tonic and made a start on the bottle of Chardonnay he had called for with the first course.

'Now, what's this about Bannock?' she insisted.

Arnold tasted the Chardonnay: it was clear, cold and crisp. He nodded approvingly. 'Well, before I tell you about him,

I should mention the curious discussion I had after I left the exhibition. You went off, you recall –'

'To my hen party.'

'That's right. When I was making my own way out I stopped to have a look at the *sudarium* exhibition and this character engaged me in conversation. He's called Sinclair. We talked about the exhibition – and Bannock's speech. It ended up with Sinclair inviting me back to his place for a drink –'

'Arnold!' she said reprovingly.

'To talk to me about matters of common interest,' he sniffed, ignoring her teasing.

'Such as?' she asked archly.

'Knights Templar. And what happened to their treasure.'

'Really?' She leaned forward, frowning, and sipped from her own wine glass. 'So what does he know about it?'

'Quite a lot, he claims.'

'A crank?'

Arnold shook his head thoughtfully. 'I wouldn't say so. Obsessive, no doubt. He's spent a lot of time on the history of the Templars. But there's nothing wrong with obsessions –'

'Look at you, for instance.'

'And he's certainly convincing in what he says. He refers to documentation, produces maps, has clearly gone into the thing in some detail and . . . well, he's kind of persuaded me to go along with him soon and look a bit more closely at some of his theories. It'll mean a foray into Scotland. Should be interesting.'

'Why you?' Jane asked suspiciously.

'Because of the *sudarium*. And because he thinks I'd be interested. And because he thinks I can help, with my own knowledge and background.'

'I love Scotland. I could have helped.'

'You weren't there. Don't be so competitive.'

'What are his theories, anyway?'

The waiter arrived. A small plate of garlic mushrooms was placed in front of Arnold, while Jane leaned forward to inspect her whitebait. They began to eat while Arnold mulled over in his mind the story that Sinclair had told him.

The red wine – a Merlot – had been opened and the Chicken Kiev was ready for him by the time he had finished telling her of Sinclair's theory regarding the route the Templar fleet had taken, and the possible use of the Templar knights at the Battle of Bannockburn.

She snorted. 'It all sounds fanciful to me.'

'Like the kind of fiction you write?' he countered.

'Which is why I could probably help him more than you. Flights of the imagination are called for in your dealings with this Sinclair man, Arnold, and no one could really claim that you are a fanciful man.'

'I'm being nice to you tonight,' Arnold complained. 'Why are you being so aggressive?'

'Because you should be inviting me to meet this man Sinclair. I'm sure I'd find him far more interesting than you do. And I'm hard-headed enough to explode his theories, treat them with cynicism –'

'A moment ago you were suggesting you're the fanciful romantic out of the two of us.'

'Well . . .' She began to attack her guinea fowl. 'Go on with your story.'

'He'd shown me the maps,' Arnold continued, 'and was very persuasive when talking about the routes the fleet might have taken. The story of the Templars at Bannockburn . . . well, it's a possibility. And it's certainly well documented that the Templars had always maintained cordial relationships with the Scots. So a lot of what he said made sense. Then there are the legends.'

Jane watched him carefully over the rim of her glass. She sipped the wine slowly. 'You're beginning to trespass into my territory,' she warned.

'What is clear,' Arnold began, 'is that legends of a Templar survival in Scotland are numerous – but tend to fall into two distinct groups. The first concerns the Strict Observance – the "restoration" of the Temple. The Preceptor of Auvergne is supposed to have escaped in 1310, to the Mull of Kintyre, where he met other fleeing Templars and re-established the Order. Possibly under the patronage of Robert Bruce, or at least with his connivance. Robert's fear of offending the French monarch would have been vanquished by his desire to secure a few capable men at arms as recruits. Then there's the second legend.'

'Which clashes with the first?'

'Somewhat. Shortly before his death, Grand Master Jacques de Molay nominated one Larmenius as his successor. Larmenius wrote a charter creating a non-Masonic, neo-chivalric institution, but one sentence in the charter states: *I lastly will say and order that the Scot-Templars deserters of the Order be blasted by an anathema . . .*'

'Nasty.'

'Power struggles in the fourteenth century tended to be sort of like that. But the statement would seem to confirm the survival of Templar fugitives in Scotland – fugitives who opposed Larmenius and tried to retain the Temple in their outpost in Scotland.'

'But still, they're legends only,' Jane demurred.

'Most legends have some basis in fact. Besides, there's the story of Simon de Goncourt.'

'Which, from the tone of your voice, is factual rather than legendary,' Jane suggested.

'That's right. Whatever the validity of the legends, there's no doubt that some Templars made their way to Scotland. They were trained fighting men – perhaps the best fighters of their age. And Robert Bruce wouldn't have been keen to turn them away. Scotland was struggling for independence and survival – she lay under papal interdict and the king himself was excommunicate. So what did he have to lose by welcoming the Templars?'

'And is there evidence he did?'

'That's where de Goncourt comes in. From what Sinclair told me, and I've checked some of his sources, the king of France sent an emissary to the English court in an attempt to enforce the rooting out of the Templars. Edward II was somewhat dilatory – he wasn't too keen on kowtowing to the French king, or to the Pope in Avignon, and he found the charges against the Templars incredible. Sinclair showed me a quotation from one of his letters to Castile, where he announced he was turning a deaf ear *to the slanders of ill-natured men, who are animated with a spirit of cupidity and envy.*'

'That's telling them!'

'So the emissary – de Goncourt – had a somewhat frustrating time. He was armed with the Pope's official Bull, but Edward acted only reluctantly. He did call on his sheriffs to arrest the Templars in England, but those who were taken were kept in comparative luxury at York, Lincoln and Canterbury. Most had time to escape. Two years later, Edward went through the formalities again, writing to his sheriffs that Templars were still *wandering about in secular habit, committing apostasy*. But it was all a bit . . . desultory.'

'A lack of zeal on Edward's part.'

'So de Goncourt thought. It was the same story in Ireland. By the time the interdict went out the Templars had disappeared. Simon de Goncourt arrived too late. He was determined to do better in Scotland.'

'And did he?' Jane asked, sipping her wine.

'The persecutions began in 1309. An inquisition was held at Holyrood, but only two knights appeared there. Simon de Goncourt then launched an attack upon what he thought would be the hotbed of Templars in Scotland – but he signally failed. His last push was towards the castle at Kilclogan, but he was faced with opposition from the Bishop of St Andrews – partly political, partly personal – and there can be no doubt that the Templars at Kilclogan had been warned well in advance of the arrival of de Goncourt. But the anger and persistence of de Goncourt seems to have been fiercer than it had been elsewhere. He raised a storm in Edinburgh: letters flew to the Pope, there was a suggestion that Bishop Lamberton himself should be excommunicated – and it seems clear that de Goncourt had thought himself close to something important at Kilclogan, only to have it slip through his grasp.'

Jane was silent for a little while, staring at her glass. She pushed aside her plate. 'The Templar treasure,' she murmured.

'That's what Sinclair concludes,' Arnold agreed. 'The Pope's emissary ranged throughout Scotland, chasing the Templars, following the trail that he sniffed out from Kilclogan, but he was frustrated at every turn: by Lamberton, by Sir Robert Moray, by a whole network of clan links.'

'Money can buy almost anything,' Jane suggested.

'I think it was rather more than that. I tend to agree with Sinclair. For the Templars to survive in Scotland, the Order would need to construct a new base, establish bloodlines, set up networks that would hold secrets, collude, cover up and redevelop. Sinclair says there's plenty of evidence that this is what happened. The holdings of the Order were kept intact, retained as a separate unity and administered by these "defrocked" Templars. The treasure was held intact – held in trust – and the controllers were a series of interlocking families who provided both a repository and a conduit. This is what de Goncourt had to face – and it defeated him. The Templars had been swallowed up into the clan system, controlled by certain major families and developing into the military formation they sponsored – the Scots Guard.'

'You told me the Templars were immensely wealthy. What happened to the Templar holdings outside Scotland?' Jane asked.

'In France, confiscation. But after the official papal dissolution in 1312, all Templar lands and holdings were granted to their former rivals, the Knights Hospitaller of St John. They'd kept their noses clean of heresy and had stayed loyal to Rome. But in Scotland things were different. When Robert Bruce gave a charter to the Hospitallers, no mention was made at all of Templar lands. After Bruce's death the Hospitallers did ask for a list of such properties, around the world. The resulting report, discovered at Valletta, says that of all the land and holdings that were Templar in Scotland the reply was – *nothing of value*. That was in 1338. In other words, the Hospitallers never laid hands on the lands or the treasures of the Temple in Scotland. They were always kept separate, handled by agents, kept in trust, even to the extent that thirty-four years after the suppression of the Templars, Temple Courts were still being held in Scotland.'

'But what exactly does Sinclair want you to do?'

Arnold shrugged. 'Help him find the treasure.'

Jane stared at him. 'Just like that?'

'More or less.'

'But hold on a moment. You just said the holdings – and presumably that includes the treasure – were swallowed up in the clan system. Over the centuries, surely, where something like that is held in trust it would become dispersed, used for Templar purposes; even taken over by these important families.'

Arnold smiled. 'Sinclair has researched the subject thoroughly. In the first instance, he believes he has some clues to the route the Templars took after Kilclogan. While the lands and holdings went into trust, he believes a large part of the treasure itself was hidden. And he believes there was a cataclysmic event, in Templar terms, some time later. It would seem there was some kind of betrayal, a defection: a betrayal of the trust. He's going to tell me about it, and the treasure. He thinks it wasn't swallowed up as such, but spirited away. He hopes to be able to find it.'

'And he thinks you can help?'

'In two ways. He needs detailed interpretation of some old buildings – a stripping away of later accretions, to decide just how old some of the inscriptions he's found really are. And then there's the other factor.'

'What factor?'

'Luck, I suppose. He believes that my finding the *sudarium* demonstrates that I possess a certain . . . flair for such things.'

Jane snorted. 'You *fell* into that chamber in Brunskill!'

'Well, yes, but I *was* probing there to begin with,' Arnold protested.

'I suppose so,' Jane conceded reluctantly. 'But I think he's being a bit optimistic. Now if I were to go along as well –'

'You could add your soaring flights of imagination,' Arnold said, smiling.

'Don't knock it!'

'I'm not, really. In fact, when Sinclair suggested I might be interested in helping him, I mentioned your name.'

'Arnold! You've been stringing me along!'

'While I don't think he's terribly enamoured with the thought he might be working with a woman, your – ah – historical credentials were enough to convince him you wouldn't get too much in the way. So you're invited as well,' he added hastily, as he saw her beginning to bridle.

'I should bloody well think so!' She was silent for a little while, toying with her glass. 'You said something about Colin Bannock, earlier. How does he tie in with this?'

Arnold shrugged. 'He does and he doesn't, really. But he made me an offer.'

'One you couldn't refuse?' Jane asked.

'One that certainly surprised me,' Arnold replied. 'And he had something to say about Sinclair, too.'

Bannock had been true to his word. He had rung Arnold and suggested they met for a drink: they'd agreed upon the Northumberland Arms in Newcastle, and Bannock had met him there in the lounge. He had been pleasant and affable; talking about things of no consequence, until after some fifteen minutes they were joined by another man. He was introduced to Arnold as Con Burnley, the librarian at Newcastle University.

He was a tall, balding man about forty years of age. His figure was spare, and he had a slight stoop to his narrow shoulders. His fingers were lean and strong, his handclasp powerful but there was a lack of humour in his mouth, and his glance was cynical. There was a disturbing intensity about his eyes that suggested to Arnold he took life perhaps a little too seriously. He was the kind of man who would not make friends easily; who viewed life with suspicion, and in whom fires of commitment would burn. When Bannock asked him what he wanted to drink, he settled for mineral water, and Bannock smiled thinly at Arnold.

'I thought it might be useful if you were to meet Mr Burnley. He has a rather longer history than I in the matter we're going to talk about, and he has probably rather more knowledge too. Where I go wrong, he can fill in and correct.'

'Go wrong about what?' Arnold asked.

Con Burnley's cold glance switched to Arnold. The councillor smiled affably. 'You'll remember I asked you the other day whether you'd ever heard of the Ancient Order of Sangréal? Well, Mr Burnley here is steeped in its history.'

Burnley glanced away momentarily, his jaw set. Arnold got the impression the man was disturbed about something – possibly the mention of the name of the Order in a public house lounge. But Bannock appeared not to notice, unless he was gently needling the man with a certain cold pleasure.

'Perhaps you'd like to tell Mr Landon all about the Order, Con,' Bannock said breezily. 'You've heard of Landon, of course. He found the *sudarium*, you'll recall.'

Burnley stared at Arnold briefly. There was an odd gleam of interest deep in his eyes, then his lids drooped and he looked at the mineral water in front of him. 'Yes, the *sudarium* . . . I'd heard. What do you want to know about the Order, Mr Landon?'

'No, no, no, that's not it,' Bannock interrupted with an edge of impatience in his tone. 'Landon isn't inquiring: we're offering information.'

Burnley did not look up, but his words were clipped and precise. 'That's not the usual way.'

'So I'm changing the rules,' Bannock said firmly. He hesitated, as though waiting for Burnley to speak, and then he turned towards Arnold. 'You've heard of the Grail,' he said abruptly.

'Of course.'

'And of the Grail Romances.'

'Yes.' The first of the so-called Grail Romances had appeared, as far as Arnold could recollect, towards the end of the twelfth century. They had spawned an immense corpus of collateral literature. They expounded a romantic concept of chivalry, and Christian rulers aspired to that concept – or sought to purvey images of themselves in that light. 'The Grail Romances are famous.'

'Quite. And you'll be aware they reflect a curious cross-fertilization – Judaeo–Christian belief, Celtic lore and legend, accretions from the Viking mythology and Norman pragmatism – but in essence, Celtic: the chivalric quest for a mysterious sacred object endowed with magical properties.'

Burnley opened his mouth, as though about to say something, but thought better of it. Bannock smiled contemptuously at him. 'We don't spend too much time these days arguing about the distinction between the Christian Grail and the earlier, pagan Grail – nor do we argue about the Judaeo–Christian superstructure which was added to the Grail Romances. There are some of us, however, who still look back to, and search for, the reality behind the legend, and the history, and the myth.'

'Are you talking about some kind of organization?' Arnold asked.

'When I speak of "us", I suppose I am. In fact, Mr Burnley and I are . . . shall we say, closely involved.'

'And what is the reality that you search for?' Arnold asked.

Burnley looked up. The deep gleam was still in his eyes. 'The blood royal,' he said shortly.

Arnold was silent for a little while. Bannock was observing him quietly, making no comment.

'Blood royal,' Arnold repeated. 'Sangréal . . . *sang réal*.'

'Precisely.'

'The blood of Christ?' Arnold asked, puzzled.

Bannock made a deprecatory gesture. 'No, of course not – that's to confuse issues with the Christian overlay. The blood royal goes back far beyond Christ. It concerns the holy blood, the true blood which is the essence of the soul of man – be it pagan-inspired, Celtic in origin, a Viking accretion . . . who knows? I suppose in one sense we have set aside all the accretions and just concentrate now on the philosophical plane. But we are an old organization. And we continue to search for truth.'

'A difficult concept – no two people agree on what might be truth,' Arnold suggested.

'All the more reason why we should look, and analyse and consider,' Burnley snapped.

'But in a sense,' Bannock interrupted, 'that emphasizes the esoteric side of the Order. There's another way of looking at us. We're a charitable organization, devoted to good works. We support schools, we make charitable donations to worthy causes. And we indulge in historical research.'

Arnold began to guess why he was being told about the Order. 'What kind of research?'

'It's wide-ranging,' Bannock said in an offhand manner. 'Celtic, medieval, Roman . . . we have scholars investigating the cults of Mithras and Sylvanus, Atys and Serapis – we circulate learned papers . . . we're a fairly liberal sort of organization. And we recruit –'

Burnley made a rumbling noise in his throat, and Bannock paused. He smiled cynically. 'Mr Burnley doesn't care for the word "recruit". He prefers that we should not open our doors until someone knocks upon them. I respect his view. I don't subscribe to it. I prefer to look for like minds; to seek out people who would enjoy being with us, would provide us with new blood, would help us in our quests. That's why I thought we should have a little chat. Had we taken Con's stance, you might never have known about us.'

'Probably not. Though some mention was made –'

'Oh? Of our Order? Where?'

'Not exactly mention of the Order.' Arnold hesitated. 'I was talking to someone at the *sudarium* exhibition, that's all.'

'The *sudarium* exhibition. Yes. Well, that's why I approached you, really. You see, I was most impressed by the work you did to uncover that historical fragment. Most impressed. And when I read your notes, talked with Powell Frinton about you . . . He's an unimaginative man . . . doesn't understand the mind that is unrestricted, untrammelled. Anyway, I thought you might be interested to hear more about us, perhaps attend one of our meetings . . .'

'I'm not a joiner, I'm afraid, Mr Bannock.'

There was a short pause. Bannock smiled thinly. 'I would have thought our Order would have appealed to you, Landon. The search for truth. The meeting of like minds. The exchange of information on a historical base.'

'Ah well, as I said,' Arnold replied uncomfortably, 'I tend to be a bit of a loner. I'm not one to join organizations – I prefer to go my own way.'

'So you're not interested in hearing more about the Order?' Bannock asked coolly.

'I'm sure it's most worthy, and well supported, but I don't feel I could offer it very much, and I –'

'There's no point in pressing Mr Landon if he's not interested,' Con Burnley said abruptly. 'I think we should leave matters there. This has been a waste of time.'

'Time is rarely wasted,' Bannock said with a tight little smile. He stared at Arnold reflectively for a few seconds. 'The *sudarium* exhibition . . . you said someone talked about the Order there.'

'Not as specifically as that.' Arnold wriggled uncomfortably. 'A comment was made –'

'By whom?' Burnley asked sharply.

Arnold shrugged. He felt he was straying into deep waters. 'A stranger . . . someone I hadn't met before. He was talking to me in the exhibition . . .'

'He was there for my talk?' Bannock asked.

'It seems so.'

'Did he introduce himself to you?'

'Well, yes –'

'His name?'

Arnold hesitated. There was an odd sharpness in Bannock's tone and Burnley too was leaning forwards, his eyes gleaming as he listened. Arnold shrugged. 'It was only a casual conversation. He didn't mention the Order by name. Just that . . .' Arnold hesitated again, realizing he was getting out of his depth. 'He told me his name was Sinclair.'

'The funny thing is,' Arnold explained to Jane as they took coffee after the meal, 'they were more than a little upset that

Sinclair had mentioned them to me. Why on earth they should worry about an offhand comment like that, when Bannock himself was making an open approach to me to join their damned organization, I don't know.'

'But isn't that a common feature of these male bonding secret society things?' Jane said, sniffing deprecatingly. 'They like to have their little secrets, don't like being talked about, want to play their silly games in private – but have to show their importance every so often, inviting notable people to join them.'

'Me? Notable?'

'You know what I mean. People who have something to offer them.'

'That's as may be.' Arnold thought for a little while, toying with his coffee cup. 'Anyway, they were both upset. And Bannock, he said something odd before we parted.'

'What was that?'

'He warned me off Sinclair.'

'In what way?'

Arnold smiled. 'Oh, quite specifically. He stopped me at the door, just as we were leaving the pub. Sinclair, he said: be careful of him. He's a dangerous man. Stay well away from him – take my advice.'

'A dangerous man? Oooh, and you're thinking of taking me to meet him!'

'I don't want to disappoint you,' Arnold replied. 'I see nothing dangerous in Sinclair – he's slightly eccentric, with his head buried in the past. But Bannock . . . now he's a different kettle of fish. *He* could be dangerous.'

A lawyer, a politician, and a member of the Ancient Order of Sangréal – but more importantly, a man with cold eyes whose tone, when he had warned Arnold, had been tinged with a real menace.

3

It had been a hard, unsatisfying day for Culpeper.

The fact that he had been forced to close the file on Frank Manley had left him with a soreness of mind that preyed on him; the disciplining of a detective-constable over his failure to keep adequate watch on a warehouse the previous evening – he'd taken twenty minutes off to get a coffee at an all-night diner and the warehouse had been done over in that period – made things worse. And when the office told him that the paperwork he'd submitted on a burglary case in Ponteland had been mislaid and would have to be done again, his temper had erupted.

For that reason when he stumped into the car park and met an equally disgruntled Detective-Inspector O'Connor he was more than receptive to the suggestion that they should have a drink together before wending their separate ways homeward.

'Bloody junior coppers,' O'Connor snarled as he thumped down two pints of Newcastle Brown Ale on the table in front of them. 'They're green behind their ears; don't know their arses from their elbows, and because they've got a degree in sociology they think they can ignore the experience of years and get all cocky to their superiors.'

'I know the type.' Baistow was of a different rank, but had the same attitude, as far as Culpeper was concerned. He watched moodily as O'Connor drained a third of his pint mug in an angry, contemptuous swallow.

'You know what the cocky young bastard said to me?' O'Connor demanded. 'He didn't see the point in the Meadow Well surveillance of the Jenkins family, because he was sure them guys weren't up to anything! In Meadow Well, for God's sake! What the hell's he know about it, five minutes on the beat? We all know that bloody family have got form as long as an elephant's prodder!'

O'Connor was a square-built, stocky man with a brutal mouth and an aggressive manner. He was coarse of language, and crude of tactics: a man whose company Culpeper was normally inclined to avoid. On this occasion, the sentiments he expressed were in line with Culpeper's. 'They're all the damn same,' Culpeper agreed, growling. 'Know-alls.'

O'Connor took another long pull at his beer and grimaced his dissatisfaction. Disgruntled still, he cocked an eye in Culpeper's direction. 'You had one of those days too, then?'

'Day?' Culpeper snorted. 'Week. Month. You name it. I'm getting pig-sick of the whole thing, I tell you. Don't seem to be getting anywhere.'

O'Connor shuffled in his seat. He frowned, and nodded. 'Oh yeah, I heard on the grapevine. You got a case pulled on you, that right?'

'Too damned right.' Culpeper scowled into his beer. He'd been aware it was the talk of the station. It made him even more resentful. 'Time was when a deputy chief let us other buggers get on with our jobs without interference.'

'S'right.' O'Connor was silent for a little while, staring at his beer. 'You think you was building a case there?'

'I think I was.'

'Talk was it was Manley again.'

'Who else?'

He caught the knowing glint in O'Connor's eyes and looked away. A small niggle at the back of Culpeper's mind suggested perhaps he was too confident in that statement; that maybe his obsession with Frank Manley was clouding his judgement. It underscored his annoyance with himself and the system. 'Whether I was or not, it wasn't right for Baistow to come in with heavy boots and close the file.'

'Yeah. Funny one that.' O'Connor shook his large head thoughtfully. 'Not the first time, though. Another pint?'

Culpeper shook his head and watched the burly detective-inspector shoulder his way to the bar. When he came back Culpeper said, 'What do you mean, not the first time?'

'Not the first time that trick's been pulled.'

'I don't follow you.'

'Happened to Sid Jenson. Just before he retired. The file was pulled. Closed. Happened about eighteen months ago, something similar.'

'I didn't hear about it,' Culpeper growled.

'There was a bit of chat around in headquarters. But Jenson was going anyway so he wasn't much bothered. He just saw it as less paperwork on his desk. But maybe you didn't hear about it. You was on that Seahouses case about that time. Tied up three months you were, as I recall.'

'I remember Jenson going. I don't recall any comments.'

'It didn't make too many waves outside the fraud detail in Morpeth, mind. I only knew about it because I was in on the early inquiry.'

'What was it all about?'

O'Connor took a long pull at his beer. He wiped his mouth with the back of his hand: there had always been something crude about O'Connor, Culpeper thought with a certain distaste. 'Chap called Stephens. Suicide.'

'Don't remember it,' Culpeper remarked.

'He ran a small insurance business at Alnwick. We got some complaints about the way it was operating. I helped out on the early inquiries. As far as I could gather at the time, Stephens had been taking the house premiums and working some kind of scam on the building loans side. Raising false papers for second mortgages, that kind of thing – it involved a fair bit of money, that was clear, but there was a bankruptcy hearing first, before we were able to get together all the paperwork. Trouble was, the hearing never took place. Stephens, he took a knife to his own wrists: did the Roman thing and bled to death in his bath. Had a pretty wife, too. She went south after that. Probably had a bit salted away anyway. Way of the world, ain't it?'

'But you said something about a file being pulled.'

O'Connor nodded. 'You know how these things work. Fact the guy was bankrupt, fact he'd topped himself, that shouldn't have stopped the inquiry. Things to be cleared up. Like who he was working with . . . who his contacts might have been.'

'And –'

'The file got closed. There were three of us who'd been working on it – we got called up to the chief's office. We were told a load of crap: it was in the best public interest that the matter should not be proceeded with. You know the formula. The CPS agreed – not enough evidence. But how could there be? We hadn't had time to do a proper bloody trawl. I always thought that was a bit . . . premature, like. Closing the file. And the same story with you, I gather. Not enough evidence.'

Culpeper frowned. 'But it was the chief who closed the Stephens file, you said.'

'That's right. But you know the chief: likes to keep above the common herd. And in the office that day, Baistow was there with him. Looking like he wanted to smirk. Cat with the cream stuff. With those fish eyes of his, you know? Another drink?'

'God, no. You knock that stuff back like a rainstorm gutter! This one will do for me.'

O'Connor lumbered to his feet. 'I got to use the can.'

Culpeper watched as O'Connor crossed the room and made his way through the door at the far end. He was gone for several minutes: moodily, Culpeper nursed his drink and thought about Baistow. They were not pleasant thoughts. O'Connor thumped down in the seat opposite to him and reached for his beer.

'Talking of other things, what exactly is it about you and that Manley guy?' he asked.

Culpeper hesitated. He knew that comments had been made from time to time at Morpeth about his seeming obsession with Frank Manley, but no one had asked him directly before. He shrugged. 'It goes way back.'

'Personal, obvious.'

'You could say so.' A fuzzy image, blurred by time, suddenly flashed into Culpeper's mind: a bloated body, fished out of the Tyne. He shook his head, as though to remove the memory. He hadn't seen that image for a long time; he kept it distant, even when Frank Manley was in his sights. It didn't help, brooding on the incident now, and he had no intention of telling O'Connor about it here in the pub. As O'Connor had said, it was personal.

'Baistow's fronting up an investigation of his own at the moment,' O'Connor suddenly said. 'Tell you, that guy's got a bee in his bonnet: thinks he'll make chief constable elsewhere by cracking cases on his ownsome.'

'It's not his job,' Culpeper growled.

'Too right. But he hauled me in and asked me to do the paperwork – dredge through and find what I could on this Coulter character.'

'Coulter? Who's he?'

'Didn't you see the report in the *Journal*? He's a local construction and property dealer, up Alnwick way. There was a splash in the newspaper about the way he called out the odds at some council committee. They was a bit careful about spelling it out, but he certainly caused some kind of rumpus. Next thing, Baistow asks me to see what form the guy's got.'

Culpeper grimaced thoughtfully. 'Who did he call in the meeting?'

'Council member. Ted Flint. You come across him?'

'No.'

'Harmless enough. Well thought of as cannon fodder: one of the faceless brigade. Bit wet, really: never takes a stand on an unpopular issue. You know what some of these councillors are like. Anyway, it seems Coulter made some wild allegations about Flint, and Baistow then asked me to start digging on Coulter.'

'Not on Flint?'

O'Connor shook his head. 'Come on, us coppers are always on the side of the angels, ain't we? If a councillor gets his arse burned, we'll rally around with new asbestos underpants! And there's always the suspicion that characters who are involved in the construction business have probably got something to hide – tax, bribes, some building fiddle or other.'

Culpeper conceded the point, nodding. 'Even so, it's odd that Baistow should intervene.'

'The chief moves in top circles. Maybe Flint caught him at the Masonic Hall and bent his ear.'

'Masonic Hall?'

'Or wherever – I don't know where they meet, the top brass. Maybe it was a pub like this. Anyway, my guess is the chief got the whisper from Flint or one of his minions, took Baistow on one side, and that creep started the investigation – asked me to dig deep.'

Culpeper sipped slowly at his beer. 'You found anything yet?'

O'Connor laughed. 'Not a lot. A couple of notes on a file: suspicion of assault, but no charges brought. A few tenants moved out at sharp notice from flats due for demolition. There's no doubt our friend Mel Coulter has been a bit of a hard man in the past – but that's common enough in the building industry. Par for the course. There was even a complaint he was using dogs to shift unwelcome squatters in some old properties he owned. But never no charges.'

'So Baistow's going to be disappointed?'

'Don't sound so bloody pleased. It's my arse on the line here. No, I don't know how badly Baistow wants the information – he was pretty laid back about it when he called me in. So whether he'll be disappointed or not, I can't tell. I might dig something up yet. Who knows?'

Culpeper leaned back in his chair and stared at his companion. O'Connor's face was slightly flushed now and his eyes seemed watery. He was finishing his glass when Culpeper asked, 'Just what did Coulter say about Ted Flint?'

'Wild, whirling words it seems. Accused him of various sorts of chicanery. There were no details in the *Journal* – they're bloody careful about libel, of course – but there was enough to suggest that Coulter was accusing Flint of meddling in a project that's dear to Coulter's heart. And pocket.'

'How do you mean, meddling?'

O'Connor shrugged. 'Involvement with some consultancy or other . . . what the hell's it called?' He was silent for a moment, dredging his memory. 'That's it. Midnorth something or other. According to the newspaper report, Coulter was reckoning Flint was tied up with this Midnorth consultancy, and in some way it was blocking his own track towards the riches of the earth.'

'But you're not looking into that.'

'Hell no, I got enough on my plate. Not my brief from Baistow, anyway. Besides, guys who shout their mouths off in public hearings like that are usually just trying to raise the stakes. They got nothing to back up their statements – they just want to scare the pants off the opposition. Some of the mud will stick, won't it – and people then back off. People like Flint, anyway. He's not known for the steel in his backbone. How the hell people ever vote for these wimps I'll never understand . . .'

Culpeper rose to his feet. Dinner would be waiting for him at home. He looked down at O'Connor: the man was clearly in no hurry to leave. His wife had deserted him, Culpeper recalled, some years ago. It was an occupational hazard.

'I'll be off.'

'See you,' O'Connor replied, uninterested.

Culpeper walked out into the street and made his way back to the car. There were few people about now: the streets were quiet. As he drove home, he again caught a brief, unbidden glimpse of a girl's swollen face, but then the other thought intruded: Baistow.

An ambitious man. A man who perhaps did the bidding of politicians. It was a thought he clung to, all the way home, turning it over in his mind, prodding it, investigating it. Tasting it for the sourness of corruption.

3

1

The village itself was small and dreary. Grey-stoned, drably-painted, it consisted of a single narrow street with a small huddle of shops and houses and a decrepit garage. At each end of the village was a pub; outside the first some wooden tables had been hopefully set, as though to persuade passing traffic that the establishment offered suitable hospitality. The passing traffic had been either scanty or unconvinced: a green mould had started to grow on the table surfaces.

Arnold and Jane had driven north through the sweeping fells of the Border Country to the rendezvous with Sinclair. The morning had been bright and the hills alive with birdsong. From the road thrusting north they had caught brief glimpses of the blue sweep of the sea, while to their left had risen the shoulders of the Cheviots, dark green against the azure, cloud-flecked sky. The gorse was bright yellow in its early summer burst and there was the occasional sharp tang of salt in the air, until they climbed over Carter Bar to see the drumlins clumped below them, and took the road north towards Edinburgh.

Some three miles south of the city they had turned into the dark valley with its steep, narrow gorge, flanked with pine and beech among the craggy outcrops of limestone. Sinclair had met them at the head of the village and after a brief introduction to Jane, suggested they drive into the valley and stop for a coffee there: he flourished a flask at them, grinning his pleasure, tinged with excitement.

The valley was a winding, narrow, mysterious place that would be the haunt of legends, and the location for stories to frighten children on winter nights. As they drove under the steep overhang to their left, Sinclair slowed and gesticulated upwards: craning to look out Arnold caught sight of a large, moss-covered rock into which the semblance of a pagan head had been carved. It caused a chill to touch his spine; glancing at Jane he saw that she had the same feeling.

Sinclair drew into the edge of the road some two hundred yards further on, bumping over tussocky grass and leaving space for Arnold to manoeuvre into a parking space behind him. He turned off the engine and got out, stretching his tall frame, and then reached back into the car for his flask. As Arnold and Jane got out, he was pouring coffee into three plastic cups. 'See the head?' he asked, as they drew near.

'Eerie,' Jane muttered, and accepted a cup of coffee.

'It's an odd place,' Sinclair agreed, glancing about him. Though the sun was high it seemed to filter into the gorge only reluctantly, touching the treetops but doing little to warm the dankness of the scrub and thick undergrowth below them. Sinclair handed a plastic cup to Arnold and gestured vaguely down towards the scattered alder and birch ahead of them. 'Down that track, you come to a waterfall. There's a sort of hollowed out cave behind it – natural enough. There's another head there, water-eroded. But no one can be sure whether the head down there is natural or carved.'

'*Another* head?' Jane asked.

'Maybe a weathered carving; maybe a natural phenomenon,' Sinclair said, shrugging. 'Can't be certain. But in a way it's symbolic of this whole place. It's got a long history, shunned by the locals, full of superstitious tales; certainly a location which would deter the curious – if they got too curious.'

'We'll be going down there?' Arnold asked.

Sinclair shook his head, and pointed to a narrow track that led away to the right. 'No, we follow that path there. It'll take us to the chapel.' He paused, thoughtfully, eyeing

Arnold with a reflective frown. 'I hope that we'll be able to make something out of what we find there. Your eyes might see things mine have failed to do so far.'

'You've been here before?' Jane asked.

'A couple of times. The first occasion, a long time ago. Its significance didn't strike me then. Later, after I'd been doing some research in Newcastle University library, I was able to trace a trail . . . and it seemed to lead to the chapel. So I came again.' He glanced at Arnold. 'That's when I first met Colin Bannock.'

'Here?' Jane asked in surprise.

'No, no. He contacted me in Newcastle – when I was at the library one day.' He seemed to expect Arnold to say something, but when Arnold was silent he challenged him. 'When you rang, and we arranged this meeting, you mentioned that you had had words with Colin Bannock.'

'That's right.' Arnold met his glance squarely. 'He doesn't like you.'

'Nor I him. But how do you know that? He said so?'

'More or less,' Arnold replied evasively. 'He tried to recruit me into the Ancient Order of Sangréal.'

'Ha!' Sinclair glanced at Jane and smiled cynically. 'I thought he might get around to doing so at some time. I should stay away from it if I were you, Landon.'

'He gave me a similar warning, about staying away from you.'

Sinclair's eyes narrowed as he looked back to Arnold. He humphed quietly to himself and began to smile. The smile faded after a moment and his brow furrowed. 'Was he explicit?'

'No. He just said he thought you were a . . . dangerous man.'

Sinclair drew his brows together as though trying to look dangerous. 'I'm prepared to be explicit about him.'

Arnold made no reply. He wasn't certain that it was any of his business. After a short silence Sinclair nodded, and finished his coffee. 'Shall we go on?'

He replaced the flask and cups in his car and locked the

car doors, then led the way along the narrow path to which he had pointed earlier. The grass was long and dank, and scrub alder and birch shrouded the path. Sinclair seemed cheerful enough, chatting to Jane – though he referred to her as Wilson – and asking her about her writing interests. He seemed in no way deprecatory about the fact she wrote historical fiction, and at one stage Jane flashed a triumphant, told-you-so glance at Arnold when Sinclair began to expatiate upon his belief that the writers of historical fiction provided a service to the public in increasing the awareness of their heritage, in a way professional historians could not.

Sinclair had made a friend, Arnold thought to himself, with a smile.

The path wound darkly through the valley, with the sun bursting through in a dappled screen from time to time among the scattering of lean trees; thrusting upwards urgently for the light. Arnold was surprised to note that the path meandered past several ruined buildings: the isolation of the valley had suggested to him that few would build here, but the cliff face itself had been quarried, and there had clearly been a local community, with several broken down huts, crudely built perhaps as shepherds' dwellings, constructed of rough limestone. Arnold suspected the valley would hold a number of prehistoric stone circle hut foundations, but he was surprised to note later constructions.

The path curved and came out into a little clearing at the foot of the cliff. Sinclair pointed: cut into the cliff face was a dressed stone window. 'Behind that window,' Sinclair explained, 'there's a whole warren of tunnels, carved out of the rock. It must have been a substantial undertaking.'

'Cliff dwellers?' Arnold asked.

'No doubt. But the tunnels were put to other uses. They could conceal a considerable number of men – and legend has it that they did, on more than one occasion. It's said that Robert Bruce himself found refuge here during one of the innumerable crises that beset his campaigns for Scottish independence.'

'Where's the entrance?' Jane asked.

Sinclair shrugged. 'You can get access through the window itself: but that's not the real entrance. I've no idea where it is: concealed in the scrub somewhere. It's been lost over the years. But do you want to go in?'

Jane shivered. 'No, thank you. Not unless it's part of the reason why we're here.'

'No, Wilson, it isn't. This is just a sideshow – though suitable for your fertile mind as a fictional location, perhaps. The place I wanted to show you is just up ahead.'

They walked on silently, the cliffs lowering above them, silent and menacing. Then Sinclair stopped, and pointed. 'The chapel,' he said quietly.

It was perched on the edge of the gorge, eerie in its silence, sad in its ruin. For a moment Arnold received the impression that it had been built like a cathedral in miniature. It was a small building, but its grey, lichened stonework was overloaded with Gothic carvings and floridly intricate embellishments. It was as though time had eaten away at its shell, reducing to its present size something much larger and more grand.

'A sort of cathedral of the valley,' Jane murmured. 'It's like a fragment of Chartres cathedral, transplanted into this gorge.'

Arnold walked forward, puzzled: his first impressions were fading as he looked more closely at the construction. The initial image in his mind, of a kind of amputated lushness in the building, was changing. The builders had lavished dazzling skills upon the stonework, costly dressed blocks of granite had been transported to the site, and many men would have worked here, deep in the valley.

But they had never finished the work.

'Can you date it?' Sinclair asked abruptly.

Arnold nodded. The stonework, and the toolmarks, the styling and the Gothic flamboyance, left him fairly certain. 'Mid to late fourteenth century, I would say.'

'Not earlier?'

Arnold shook his head. 'No. That scrollwork there was developed by a mason named Luther – it was much copied for about fifty years and then faded into disuse. I would date this building to about 1350, give or take twenty years.'

Sinclair sighed, as though in gentle satisfaction. 'It was never finished.'

'That's right. It was an expensive construction,' Arnold said. 'Maybe they ran out of money. Or maybe they began to question why the hell they were building the chapel in this lonely valley anyway.'

'To be closer to God?' Jane asked.

Arnold shrugged. 'I don't know. It's clearly designed to be something larger, part of a grander construction. Look at that west wall, for instance. You see how the massive granite blocks thrust out, jutting away from the main wall? They were put there, waiting for other blocks that, it seems, never arrived.'

'It was designed,' Sinclair pronounced sonorously, 'to be the Lady Chapel of a vast collegiate church, a full-sized cathedral on the French style.'

Arnold looked at him, puzzled. 'How do you know that?'

'Library research. There are several books written about this chapel – but none within the last eighty years. The Victorians had a brief fascinated flirtation with it – they were passionate about antiquities, but usually got things wrong. It was eventually put down as a sixteenth-century folly: a deliberately built half ruin. The Victorians themselves liked that sort of thing – romantic ruins. So trippers used to come here with their parasols and crinolines. Can you imagine it!'

Jane shuddered. 'Hardly.'

'But they got it wrong,' Sinclair repeated. 'Come.'

He led the way across the clearing and began to climb, scrambling over broken, overgrown stone steps. Invasive scrub had crossed the path since the Victorians had come here, and the stones were slippery and damp under the arching trees. They made their way into the open portico and stepped through the tall, crumbling doorway, festooned with rank growth, and then Arnold, bringing up the rear, heard Jane gasp.

He moved in beside her and looked around him with a sense of wonder.

The roof was broken and open to the sky. Shadowed by trees, there was yet enough light to see clearly inside the chapel and stray beams of sunlight illuminated the dark corners, casting a faint bloom on the stone, a gentle luminescence on the fluted pillars. To Arnold's amazement, the interior of the chapel was like a fevered hallucination in stone: a riotous, ritual explosion of carved images and geometrical configurations. Arnold stepped forward in quick excitement, running his hand over the cold, gleaming stone; noting how the configurations were interlinked, piled one on top of the other, flowing and lapping; overlapping in a sinuous movement of rolling carvings. The pillars seemed to writhe with symbolic beasts; the vaulting was a rolling sea of carvings, geometric symbols, latticework extended along the base of the half-finished windows and intricate scrolls appeared along the fluted pendants.

'This is . . . amazing,' Jane breathed.

'Others have found more resounding phrases to describe it,' Sinclair intoned. 'Such as . . . a petrified compendium of esoterica.'

'Esoterica? What do you mean?' Jane asked.

Arnold had already seen it. He pointed. 'Motifs. They're everywhere. Look there: the angel indicating the breast and right calf; the Creator as the Divine Architect of the Universe; arabesques, the arch and the pillar; the whole range of the so-called "sacred" geometry. This chapel isn't just Gothic in its style: the interior is crammed with esoteric motifs. This place must always have been a focus for secrets and legends. Many of these motifs have been adopted by Freemasonry –'

'But many predate that secret society,' Sinclair added. He eyed Arnold thoughtfully. 'Have you heard the story of the murdered apprentice?'

'*I* haven't,' Jane said quickly.

'Then I'll tell you, Wilson. There is a tradition that there was a beautiful pillar in Rome that was much admired. A copy was made of it and sent to Scotland. The master mason was unwilling to start work on the copy until he himself went to Rome to inspect the original. While he was off doing that, an apprentice finished the pillar in Scotland; the master mason, on his return, saw the pillar exquisitely finished, and was so incensed and stung with envy that he killed the apprentice who had executed the work.'

He turned, glanced at Arnold, and then motioned towards the west door of the chapel. Arnold walked across and looked up to the lintel above the door. Carved there was the head of a long-haired young man, flowers wreathing his brow. He had a gash in his right temple. Opposite the carving was another head: a bearded, heavy-browed man with serpents writhing above him.

'The apprentice?' Sinclair asked quietly. 'And perhaps the man who killed him?'

But Arnold was staring at a third carving, a woman: her face, half-veiled, was sad; her body delineated, clothed in sombre garments. 'The Widow,' Arnold said quietly.

'Exactly.' Sinclair's voice seemed to echo hollowly in the chapel, and there was a scrambling, scuttling sound in the broken stones above their heads; a rodent or a bird seeking safety from the intrusion. After a little while, Jane broke the silence. 'What's all that supposed to mean?'

Arnold sighed. 'I'm sorry. Sinclair's seen the significance as I have. He's right about esoterica. The interpretation I'd make of these carvings is that we have here the murdered apprentice, the master mason who killed him, and the grieving mother of the apprentice.'

'The Son of the Widow,' Sinclair added.

'So what?'

'The phrase – *Son of the Widow* – is one that's familiar to all Freemasons. It was borrowed by them in the seventeenth century from much more ancient rituals and beliefs. It ties in with the story of Hiram and the building of Solomon's temple – a Judaic thread in seventeenth-century Freemasonry. But, oddly enough, the same phrase was also used to designate Percival, in the Romances of the Grail.'

'Exactly. The Masonic connections of this chapel are clear,'

Sinclair agreed. 'The connotations and the symbolism cannot be coincidental.'

'The Grail . . .' Arnold muttered, almost to himself.

Sinclair turned to look at him, almost owlishly. 'Another connection?'

'Colin Bannock's Ancient Order of Sangréal.'

'That's right. That's why he asked me to join his Order – he heard of my interest in this site, knew about my researches. And maybe that's why he warned you off me – called me a dangerous man.'

'I'm afraid I'm getting completely lost,' Jane announced firmly. 'So will someone please elucidate?'

'I beg your pardon, Wilson,' Sinclair said gravely. 'I have been amiss: my excuse is that I wanted Landon to confirm my own interpretations, which he has done. But it also gives me an opportunity to tell you both about Bannock. You are aware he is *Master* of the Ancient Order of Sangréal?'

Arnold shrugged. 'He approached me, so I presume he had some official standing.'

'Was he alone?'

'No, there was a man called Burnley with him.'

'Ah, yes.' Sinclair nodded as though his guess was confirmed. 'Well, I may as well tell you that you had there the two senior members of the Order in the north – Bannock is Master; Burnley, Deputy Master.'

'Burnley seemed not too pleased by the approach.'

Sinclair nodded. 'That does not surprise me, Landon. I obtained the impression that Burnley is deeply committed to the Order, its traditions and all he believes it stands for. Charity, good works, esoteric mysteries, the search for truth –'

'And Bannock?'

Sinclair permitted himself a wintry smile. 'I understand that Bannock is a more . . . political animal. I suspect he sees the Order more as a tool to be used for purposes other than those in Burnley's mind. But that's their problem. What both are committed to is the legend of the Grail, which they relate not just to the search for truth, but also for their roots. And like so many of these pseudo-religious, pseudo-historical cult organizations, they believe their roots lie buried deep in the history of the Knights Templar.'

'All modern quasi-Masonic cults look back to the Templars or the Hospitallers,' Arnold agreed.

'Perfectly true. But in Burnley, the Sangréal people have a man who – perhaps from his vocation as an academic librarian – has always been interested in the research that produces information about his sect. And that is why Bannock approached me.'

'I don't understand,' Jane admitted.

Sinclair glanced at her thoughtfully. 'My research has led me down many esoteric backwaters. But I eventually worked in the university library on some translations of old documents relating to the Seton family in Scotland. In so doing, I enlisted the aid of Burnley. He was most helpful. What I didn't realize was that I had stumbled on something of great interest to him.'

'In what way?' Arnold asked.

'In two ways, actually. The first involves Seton himself. He was one of the founders of the Ancient Order of Sangréal. The second matter of interest is the treasure of the Templars.'

'I don't see the connection.'

'There is one, believe me. For the moment, suffice it to say that my work led Burnley to watch me carefully. He must have told Bannock about it all, for Bannock's approach was more direct. He simply invited me to join the Order. I was interested, as I am in all secret societies, but after a few meetings with the pair of them, and after talking at some length with Bannock, I became . . . shall we say, disenchanted? I don't believe Bannock's aims are really those of the Order . . . and both he and Burnley are too interested in the treasure.'

Jane giggled. 'How can you be *too* interested in treasure?'

Sinclair sighed. 'One must always remember that the word "treasure" did not necessarily mean, in medieval times, what we would connote today. You have already had some experience of that, in your discovery of the *sudarium*. It could be regarded as merely a worthless piece of old cloth. But in Bannock's heart and maybe that of Burnley too, the treasure is real. Bannock has other motives, of that I'm sure, in his use of the Order; Burnley is less . . . worldly. But both put pressure on me to tell them what I knew, and also, when I resisted entering their Order, to desist from the search. They claim it is their truth, not mine. They were rather . . . positive about it.'

'How do you mean?'

'Threats,' Sinclair replied mildly. 'Subtle from Burnley . . . rather more direct, as might be expected, from Bannock.'

'So you think Bannock approached me –'

'Because he sees in you what I do. A man well versed in the . . . unusual skills. And one with a precious commodity in the search for ancient "treasures" – luck.'

'You're overestimating my powers,' Arnold said, shaking his head.

'But you *did* refuse to join the Order?'

'I did. I said I wasn't interested.'

'And Bannock warned you about me.' Sinclair thought for a moment. 'He would certainly be concerned that you are helping me now.'

'I don't see my activities as any of his business.'

Sinclair shrugged. 'Well, he warned you about me. Let me warn you about him. I think Bannock is a powerful and dangerous man. He has many tentacles of influence, overt and covert. I'm not sure which are the most dangerous. And you *do* work for the local authority. He is a politician, Landon, so be wary of him.'

'I'll bear that in mind,' Arnold replied, moving away. He was getting rather bored with Sinclair's sententious warnings. He could see no harm in pursuing his own hobbies, and couldn't see in what way they might impinge upon Bannock. He walked over the rough, broken floor, picking his way with care as he stared up at the ceiling. After a moment, he stopped. 'Have you seen this here?' he called out to Sinclair.

Jane came forward with Sinclair and they both stared at

the carving above Arnold's head. It comprised a canopy of writhing leaves, under which a young man drew a girl by the hand, while at the edge of the canopy a small group of animal-headed figures pranced. 'Have you considered this?' Arnold asked.

'I can't say I've paid it much attention. I've concentrated on the Masonic symbols.'

'It's odd it should be here, in the chapel,' Arnold suggested.

'Why?'

'It's Robin Hood.'

There was a long silence as all three stared at the carving. At last, Jane remarked, 'I can't see any connection between that carving and the medieval outlaw of legend.'

'You must go further back,' Arnold explained. 'Robin Hood as an outlaw was a later accretion. Robin Hood was derived from the fairy of old Celtic legend; he also became the Saxon god of fertility or vegetation. He was interchangeable with Green Robin, Robin Wood, Robin Goodfellow, or Shakespeare's Puck. The legend provided a handy guise whereby the fertility rites of ancient paganism were introduced into a nominally Christian Britain. May Day was a pagan ritual: the Maypole was a symbol of the archaic goddess of sexuality and fertility. Every village virgin was really Queen of the May – many of them were ushered into the greenwood where they would undergo sexual initiation at the hands of a youth playing Robin Hood. May Day was a day of orgy, producing an annual crop of children.' Arnold smiled briefly at Jane. 'Have you never wondered where the surname Robinson originated?'

'Are you pulling my leg?' Jane demanded.

'No,' Sinclair said harshly. 'You strike a chord in my mind, Landon. In this valley, at the village, a play was enacted every year – Robin Hood and Little John – by strolling players, with an orgiastic Abbot of Unreason –'

'Friar Tuck,' Arnold supplied.

'And a Venus-like Queen of the May. It was regarded in the sixteenth century as a pagan fertility rite, and was banned by the Calvinists and Roman Catholics.'

Arnold looked up again at the carving. 'They no longer needed their links with the past. Yet it's here, in the chapel.'

'It can only mean that the builders actually sanctioned such practices,' Sinclair said quietly. He stood silently for several minutes, his mouth working. Then he spun on his heel. 'Here, come with me.'

He scrambled across to the west door. He pointed upwards with his finger. Arnold stared. Sinclair was already walking away to the far window, and pointing again; whirling away he jabbed in the air with his forefinger again and again, pointing, and Arnold saw what he meant.

'They're everywhere.'

'Yes, but their significance?' Sinclair demanded, almost exultantly.

They had been concentrating on other things. But now that Arnold looked again, he could see that it was a dominant figure in the chapel. At almost every turn, the carving appeared, a human head with vines issuing from the open mouth, sometimes from its ears, sometimes from the eyes of the figure. The vines came forth and then spread wildly, a tangled proliferation into the columns and the walls, the pillars and the lattices. The head seemed to be everywhere, peering from corners, hiding behind the lianas that issued from it, the tendrils that the head itself engendered.

'What is it?' Jane asked, puzzled.

Never a body, only the head. 'It's the Green Man,' Arnold replied quietly.

'The severed head of ancient Celtic tradition, the talisman of fertility . . . of course!' Sinclair exclaimed. 'I hadn't realized it, until you pointed out the symbols the sixteenth-century Church regarded as subversive.'

'I still don't see the significance of the Green Man –' Jane began.

'It's the juxtaposition,' Arnold interrupted, feeling the excitement rise in his own chest, to match that which was clearly affecting Sinclair. 'This is a fourteenth-century Christian chapel, and yet we have carved within it the geometric symbols of the Templars as well as the symbols of the archaic Celtic kingdom.'

'A kingdom which Robert Bruce sought to restore in Scotland!' Sinclair added, his face flushed and excited.

'But who built this chapel, and why?' Arnold asked. 'What have your researches disclosed – why did you come here?'

'I can't be sure, but there's a link with the family of Seton – who had a part to play in the story of the Templar treasure. I found the original hint in an old satirical poem that is dated to the fifteenth century. I know it by heart . . .'

He closed his eyes for a moment and thought, then in a sonorous tone that boomed eerily in the confines of the chapel he began to recite, in a heavily accented voice, the ancient verse he had memorized.

> 'Fye upon the churle quhat solde
> Haly erthe for heavie golde;
> Bot the Tempel felt na loss,
> Quhan David Setoune bare the Crosse.'

There was a short silence. It was broken by Jane. 'I like the Scottish brogue, but what's the doggerel supposed to mean?'

Sinclair swivelled on his heel to stare wildly about him, shaking his head. 'The signs are there, I know it! It's the interpretation that is important. It's all here, I feel it in my bones!'

'Who was David Seton?' Arnold asked quietly.

Sinclair stared at him, his eyes gleaming. 'It depends on what you read – either the saviour, or the thief, of the treasure of the Templars!'

'What's your interpretation?'

'At this length of time, it's difficult, of course. The facts that I'm *convinced* of are that the Templar fleet successfully escaped down the Seine and eventually reached Scotland. The Templars determined to bury themselves in the clan system and remain underground. But they certainly converted some of the treasure into landholdings: there's a chartulary for *Terrae Templariae* which documents five preceptories and almost five hundred other Templar properties in Scotland: crofts, fields, farms, castles. So the Templars remained powerful and rich.'

'But something happened?'

'A falling out. A dispute arose about who was to succeed as Grand Master. The details are vague, but it all came down to a confirmation by the Grand Master of the Hospitallers in Malta. The succession was confirmed in the name of James Sandilands. He was a survivor, was Sandilands: he supported whichever side seemed more likely to win in the political and religious upheavals that racked Scotland, and when the pressure became too great he found his own solution. A royal decree annulled the rights of the preceptories, but when they were taken away this Grand Master came out smelling of roses. By the simple expedient of handing over to the Crown all the Templar lands.'

'*Holy earth for heavy gold,*' Arnold murmured.

'As the old poem has it,' Sinclair agreed. 'Sandilands got ten thousand crowns, an annual rent and a perpetual leasehold on the properties for himself. And he got an hereditary title, as Baron Torphichen.'

'He displayed an entrepreneurial spirit: the city yuppie of his day, maybe,' Jane suggested sarcastically.

'He had certainly swindled the Temple – disposing of their lands and enriching himself in the process.'

'And Seton?'

'Ahah! Altogether more mysterious. He is nowhere so clearly delineated in history as is Sandilands. But he clearly played an important part – in my view a crucial one – in the final disposal of the Templar treasure.'

'But you said it had been converted into land,' Jane protested.

'Not so. A large part of it had been used to purchase properties, but a significant part of it would still have been held within the Order for commercial as well as ceremonial purposes. And throughout the story of the Scottish Templars, there runs the theme of the Treasurer – never named, but a powerful figure who was regarded as the protector of the most arcane secrets of the Temple, of its ceremonial, and of its treasure.'

Arnold was silent for a little while. Then he asked, 'Do you have any evidence to link this Treasurer with David Seton?'

'Not directly. But do you remember me telling you about the Scots Guard, and the close links with the Templars? They are really the inheritors of the Templar military tradition. There were various families which contributed strongly in terms of manpower to the Guard: the Montgomeries, for instance – and the Setons. The Scots Guard declined as a power but it remained a neo-Templar organization until the seventeenth century and served as a vital conduit of transmission. And there is a document which purports to tell of the history of the building of this church. The main endowment came from the Seton family.'

'They must have had a hell of a lot of money,' Jane murmured, looking about her.

'Money . . . and a sense of history, a feeling for the past, and a need to signal their origins.'

'You mean,' Arnold said slowly, 'the Templar motifs, the Celtic background Bruce tried to recreate, all tied in with a religious order?'

'Precisely,' Sinclair said in a positive tone. 'What we have here, in this church, is the beginning of an investment for the future. But it eventually became a breakaway movement, because of the despoliation of the Templar holdings by Sandilands. The funds dried up, and what remained was spirited away. Of this I am certain. The remains of the Templar treasure still exist, after the Sandilands depredations, but they were held in trust by the Setons, following the example of David Seton. That is what the doggerel means: that is where the truth lies!'

2

Culpeper knew it was the wrong thing to do.

The resentment that had built up within him at having the file on Frank Manley closed rumbled on in his chest. It weighed on him during his working day and it caused him to toss in his bed at night. The resentment did not pass with time: it grew cancerously, churning over in his mind and poisoning his thoughts. He knew he was being obsessive about it but he was unable to control himself over the matter: there were times when he sat at his desk and stared out of the window and tried to tell himself he was making a bad mistake, simmering on like this about Baistow.

But there was always the sustaining thought that Baistow had behaved badly too – and suspiciously, as far as Culpeper was concerned.

And finally, even though he knew it was the wrong thing to do, he called in Detective-Inspector Farnsby.

Vic Farnsby was in his mid-thirties, a tall lean man who had achieved quick promotion through the accelerated graduate scheme. His features were saturnine and though he was intelligent and quick-witted, Culpeper had never liked him. They had worked together on the Bloodeagle investigation, however, and in spite of his prejudices against the young man with the pale, washed-out blue eyes, Culpeper had come grudgingly to accept that Farnsby had qualities that the chief constable at least had recognized early. And in an odd way the problems that Farnsby had had to face in his marriage, and the manner in which he had struggled to overcome them while sticking to his job, had also impressed Culpeper. The man was separated from his wife now, and seemed more in control of himself at work.

Even so, Culpeper knew he was taking a chance discussing the matter that bothered him with Farnsby: if Farnsby felt his loyalties lay elsewhere, Culpeper could be in trouble. Because of this he prevaricated for a while, discussing nothing of importance with Farnsby, over a cup of coffee, until at last he blurted out, 'Have you heard that an investigation has been started on a local businessman called Mel Coulter?'

Farnsby shook his narrow head, his pale eyes fixed on Culpeper. 'Can't say that I have, sir.'

'O'Connor's handling it.' Culpeper paused, considering, almost unwilling to go on. 'I think it's rather an . . . odd inquiry.'

'How do you mean?'

Culpeper shrugged. 'I was told that there was a flare-up in one of the council committees the other day. This man Coulter – a builder by profession – started calling names, making threats. I read the newspaper reports after my attention was drawn to it.'

'And now we're looking at Coulter?' Farnsby frowned. 'Who started the inquiry?'

Culpeper hesitated, then took the bull by the horns. 'The deputy chief.'

'Baistow? Why would he do that?'

Culpeper shrugged, but a small knot of anxiety began to unravel in his chest. 'I don't know. It seemed a bit odd to me, unless Baistow has information – or suspicions – that we don't know about. It's pretty unusual for the deputy to get involved like that. Anyway, he's set O'Connor on to the thing, and . . .'

His voice trailed away. Farnsby sat impassively, watching him, but there was a calculating gleam in his eyes. At last the detective-inspector said quietly, 'You and I haven't got on too well, sir.'

Culpeper was somewhat taken aback. He shrugged. 'You could say that.'

'That doesn't mean that I thought Baistow was right, closing that file on you.'

'You've heard about it?'

'Who hasn't?' Farnsby smiled, a little wolfishly. 'Gossip says that you might have got your hands on Frank Manley at last.'

'Baistow put a stop to that,' Culpeper snapped, in spite of the warnings in his head.

'But what's that got to do with the Coulter investigation?'

'I didn't say it had anything to do with Coulter,' Culpeper replied quickly, but felt the flush rise in his face. Farnsby was quick-witted, he realized. 'It's just that . . . it's just the one thing coming on top of the other. Something odd's going on. And O'Connor tells me . . . it's not the first time an inquiry has been halted recently.'

'Is that right?' Farnsby asked coolly.

Culpeper frowned. He was losing control of the interview. He humphed, and leaned forward, elbows on his desk. 'Yes, that's right. It's one thing to have the Manley case set aside, but it's another when inquiries are started which seem to start out of nowhere, to have no reason . . .' He was floundering. He gritted his teeth, took control of himself. 'What have we heard about Coulter? Nothing that can give us reason to start an investigation. Unless we've been given information by someone . . . maybe someone who feels under political pressure. And if that's the case, what the hell are we doing, jumping to the crack of a politician's whip?'

There was a short silence. Farnsby was watching him, with careful eyes. 'What exactly do you want from me, sir?'

Culpeper shrugged. 'I don't know. Maybe I just wanted to use you as a sounding board. Or maybe . . .'

'Maybe you thought that I could keep my ear to the ground in a way you can't . . . sort of take a watching brief, if I can mix the metaphor.'

Culpeper didn't know about metaphors. Bloody graduates. But he sensed that Farnsby wasn't averse to doing what was being hinted at. He nodded. 'Something like that. I'd just like to find out a bit more about why we're investigating Mr Coulter, and maybe a bit more about what was said at the building sub-committee meeting, this Midnorth thing and so on. Let's find out if there was any substance behind Coulter's bluster – while O'Connor finds out if there's any dirt to be dished on Mr Bloody Coulter himself.'

Farnsby stared at him with cool eyes. He seemed to be weighing something up in his mind. 'I take it this . . . inquiry we're making is sort of . . . ah . . . unofficial, sir?'

Culpeper felt uneasy. He nodded. 'In the first instance, we should keep it to ourselves.'

'Just you and me, you mean.'

Culpeper nodded. 'For the time being.'

Farnsby nodded, then slowly finished his coffee. He stood up, looking down at Culpeper. Seated, Culpeper felt oddly at a disadvantage. He glared up at Farnsby but the man was unconcerned: he smiled thinly. 'You can count on me, sir. I'll ask around, but I'll keep things discreet. And I'll report to no one but you – before we decide whether to go further.'

We decide.

Culpeper caught the stress. He watched as Farnsby turned and left the room. He was vaguely angry with himself: he had the feeling that in some way he was going to end up beholden to Vic Farnsby, and it was not a situation he cared to be in.

Driving south to Newcastle, Arnold Landon was also angry.

The A1 was busy, and he guessed he would have trouble parking in the city; had he been able to leave earlier he could have driven into one of the town car parks but now he guessed he would be better advised to stop at Kenton Bank Foot and pick up the Metro: the railway would take him within walking distance of the library. But this should have been a full day's leave he could have spent following up some of the leads Sinclair had given him: instead, he had been forced to waste half of the morning undertaking one of Brent-Ellis's unpleasant little chores – one the DDMA was unwilling to undertake himself.

Arnold's mistake had been to call into the office to drop off some files on his way to Newcastle. He'd received a message immediately, to go to see the DDMA.

'I see you've put in for a day's leave,' Brent-Ellis intoned, and twisted his moustache-end between thumb and finger.

Arnold nodded, standing stiffly in front of the DDMA's desk, aware of the eyes of the *gauleiter* secretary drilling into his back. 'That's right, sir. I have some leave due to me.'

'It's not the best of times,' Brent-Ellis grumbled.

'It never is,' Arnold replied boldly.

The secretary, still waiting to take dictation, stirred in her chair as though wishing she had a whip to curl around Arnold's neck for this garotte-worthy insolence. Brent-Ellis shuffled his feet under the desk, in a futile tattoo of irritation. 'That's as may be, but the last time you had leave –'

'You cancelled it. But there's nothing really important on at the moment.'

'I hear the Ogle committee meeting didn't go smoothly,' Brent-Ellis protested vaguely. 'Mr Flint was telling me . . .' His voice tailed away in uncertainty, as though he took wiser counsel and decided not to repeat to Arnold what Flint had said to him.

'Matters were resolved at that meeting,' Arnold replied firmly, 'in favour of the archaeology submission. That seems to have ended the matter for the time being and it's not really anything to do with our department, anyway –'

'Not so, I'm afraid,' Brent-Ellis interrupted, and ground his teeth unhappily. 'A Mr Coulter is in the building. He wants to see me. And now I hear you're wanting to take a day's leave just when I –'

'I was planning to go to Newcastle –'

'Well, I'm afraid you'll have to wait until you've seen this Coulter fellow,' Brent-Ellis insisted, a touch of colour appearing in his cheeks. 'I simply don't have time to deal with the matter – and you know more about it in any case, since you were at the meeting . . .'

Which Brent-Ellis had forced on him, Arnold thought wearily. But there was no point in arguing. 'Where exactly is he waiting, Director?'

Coulter had been seated for some time in a small, airless interview room. He was sweating, and angry at having been kept waiting. He was also angry to see Arnold.

'You were at the committee meeting.'

'That's right.'

'I wanted to see Brent-Ellis.'

'I'm afraid he's busy.'

Coulter scowled and hunched his powerful shoulders. He

sat there like a belligerent gorilla and his voice came out in a growl. 'Not too busy to hobnob with Ted Flint, is my guess. Or that bloody weasel Santana! I suppose you're into the same game, are you?'

'I don't know what you mean.'

Coulter jabbed a stiff finger in Arnold's direction. 'You've been sent in here to ward me off. It's not done too easy, believe me! But if I can't get to see Brent-Ellis, I'll tell you and you can scuttle back to him and give him the bad news, since he's too scared to see me personally. I know exactly what's going on in this rat-hole. I know Ted Flint's got this planning business all tied up, and I know that dragging in the Museums Department is Brent-Ellis's idea –'

He was certainly wrong there, Arnold considered, remembering the DDMA's penchant for leading a quiet life.

'– to try to delay things further. Well, it won't work! I've started collecting information on the Midnorth fiddle, and it won't be too long before I'll have enough to nail all you bastards to the wall. And don't try to tell me you know nothing about Midnorth: I know damn well that County Hall is up to its neck in –'

'Mr Coulter,' Arnold said wearily, 'it really is of no concern to me just what you're up to or what you think you know. I have no knowledge of, or information about, this Midnorth business, and our department is simply not involved, other than peripherally in view of the Santana submission, in the whole matter.'

'Do you know how much money I've got tied up in this venture?' Coulter hissed angrily.

'I don't know, and I don't want to know,' Arnold replied firmly. 'Now, if there is something specific, relating to this department's work, that you want to know about, I'll try to help you. Otherwise, if you've come in just to let off steam about the inquiry before the building sub-committee, I'm afraid you've come to the wrong place.'

Coulter stared at him fixedly for several seconds. Then, suspiciously, he asked, 'Do you know Ted Flint?'

'I know him slightly, in a professional capacity.'

Coulter snorted his contempt. He continued to eye Arnold warily, a gleam of doubt in his glance. 'You're not too happy about this . . . involvement, are you?'

Arnold shrugged. 'My feelings are irrelevant. But . . . it's not really anything to do with us.'

'That's the trouble . . . finding out who it *is* to do with!' Coulter hunched his shoulders in barely subdued anger. 'I'm not a violent man, but I know my rights and I know when I'm being given the runaround . . . and then I can get vicious. Once I know who's responsible.' He wrinkled his nose as though he smelled something unpleasant. 'This Flint character doesn't impress me. How does he strike you?'

'I really don't want to discuss –'

'He's a bit of a wimp, really,' Coulter went on, almost reflectively. 'A yes-man: a grey character who fronts up things, takes no real decisions himself – a party hack. But he's been surprisingly firm about Midnorth.'

He shot a quick, suspicious glance at Arnold, as though seeking confirmation. When Arnold gave no reaction, he went on, 'And he's not been afraid to outface me. There are those,' he added in a threatening tone, 'in the past, who *have* been afraid.'

'That may be so, Mr Coulter,' Arnold said, 'but this conversation is getting us nowhere.'

Coulter's eyes were glazed now, as he stared at Arnold. 'I'd heard Brent-Ellis isn't the kind of man who likes . . . disturbance. You, I've heard nothing about. But I'll tell you this, and you can pass it on to your boss. I think Ted Flint is covering up a scandal over Midnorth and I'm being blocked in my project. But I also think that Flint isn't muscular enough to do that on his own. Someone's behind him: there's a puppet master pulling his bloody strings. I'd hoped I'd learn something here today. No matter: I'll find out, in my own way. And when I do find out . . .'

His features were suddenly suffused with blood – a quick, uncontrolled violence rising to the surface. He clenched his fists as he rose to his feet and strode towards the doorway. At the door he paused, and glared back at Arnold. 'You tell your bloody boss. When I find out just who's pulling Flint's strings – I'll break his bloody back!'

The threat was still on Arnold's mind when he boarded the Metro and took the short journey from Kenton Bank Foot into Newcastle. He had not reported back to Brent-Ellis, for several reasons: there was little really to report. Brent-Ellis wouldn't have relished hearing about threats, and in any case the DDMA had already left the office for one of his golfing jaunts. It concerned Arnold somewhat that Coulter was still insisting there was some kind of chicanery behind the Santana archaeological submission, but his own conscience was clear: he had advised the committee as to the validity of the submission and the importance of the site, and that was as far as he was called upon to go.

Council corruption – if it existed – was nothing to do with him.

It was only a short walk from Grey Street to the university library. Arnold came out of the Metro station to find the streets were crowded: in spite of recession there still seemed to be plenty of people shopping in the city centre. The university library itself was almost empty: students had already gone down after the early summer examinations. He had a few words with the sub-librarian, explained who he was, and after filling in a card was allowed to enter the stack room where she assured him he should be able to find the volumes Sinclair had advised him to check.

She made a list of the books he required, for security reasons, she explained, and then allowed him to enter the stack room where he would be able to make use of one of the carrels.

He worked there for the rest of the morning. At twelve-thirty he managed to get hold of some ancient county volumes relating to the Borders, and some old genealogical tables that Sinclair had not mentioned. There was also a history of the Scots Guard, written in the 1830s, which he found tucked away in a dark corner. It was dusty, and clearly had not been used for some time. At two o'clock he decided he'd better get some lunch.

He was tempted to walk down through Grey Street to the Quayside, where Jane Wilson would probably be at work in the bookshop she had inherited from her uncle – Arnold's old friend Ben Gibson. He bought himself a sandwich instead, and sat on a bench near Amen Corner, thinking about what he had been reading.

The arrival of de Goncourt, according to Sinclair, had startled the Templars and caused them to flee. The Setons were probably involved. And at a later date, when James Sandilands betrayed his trust, it was David Seton who had 'borne the cross'. But where had he carried it – and from whence had he taken it? The first problem to face was – where had the Templars gone when they left Kilclogan?

When he had finished the sandwich he crossed the road, and went down the side street to a small second-hand bookshop he knew: he soon found what he wanted there. The old map of the Border Country cost him five pounds. He took it back with him to the library.

For the rest of the afternoon he worked quietly in the stack room. An occasional sub-librarian disturbed him, walking past on some errand or other. And at one point the footsteps that seemed to be moving past stopped, and Arnold was aware of someone staring at him.

Arnold looked up. The face was familiar: it was Colin Bannock's companion, from the pub.

'Mr Landon. Are you finding what you look for?'

'Hello, Mr Burnley. Your staff have been most helpful,' Arnold replied non-committally.

Burnley hesitated, glancing at the volumes surrounding Arnold on the narrow desk. He wrinkled his nose, as though sniffing for trouble. 'You're researching into the Border Wars?'

'Not exactly. But I must say you have an interesting and eclectic collection . . . for a university library.'

'We have all sorts of demands made upon us here,' Burnley replied vaguely. There was an odd hostility in his glance as he stared at Arnold: it was as though he resented the fact of Arnold's presence. Or perhaps it had something to do with Arnold's refusal to join the man's precious Order of Sangréal.

'Well, I won't detain you longer,' Burnley said after a short silence.

Arnold went back to his studies.

He was pursuing two lines of inquiry. The first related to the history of the Scots Guard, and the part played in its formation and later history by the Seton family. It was quite clear they had been central to its organization. Arnold read about the links with France: uniquely Scottish, the Guard had yet played out their early years in France, and this led to a paving of the way for the refuge which the last Stuarts found in France. It also led, in Arnold's view, to the kind of Jacobite Freemasonry – a Templar-orientated Freemasonry – which coalesced around them.

The Setons were closely involved and he was able to trace their later history from a nineteenth-century text which had been produced in a private limited edition, detailing the genealogy and the holdings of the Setons. There was only one reference to David Seton himself: an obscure one to Seton of March.

When he found himself getting bogged down in that inquiry, Arnold turned to the other line. Sinclair had sketched for him the likely events that had followed the arrival of Simon de Goncourt at Kilclogan. The inquisitor, furious at having lost the trail of the Templars, and at the lack of support he received from the Bishop of St Andrews, had inveighed in Edinburgh and London loudly, but to little avail. On the other hand, there were scattered clues in the volumes recommended by Sinclair: Arnold was able to note the routes and trails that de Goncourt had followed and the castles and churches he had visited, albeit unsuccessfully.

But he learned little from that. It was only when he began to trace the ancient roads on the Borders map, and check them with known presbyteries and churches, preceptories and castles, that the beginnings of a thesis came into his mind.

He explained it later that day, when he finally walked

down to the Quayside bookshop and persuaded Jane to make him a cup of tea.

'It's the theory of the fox,' he suggested as she poured his tea.

'What the hell is that supposed to mean?'

'It's the thought that when chased hard, the fox will often double back on his tracks, lay false trails – and then go somewhere, a safe haven, which the hounds would not return to. One maybe they'd already checked.'

Jane sat down and sipped at her own tea. 'You think the Templars may have gone back on their own tracks while de Goncourt was at their heels?'

'It's possible. Look here.' Arnold dragged forward the map he had bought. 'Here's the site for Kilclogan Castle. That was the last chance de Goncourt had to catch them and he blew it. Then he harried them throughout Scotland, not helped by the Bishop's intransigence, but he never caught up with them, apparently. Maybe it was because they were no longer there.'

'In Scotland, you mean?'

'That's right. Maybe they'd left Bruce's domain, and gone back south.'

'To England? But that would have been playing right into de Goncourt's hands! To land themselves under the jurisdiction of Edward –'

'Why? The English king had already shown himself reluctant to enforce the papal decrees! And with de Goncourt chasing around Scotland, making a fool of himself . . . Look, you see this pattern of roads marked here – they are the ancient tracks and roads that were in use, as far as we know, in the fourteenth century. They follow the obvious lines of the land, so there's no problem there. The inquisitor did not have the political strength to close those roads, and he was too late anyway . . . but what was to prevent the Templars from running south again, away from Edinburgh and danger? Robert Bruce would support them, of course, but a little discreet tucking away for a while . . .'

Jane shook her head. 'Seems thin to me. What would you be looking for, then?'

'I'm not sure.' Arnold pursed his lips. 'But, for a start, maybe a Templar foundation that post-dated de Goncourt's search. A property – a church maybe, or a castle, which would have Templar connections, and was certainly later a Templar holding. And one located in the Border Country – not Scotland, but under the sway of Edward . . . Remote, where too many questions wouldn't be asked.' Arnold leaned back in his chair. 'When I've finished my tea I'd like to have a look on your top shelves. Ben used to keep all sorts of old stuff up there, on churches and foundations and medieval holdings. He had some funny tastes.'

'He was *your* friend,' she snorted.

After two hours poring through the top shelves, Arnold had found nothing that seemed of any assistance. When he expressed his disappointment, Jane chided him. 'You don't even know what you're looking for. When Sinclair said he was relying on your luck that's one thing – but now *you*'re beginning to rely on it. You might just as well pick any old route guide, or general genealogical table – and we've got a few of those – and hope for the best! You should know, Arnold, it's hard work, not luck, that brings dividends.'

He stared at her, slightly discomfited. 'Well, why don't we do just that?' he suggested. 'Let's look at some old genealogical tables. I don't suppose you have anything on old Scottish families!'

'Ben kept something on everything,' she replied sarcastically. 'Try under "S". He also had an idiosyncratic filing system!'

Arnold laughed and turned back to the shelves. He snorted. 'Well, I'm damned, you're right. He did keep tables of the Scottish nobility under "S".'

He brought the heavy volume down and placed it on the table in the back room. He opened it and dust drifted about them, fine and irritating. Jane sneezed.

'Here's the Setons,' Arnold said.

'And there's David Seton,' Jane added, pointing, with her finger touching the heraldic device. Arnold pushed the finger aside and peered more closely at the device. 'What is that?' he wondered.

'The armorial bearings,' Jane replied.

'Yes, but look closely at them. The sword in the corner.'

'So?'

'It's a Templar sword.'

'Is that unusual?' she queried.

'No . . . but I've never seen it allied to . . . what is that? A cornucopia?'

Jane leaned over him, her hands on his shoulder as she peered closely at the bearings. 'Wait a moment, while I get my sewing glass.'

She came back a few minutes later with a plastic magnifying sewing glass. 'We're none of us getting younger,' she said defensively.

Arnold ignored her, took the glass and inspected the armorial bearings. 'It's a cornucopia, right enough. The horn of plenty. But there's something else. Look.'

For a moment, she saw nothing, then she muttered under her breath. She looked at Arnold, frowning. 'Vine leaves, writhing out of the horn, and down to its base. Are you suggesting . . . ?'

'A link with the chapel? I don't know yet. Let's check the bearings in the index.'

Carefully, he turned the old, yellowed sheets until he reached the index. He sought out the name, then read it aloud.

'David Seton, of March . . . That's what it said in the book I looked at in the library. But where the hell is March?'

They checked the maps they had in their possession, including the one Arnold had bought. They found no mention of March. Finally, Arnold rang Sinclair and told him of their puzzlement. He was silent for a long time at the end of the phone, and when he finally spoke there was an odd reluctance in his tone.

'I'm not sure what you've found, but there's only one way

to check it, as far as I can see. The university library has a copy of the chartulary of the *Terrae Templariae*. It might be worth checking there. I'd do it for you, but I'm not exactly *persona grata* there.'

'I don't understand,' Arnold puzzled.

'The book is old and rare, even as a copy. It can be accessed only with permission. Mr Burnley would certainly bar me access to it.'

'Would he refuse me?' Arnold asked.

'He is very protective . . . and if he thought it had anything to do with the Order of Sangréal –'

'Which it doesn't.'

'The suspicion would be enough.'

'I am not without friends in the university,' Arnold said pompously.

'Pompous ass,' Jane said when he replaced the phone.

3

Professor Vidal Santana was a birdlike man with all the quick nervousness of the species. His features were sallow and his hair was dark and carefully parted; his eyes were black and sharp, and his nose had the lean, curving narrowness of a predatory beak. He wore a neat jacket and dark grey slacks: his bow tie was the only startling incongruity about him: an affectation – it served to demonstrate that he was not a colourless husk of an archaeologist, but was a man who could make statements.

'You don't know the trouble I've had, Mr Landon,' he stated.

'I'm sorry if I've caused you problems,' Arnold replied as he seated himself in the professor's office. 'But what sort of trouble do you mean?'

Santana gestured towards the thick volume on the leather-topped desk in front of him. 'It wasn't easy getting hold of that.'

'I can't imagine why.'

'Nor I.' Santana peered at the leather cover. '*Terrae*

Templariae. From the librarian's attitude you'd think it was one of the keys to heaven. What's so important about it?'

'It's a copy of a rare book.'

'The library's full of rare books.' Santana tugged at his bright bow tie. 'Getting access to them isn't normally like getting access to Fort Knox. Some librarians seem to believe the library is their own special preserve.'

'It's an important job,' Arnold offered.

'And I hold a professorial post in the university.' Santana sniffed, his sallow features taking on a lugubrious air. He eyed Arnold from behind his beak of a nose. 'I got a message from the head of the department – I believe you know him.'

'Professor Gregory. Yes. We've worked together from time to time.'

'Hmmm. He said that you'd been refused access to this document. Why was that, Mr Landon?'

'I applied to the librarian – Mr Burnley. I was told it was a matter of university policy not to give access to non-university members,' Arnold replied coolly. 'But I've always understood that the encouragement of research was a matter of university policy – not its prevention.'

'Quite so,' Santana said, after a short pause. He seemed to be weighing up Arnold. 'So you made use of your contacts . . . approached Professor Gregory.'

'That's right. I was told that as an outsider I couldn't have access. So it seemed simpler to gain access through a member of the university.'

Santana sniffed again. He seemed doubtful. He eyed the volume as though it were covered in snakeskin. 'I can't understand what all the fuss is about, but Professor Gregory vouches for you and I see no reason why I shouldn't help. I must say, though, the form filling that went on surprised me. The librarian made me agree to an indemnity, ensuring that the volume did not leave my custody. It's almost as though he feels you'd be interfering in his own researches or something. Academics can be like that, you know – protective of their own patch.'

'So I can't take it away from this office?'

'I'm afraid not.' Santana inspected the volume again, gingerly. 'I really cannot see why not, but I gave the guarantee . . .' He twitched his bow tie again. 'However, the arrangement I've agreed with Professor Gregory is that you could undertake your . . . ah . . . reading of the volume here in my office. I'll be working here today so if you can agree to those conditions, there's no reason why you can't use the book.'

'I see no problem with that, Professor,' Arnold said gently.

Santana picked up the book, hefted it in his hands for a few seconds and then walked across to the small writing desk placed in front of the window. 'You can look at it here. I'll be working at my desk and I shouldn't interrupt you. I've got some rather long papers to read on archaeological matters.' As he spoke, his eyes suddenly clouded, and he looked again at Arnold, carefully. But he said no more.

When Santana sat down, Arnold took the place allocated to him near the window. He caressed the ancient leather of the book before he opened the covers: the copy was seventeenth century in origin although the original, which Sinclair had told him had been discovered in Malta, would have been fourteenth-century.

It had been written in Latin, of course: the lingua franca of the medieval world, before French had taken its place. Arnold had not received a classical education, although his interests in adult life had forced him to make a study of the language. He was not proficient, however, but he had brought in his briefcase a Latin dictionary which he could use to decipher any phrases that presented particular problems.

He began to work his way through the index.

The book consisted of a long list of place names, with a brief explanation of the holdings associated with the location. There was no map, but Arnold had his own map to refer to, and soon found that he was able to trace the more obvious locations. He also discovered that the descriptions of the holdings included the names of families associated with them on occasions, and he was able to make a note of names such as the Montgomeries and the Setons from time to time, while the Latin dictionary proved useful with some of the more esoteric words he came across.

It was long, dusty, detailed work.

From time to time Arnold heard Professor Santana sigh and shuffle his feet in frustration at what he was reading; on a couple of occasions Arnold looked up to catch Santana staring at him, but there was a vagueness about the glance that made Arnold guess the archaeologist was not really seeing him, but concentrating on matters in hand.

Almost two hours sped by. There was a light tap on the door and a middle-aged woman in a brown cardigan looked in. 'Professor Santana, would you like a coffee now?'

'Please, Geraldine; and perhaps . . . Mr Landon?'

'That would be most welcome.'

The woman withdrew and Arnold went back to his work. Several minutes elapsed, and then the door opened again, and Geraldine backed her broad posterior into the room with two cups in her hand and a package under her arm.

'The post has arrived too, Professor Santana –'

At that moment the package slid as the pressure from her elbow relaxed, she jerked sideways in an attempt to prevent it falling, and spilled part of the coffee in one of the cups.

The package fell to the carpet. 'Oh dear!' she exclaimed and stood there helplessly as Arnold rose from his seat and picked up the package. 'I'm terribly sorry. I'll make another cup, if you'll just wait a few minutes. I can easily put the kettle on again.'

Arnold smiled. 'There's no rush.' He placed the package on Santana's desk, inadvertently glancing at the label as he did so. The sender was named as the Midnorth Consultancy Group. He looked up. Santana was staring at him again. His beaky nose seemed to quiver.

Geraldine placed Santana's cup down, bobbed her head to Arnold and left the room to make a fresh cup. Arnold went back to his seat. Santana said nothing, but there was a sudden edginess in the atmosphere. Arnold went on with his work, moving onwards down the page, reading through the list of

Templar holdings and attempting to identify them on his map.

After a little while, the broad-beamed Geraldine came back with the second cup of coffee. She apologized profusely to Arnold as she placed it in front of him. After she had gone, he sipped the coffee and looked up, to meet Santana's glance.

The sallow-faced professor seemed uneasy. He blinked. 'Mr Landon . . . You work in the Department of Museums and Antiquities at Morpeth, I understand.'

'That's right.'

There was a short pause. 'You wouldn't have been present at the recent building sub-committee meeting, would you?'

'I was there, yes.'

Santana grimaced nervously. His black eyes were evasive. 'I'd heard that there was a representative from that department . . . I had a submission going there, you see.'

'I know.'

'So it would have been you, Mr Landon, who spoke up in favour of the submission before the committee.'

'That was my function,' Arnold agreed. 'I was briefed to do it. But I was happy to support it. The Ogle excavation is an important one: I am quite sure that we have a great deal to learn yet from further work there.'

'Of course . . .' Santana frowned, thinking, until light suddenly dawned. 'Landon . . . You will be the man who found the *sudarium*,' he said abruptly.

Arnold made no reply, but sipped his coffee. Santana wriggled in his seat. 'Anyway, both Professor Gregory and I were grateful for the support you gave the department over the matter. In the face of . . .' He hesitated, looking away, studying his notes for a moment, clearly wondering whether to go further. 'That was a remarkable outburst in the committee, I understand.'

'Outburst?' Arnold asked unhelpfully.

'From Mr Coulter.' Santana's reply was quick. 'I gather he raised all sorts of comments . . . threats, even. The man is clearly deranged . . . a persecution complex, or something like that.' His eyes strayed inadvertently to the package on his desk. 'I gather my name was brought up.'

'It was your submission, Professor Santana.'

'Yes, but I mean Coulter said . . . certain things. I've made no secret,' he added in a defensive manner, 'of my connection with Midnorth. It's a matter of university policy . . . we are encouraged to do outside work that increases our efficiency . . .' He was beginning to flounder. He gestured almost angrily towards the package in front of him. 'I've had a consultancy with them for years. I'm a qualified architect as well as archaeologist. So there was no reason for Coulter to make those wild accusations. It was slanderous.'

'Someone there actually made that point,' Arnold replied gently.

'But what did the committee make of it, do you think?' Santana asked.

Arnold shrugged. 'I don't know. They agreed to support your submission. Coulter left the room and no further discussion took place about the . . . issues he raised.'

'Were they seen as that, then? *Issues?*'

There was a sharp, fearful edge to Santana's tone. Arnold shrugged. 'I really can't say.'

'My conscience is absolutely clear,' Santana said, staring directly at Arnold.

The insincerity in his tone was matched by Arnold's own. 'I'm sure it is, Professor Santana.'

Arnold returned to his study of *Terrae Templariae*. He was oddly disturbed. There was no reason why Santana should have reacted the way he did to Arnold's catching sight of a package from Midnorth, addressed to the professor. There was no reason for him to defend himself to Arnold. It could only mean that the professor himself was uneasy about the relationship with Midnorth, that he was compulsively eager to defend himself against even imagined dangers – but it was none of Arnold's business, and he did not want to get involved with political matters such as the Coulter–Santana affair.

He had enough on his plate as it was.

The two men worked on in silence. When Arnold left to get some lunch the volume remained in Santana's office; the professor ceremoniously locked the door behind them. 'I'll be back at two,' he said, but did not meet Arnold's eye. It was clear he was regretting the display of nervousness he had shown earlier.

Santana was already back at his desk when Arnold returned a little after two o'clock. They did not speak: each got down to the work in front of them. As Arnold continued to plough through the lists, he found little that was useful, and he was beginning to believe that it was a waste of time. It was three-thirty before he picked up the name David Seton for the first time. He went rapidly down the page: the name cropped up on a further four occasions in the list of holdings. He had clearly reached a section in which the Seton family had been connected with a list of Templar lands. There were two crofts, a preceptory, a manor house, and a chapel. All Templar holdings, all named, and all allocated to David Seton.

But none were called March: the manor house, on the other hand, was stated to be Marchment.

Arnold sat back in his chair and stared out of the window. He wondered whether the later writers had slipped up – made an error in describing Seton as being of March, rather than Marchment. He turned back to the volume, moved on through the next few pages and then came upon the name again.

David Seton: the living of the Church of the Holy Cross, Temple Marchment. Arnold turned quickly back to his map: there was no sign in the Border area of a village called Temple Marchment, or of a church in such a location.

But that did not mean it had not existed, in the fourteenth century.

Abruptly, he rose to his feet.

'You've finished?'

'I think so. I'm grateful for the use of your office, Professor Santana.'

'You found what you were looking for then?' Santana asked curiously.

'I believe so. The book –'

'Don't worry about it.' Santana's glance strayed towards the *Terrae Templariae*. 'I'll see to it that it gets back safely to the university library. Huh, it would be worth more than my life if I didn't . . .'

'Give my thanks to Professor Gregory. This has been a great help.'

'All in the interests of research,' Santana said gravely. Arnold nodded and made his way to the door. As he looked back, closing the door behind him, he saw Santana begin to open the package he had received from the Midnorth Consultancy Group.

The next few days were busy for Arnold, and the files he was dealing with at the office meant work at home as well: he suspected that his insistence on having a day's leave, to investigate the Templar leads, had led to Brent-Ellis taking revenge, placing some urgent matters on his desk so that he was kept more than fully occupied.

Towards the end of the week he did manage a telephone conversation with Sinclair where he was able to give him the results of his researches, and his study of the *Terrae Templariae*. He also mentioned the obstructive tactics employed by Burnley.

Sinclair humphed. 'You don't surprise me. I told you Burnley was committed to this Order of his; I've no doubt he believes that the *Terrae Templariae* is private property. Private to his Order, I mean.'

'But it's university-owned, and has nothing to do with the Ancient Order of Sangréal, anyway.'

'That's not how he would see it. Anything to do with Templar research would, in his view, touch dangerously upon the secrets of his society. And I've no doubt he'll have talked it over with his Master, as well. Never mind – stuff them! What about this Marchment place?'

'It doesn't appear on the maps, but I've ordered a copy

from the national library at Wetherby of a research volume on *Deserted Medieval Villages*. There's the possibility that Temple Marchment – which certainly is catalogued in *Terrae Templariae* as a Templar holding – might have disappeared as an entity in the sixteenth century. There are many such deserted villages scattered throughout Northumbria, and they don't appear on the maps.'

'It's a possibility.'

'I should get the book by Friday. If I do turn it up, I'll get in touch, and maybe we can visit, to see what we can find.'

'With Wilson in tow?' Sinclair asked lightly.

'She's always interested in old locations she might use in her fiction,' Arnold replied.

On the Friday morning the book arrived, as he had anticipated. Arnold put it on one side, to check through that evening when he got back from work. He drove the car out of the garage to make the short journey into Morpeth. He turned on the radio for the local news broadcast.

He learned that early that morning the body of an unidentified man had been dragged from the Tyne at North Shields.

4

Culpeper scowled up at the hazy sun, and hunched his shoulders against the cool breeze that swept up from the mouth of the Tyne. From where he stood on the steps leading down to the murky waters, he could see the outline of Tynemouth Abbey, its ruined shell fingering gauntly against the sky; beyond was the fading hull of the North Sea ferry, disappearing in the haze on its way to Bergen. It was a trip he'd always vowed to take, but had never actually made. For that matter, Newcastle itself was almost Norwegian at weekends in Marks and Spencer, he grumbled to himself, with all the shoppers coming over for cheap, quality goods.

But there'd be no chance that the guy they'd hauled out at the foot of the steps was an itinerant seaman or weekend shopper. A businessman, and local, more like, from the way he'd been dressed. As for his being here, near the mouth of the Tyne, Culpeper knew enough from his experience of suicides in the Tyne that the body had been in the water for a couple of days at least, and had probably been dumped into the river further upstream. The current had a way of tumbling a corpse down this way, or across to Jarrow Slake.

The body had been found early that morning, by some bright spark who had made two phone calls – one to the police and one to the newspapers. That was something Culpeper could have done without: media attention was the last thing he wanted at the beginning of an investigation. His relations with the local pressmen were not of the best. When Culpeper had been assigned to the case he had decided he'd take the chance for some fresh air and come out to view the scene of the crime.

The unit had practically finished by the time Culpeper had arrived, and the corpse had been taken back to Gosforth in a shell, to the forensic laboratory there. All Culpeper had seen was the man's clothing and the fish-nibbled, swollen, unrecognizable face, before they'd carted the corpse off to Gosforth. Farnsby had gone along with it: let him inhale formaldehyde for a while. Culpeper would settle for ozone.

He began to climb back up the steps to the car. His driver was waiting, a fresh-faced constable who was still wet behind the ears. He seemed pleased to be involved, even if only peripherally, in a murder investigation. He'd learn better, in time, Culpeper considered grimly: there was no glamour in death. Culpeper nodded to him. 'Back to HQ, and let's get started on the paperwork, son.'

As he climbed into the car the radio crackled. The driver looked questioningly at Culpeper. 'Go ahead, son.'

The message was brief. It was from Vic Farnsby.

'We've got a make on the dead man, sir.'

'Papers?'

'It wasn't a mugging, or a robbery with violence, sir. Wallet untouched. Credit cards still there. But that's the good news.'

'Tell me.'

'It'll hit the headlines, this killing. He's well known in important circles.'

Culpeper groaned. 'Let's have it.'

'He's a politician; a lawyer. Well known. His name's Colin Bannock.'

Culpeper started. Bannock. He had a brief momentary glimpse, in his mind's eye, of a suave man standing up in a committee room, speaking smoothly, persuasively . . . then there was the recent image of white, bloated flesh, picked at and torn. Culpeper thrust the image aside and stared gloomily out of the window as the car headed back along the river to Newcastle.

A politician – and a lawyer. For screaming headlines, Culpeper could hardly think of a worse combination.

Colin Bannock's cottage was in the high street in Warkworth, halfway up the steep rise towards the castle. Culpeper had been up to the ruins of the favourite residence of the Percys a few times as a tourist with his wife: they'd walked around the great motte and bailey with their son when he was young, and taken the boat trip along the loop of the Coquet to visit the fourteenth-century hermitage and chapel.

And he liked the village itself. The borough had been established in the twelfth century, stretching down from the castle to the bridge over the Coquet. The bridge was still there, defended by a gatehouse, one of the few fortified bridges left in Britain, he understood. Now swallows and martins flew low under its parapets, nesting in the stonework. And the steep street houses fetched stiff prices, from businessmen in Northumberland or second home owners further south.

The cottage was similar to the medieval houses it shouldered: a burgage plot, a long garden at the rear running down to where the Coquet curved in its long loop around the castle towering above. The cottage itself was eighteenth-century, however: there had been some major reconstructions at that time.

It held three bedrooms but only one of them seemed to have been in regular use. Three reception rooms downstairs were expensively furnished: two as sitting-rooms, one as an office. It was from here that Colin Bannock had managed his professional life: he had his lawyer's office in Morpeth but the story was that he rarely used it of recent years, leaving the business to his partners as he came more and more to concentrate upon his political activities.

Culpeper prowled around the sitting-rooms, taking down a photograph from the mantelpiece. It showed a woman in her late thirties, smiling vaguely at the camera. Farnsby moved to his shoulder; Culpeper gestured to the photograph. Farnsby nodded.

'It's his wife, I believe.'

Culpeper looked around him. He was a married man; he knew what the house of a married man looked like, and smelled like. This didn't: it had a bachelor air about it, self-indulgence, a lack of frippery, a solid, heavy practicality that suggested no woman's touch.

'She died about eight years ago, it seems,' Farnsby explained. 'Cancer. She left him a fair bit of money. It's when he took up politics seriously.'

'Where'd you get that from so quickly?' Culpeper asked in a nettled tone.

'Newspaper obituary. They had a file on him. The *Journal* editor let me have a copy.'

'Don't believe all you read in the newspapers,' Culpeper growled. 'You got someone going through the office papers in there?'

'Yes, sir. Nothing so far.'

'Not even theories?'

Farnsby ran his tongue around the roof of his mouth and shrugged. 'Not a mugging, or a robbery, that's clear. Maybe someone he knew. Maybe a political motive – or a legal one. We do have someone who's being interviewed right now; made a statement about seeing a quarrel between two men the other evening, on the Quayside – but quarrels down there, even with the sound of a splash afterwards, are common enough. Newcastle police came up with that one for us. Bannock being found near Shields, though, means it's still in our bailiwick, wherever the killing took place.'

'Did Bannock visit Newcastle often?'

'He had a subsidiary office there. Enough reasons to be in the city. And plenty of acquaintances.'

'Diary entry?'

'No diary yet. People in the office have been questioned – preliminary. They reckon he didn't keep them regularly informed of his movements: just told them when he was coming in. And he didn't keep an office diary.'

Culpeper walked through into the room used as an office. It was a large room, holding two filing cabinets and a broad, reproduction Georgian desk. A leather swivel chair stood in front of the desk. There was a picture of the Queen on the wall, and one of Cambridge University behind the door. The detective-constable standing beside the filing cabinet was taking out files and placing them carefully in a box.

There were only a few scattered papers on the desk itself. 'No diary, hey?' Culpeper murmured to himself.

'We've cleared the drawers – except that one,' Farnsby pointed. 'It's locked. No key to be found yet.'

'And no imagination,' Culpeper scowled. 'All right, son, take a break,' he suggested to the constable. When the young man stepped outside, Culpeper drew a small penknife from his pocket. 'When you come up through the system the way I did, you learn all sorts of villainous tricks.'

'Do you think that's wise, sir?' Farnsby asked evenly as Culpeper advanced towards the locked drawer.

'You can look the other way if you like, Farnsby,' Culpeper replied, and applied himself to the lock on the drawer.

It took no longer than thirty seconds. 'There you are, not a scratch. Now, if it had been a real Georgian desk,' Culpeper breathed, 'I bet I'd have had more trouble than that. Still, let's take a look, shall we? When a man locks a desk, he's usually got something to hide . . .'

Carefully, Culpeper emptied the desk. He placed the small, leatherbound book to one side, almost with anticipatory delight, while he worked his way through the scattered papers he found underneath it. They looked interesting: legal papers relating to some committee activities in the council, reference documents regarding various business commitments Bannock seemed to have entered, and a few private letters.

'We'll read them later,' he suggested. 'Pack them up with the rest. But meanwhile, let's see what we can see . . .'

He opened the leatherbound book. It was an address book. Slowly he read it, page by page. Some of the names he recognized as councillors, businessmen, important people in the county. Others were the names of firms, legal contacts, the detritus of a public and professional life. Then he paused, and sat staring at the page in silence, his face draining of colour.

'You found something, sir?' Farnsby asked in a husky voice.

'Found something?' Culpeper seemed almost dazed. 'Yes, you might say that . . .' His hand was shaking slightly as he gently closed the book. 'You might even say we've hit the bloody jackpot!'

4

1

Deputy Chief Constable Baistow strode into the conference room and took the seat at the end of the polished table. His shoulders were squared, and his brow furrowed with resolution as he tidied the papers he had carried in with him, but he was pale, and Culpeper thought he could see lines around the man's mouth that he had never noticed before.

There were five officers in the room: apart from Culpeper and Baistow, Vic Farnsby was present, together with Detective-Inspector O'Connor and a detective-sergeant called Hargreave. The meeting had been called urgently that morning, by the chief constable, but it was Baistow who took the chair.

'The chief asked me to convene this meeting,' Baistow began, in a low, controlled tone, 'so that we may forestall any problems that are likely to arise during the next few days of the Bannock inquiry. This week is almost certainly going to be hairy; after that, we can hopefully expect the noise to die down somewhat. It's necessary that all of you now drop whatever else you're doing – O'Connor, for instance, you can leave off the inquiry you're presently on and assist Culpeper – for the time being at least – with the Bannock killing.' He paused, looked slowly around the table, staring at each man in turn. 'It's also been decided that we need top level involvement on this one, so all reporting will be done directly to me.'

Culpeper cleared his throat. Baistow glared at him, as though expecting an argument. Culpeper said nothing, but perhaps the look in his eye made Baistow decide to justify the stance.

'I appreciate some of you might regard that as an unusual step. But the fact of the matter is, we have an unusual situation. Colin Bannock wasn't just a local businessman; he was a local politician who was well known in the county, and had made quite a reputation for himself. Now, the press are going to be wanting answers soon, and we're likely to be well hounded. If we're not extremely careful we could be pushed into statements that might be . . . embarrassing. With me in charge, it means I can deal with any issues that arise.'

'What kind of issues, sir?' Culpeper asked, his mouth oddly dry.

Baistow hesitated. 'Bannock was a politician. There's the chance that some . . . delicate matters might get aired. Before anyone goes talking out of turn, it's as well that clearance is obtained.'

'From County Hall, you mean?' Culpeper persisted.

'From relevant sources,' Baistow snapped. 'We don't want any scaremongering here, and we don't want libel suits being slapped around the place. We have to tread delicately in a case like this, so the chief and I have decided that I'll handle press matters. That was the first reason for calling this case conference: to make the position clear. The second is to confer amongst ourselves – to determine just what we've got. Farnsby, I believe you've been dealing with detail?'

Vic Farnsby nodded. He leaned forwards in his seat. 'The preliminary forensic report is in, sir. It discloses that Bannock was killed by several blows to the head, at least two from behind. It might have been someone he knew, for it clearly was not a robbery situation. Nothing of consequence seems to have been taken from the body.'

'Any thoughts about place of death?'

Farnsby glanced at Culpeper. 'Though the body was found near Tynemouth, on the North Shields shore, we don't think the murder took place there. The likelihood is that he was killed further upstream – maybe even at the Quayside –'

'Supposition?' Baistow snapped.

'We have a report of an altercation three nights ago, and the sound of a body falling into the river.'

'Witness?'

Farnsby shrugged. 'Not terribly reliable. Can't identify the individuals, didn't really see much, was coming out of one of the local pubs . . .'

'If Bannock was killed at the Quayside, there's a strong possibility the body would have been swept by the tides around to the point we found him,' Culpeper added.

Baistow eyed him coldly. 'Local knowledge?'

'Long experience.'

Baistow was aware of the gibe; his eyes narrowed. 'All right, what else have we got?'

'No office record of his movements,' Farnsby continued. 'He'd spent little time at the firm of late; wheeling and dealing with the council most of the time –'

'What do you mean, wheeling and dealing?' Baistow demanded, sitting up.

Farnsby's eyes widened. 'Just a phrase, sir. I mean . . . he's been mainly on council business.'

'That's the kind of careless remark that can cause trouble,' Baistow said coldly. 'Go on.'

'There is a sub-office for Bannock's law firm in Newcastle, and there's the possibility he went there on the day he was killed. But again, no record. He seems to have kept his movements very much to himself.'

'Did he use a pocket diary?' O'Connor asked. 'Most businessmen keep pocket diaries.'

'It wasn't on him. It might have been the one thing that was taken,' Farnsby replied.

'To wipe out the record of his movements – and maybe the identity of the person he met,' Baistow said. 'What about his house?'

Before Farnsby could reply, Culpeper intervened. 'I was with Farnsby when the house was searched. Bannock had an office there – we gave it a good going over, and brought in piles of documents for investigation here.'

'I'd like to have a look at those myself,' Baistow said,

unexpectedly. Culpeper felt something move in his chest as he stared at the deputy chief constable: Baistow's eyes were hooded, yet watchful, and there was an odd nervousness about his mouth. 'Are they boxed up in the inquiry room?'

'Yes, sir.'

'I'll take a quick look through the papers after this meeting. Anything else?'

Culpeper leaned back in his chair. He folded his arms. 'No diary, for certain. The papers you'll look through might give us some leads, about enemies, business problems, the shenanigans Bannock was up to, that sort of thing. I was going to set Farnsby, and now maybe Hargreave here, to go through them this morning –'

'I'll take a preliminary sift myself,' Baistow insisted. His lips were pale: he was not enjoying this. 'Was there anything else turned up at the house?'

Slowly, Culpeper shook his head. 'Not so far, sir.'

Farnsby stiffened beside Culpeper and began to turn his head; he thought better of it and did not look at the senior officer. Nevertheless, Culpeper felt the tension rise in the room.

'Nothing at all?' Baistow asked.

'No. There are a few lines of inquiry I shall be following, of course . . .'

'Such as?'

'Too early to say, really,' Culpeper replied cheerfully. 'Certainly, too iffy at this stage to take up *your* time, sir.'

Baistow glared at him, his mouth working silently. There was something he wanted to say, but Culpeper guessed he dared not say it. At last, Baistow ground out, 'You'll keep me informed, of course.'

'Of course, sir,' Culpeper assured him in a placid tone.

Baistow rose abruptly to his feet. 'Well, if there's nothing else . . . Hargreave, you come with me. I want to have a quick look through the documentation that's been gathered, so I can familiarize myself with the possible issues that might arise. Gentlemen . . .'

He nodded grimly to them as they stood, and the meeting

broke up. Hargreave followed the deputy chief constable out of the room and Culpeper grimaced at Farnsby. Detective-Inspector O'Connor shuffled across the room to stand near Culpeper, peering at him suspiciously. 'So what was all that about?'

'I don't know what you mean.'

'You was needling him. What's going on here?'

Culpeper shrugged. 'You're reading something into nothing. What you really ought to ask is why the hell the top brass are getting involved – again – in basic investigations.'

'Maybe it's just Baistow's way,' O'Connor muttered.

'Checking through the documentation from Bannock's house? Or sifting it, as he says. More likely, weeding it for embarrassing material! Anyway, you're in the big league again now, O'Connor – away from back street investigations into doubtful building contractors and on to the investigation into the murder of a local bigwig.'

O'Connor grinned. 'That's right. Baistow pulled me off that quick enough when Bannock got chopped. He's taking this Bannock thing seriously, isn't he?' He paused, squinting suspiciously at Culpeper, wondering whether he was being diverted from something. 'Are you sure you're not holding back on some information?'

'You know me better than that,' Culpeper evaded him. 'Did you get anything interesting on Coulter?'

O'Connor snorted. 'Nothing you could haul him into court over. Plenty of suspicious thumpings, a hint of tax fiddles with the casual labourers, that sort of stuff. But mainly a waste of time. He's clearly got his knife into Councillor Flint, that's for sure, making all sorts of wild accusations, but I wasn't able to give Baistow any real dirt to throw at the guy. A hard case, a tough nut – a guy I wouldn't like to meet in a dark alley and a character with a real violent temper – but a crook? Nothing I could pin down.'

'Well, now you can concentrate with us on Bannock,' Culpeper said cheerfully, 'and see what we can pin on someone else.'

O'Connor grinned, ducked his head and made his way out

of the conference room. Culpeper started to gather up his papers. Farnsby stood staring at him quietly for a moment. At last he said, 'You're taking a hell of a chance.'

'Oh?'

'Not telling Baistow about the address book you found in Bannock's study. He specifically said –'

'To hell with what he said.'

'If he finds out –'

'Sod him. As far as I'm concerned, I'm following an interesting lead, and there's no reason for him to be involved. Besides, don't you think it all smells a bit? Baistow is running scared – didn't you see his face? But scared of what?'

'I'm not so sure that –'

'Pressure,' Culpeper interrupted. 'He's under some kind of pressure, the same kind of pressure he was responding to when he started fussing about the Coulter thing with O'Connor. But that's small beer now, because Bannock's been killed and someone is getting rather nervous. I mean to find out why. And I don't think that'll be made easier by my telling Baistow about the book. Let the bastard sweat a bit more!'

Farnsby followed Culpeper out into the corridor. His voice was edgy. 'All hell could break loose if he knew –'

'Who's going to tell him?'

'But if he finds out –'

'Finds out?' Culpeper challenged.

'Just who you've had brought in today.'

Culpeper stopped, turned, and grinned wolfishly at the younger man. 'By the time he does find out it'll be too late for him to interfere. By then, I think we'll have cracked the whole case!' He walked on jauntily, calling back over his shoulder, 'You can sit in on this one with me, if you like.'

When they reached the interview room he pushed open the door and smiled at the man seated in the chair behind the table. 'Hello, Frank,' he said genially. 'Nice to see you again!'

Frank Manley was sprawled easily in the hard-backed chair, making a show of bored confidence. His black shirt was open at the neck, displaying a tanned throat, and the fingers of his left hand were hooked into his belted slacks. He was smoking, dark eyes narrowed against the drift of smoke as he stared up at Culpeper. 'I thought you might be responsible for this,' he said harshly.

'*Might?* You should have been confident enough to count on it! How are they looking after you?'

'I've been here forty minutes. I want to leave as soon as possible. But –' Manley smiled thinly, confidently, '– I'm also interested in what the hell you've dragged me in here for.'

'Just a chat, Frank. Old times' sake.'

The reference to old times was not lost on Manley. He dragged on his cigarette, then stubbed it out deliberately in the ashtray in front of him. 'So what's this about?'

'You been busy lately, Frank? Haven't heard too much about you on the street.'

'Maybe you've been talking to the wrong people. I keep busy.'

'I bet.' Culpeper grinned sarcastically. 'But your kind of busy can be a bit . . . tricky, from time to time. Kind of on the dark edge, you know what I mean?'

'You been trying it on with me for years, but you still got nothing on me, Culpeper.'

'That's as may be.' Culpeper drew up a chair and sat down, as Farnsby moved to lean against the far wall, nodding to the constable on duty that he could leave. After the door closed behind him, Culpeper said softly, 'But I'm not really too interested in what you've been up to, actually. It's small beer now, isn't it?'

'What's that supposed to mean?'

Culpeper shook his head. 'I envy you; I really do. You must have had it made. Friends in high places . . . it's the kind of thing a petty villain like you dreams of. If you pull a caper, and the fuzz get wind of it, who cares? You can get it greased. Was that the way of it, Frank?'

'What the hell are you talking about?'

'Influence. Friends in high places. Power pays.'

Manley was silent for a little while. He sat glaring at Culpeper, thinking hard. He was edgy, but that could have been the influence of the surroundings; he was certainly worried about something, Culpeper was sure, but he was a long way from breaking.

'Can you give us an account of your whereabouts these last few nights?' Culpeper asked. 'Starting with . . . Tuesday, say?'

'Why?'

Culpeper spread his hands wide. 'Helping police with their inquiries, what else?'

'I know you, Culpeper. You'd love to fix one on me. But it's no go. I don't know what you're on about, I don't see how I can help you –'

'You could start by giving me a list of your friends and acquaintances.' Culpeper held up a hand. 'Not your run of West End villains who call themselves your muckers, I mean – but, well, other people. Sort of important people. *Prominent* people.'

Something moved deep in Manley's black eyes. He glanced across to the silent Farnsby, then back to Culpeper, calculating. At last he said, 'I don't have to take any of this. You want to tell me what it's all about, maybe I can clear things up. Otherwise –'

'You trying to persuade me you don't have influential friends? Aw, come on, Frank. Let me put it to you like this . . . A little while ago I knew I was on to something. You know damned well I was getting close on your little operations – the car scam. Then I get told I'm out of line: I should stop hassling you, the file was closed for lack of evidence. Who's kidding along here? Lack of evidence? Everyone knows about you in this nick, Frank, and I'm told to stop chasing you. Now that means, somewhere, you got friends.'

'You're pissing in the wind, Culpeper.'

Culpeper ignored the provocative scorn in Manley's tone. He leaned back, eyeing Manley with enjoyment. 'Not so. I got evidence.'

'About what?'

'About who your friend in high places was.'

Manley frowned, seemed about to laugh, but thought better of it. He straightened in his chair. 'Was?' The thought disturbed him, wrinkled his brow. 'I think it's time I was out of here.'

'Now be reasonable, Frank –'

'I know my rights. You want to ask me straight questions, maybe I'll answer them; or maybe I'll get my solicitor to sit in here with me. But this kind of chat doesn't go down with me. I want out.' He glowered at Culpeper sourly. 'Unless you want to tell me what this is about.'

Culpeper feigned consideration. 'Well, I'm not sure about that, because I still haven't got the picture clear myself, yet. But let me put it this way to you.' He paused, watching Manley carefully. 'How long have you known Colin Bannock?'

There was a long silence. Various emotions chased across Frank Manley's face. Initially, he was shaken, probably at the linking of his name with Bannock's, then by the realization that this interview was linked to a murder investigation. Culpeper saw the traps of his mind close, shutting out the pressure, clearing his mind of extraneous emotion; concentrating. Manley leaned forwards, one elbow on the table. 'Bannock? I never met the guy. That the one they found dead?'

'You knew about that? When?'

'Saw it in the paper.' Manley gritted his teeth scornfully.

'Weren't you sad, losing a friend?' Culpeper asked softly.

'I told you, never even met him.'

'You don't have to meet someone to know you've got a friend,' Culpeper replied. 'And are you sure you never met him – I mean, positive no one could ever say they saw you together?'

'I already told you – I never met him, and I didn't know him. What the hell is this? Are you trying to find some way to tie me in with his killing? That's crazy – I tell you he was a stranger to me!'

Culpeper smiled wolfishly. 'So how come your name appears scrawled inside his personal address book?'

The black eyes widened, then were slitted again in a sudden panic. Frank Manley took a deep breath and tried to relax, leaning back in his chair, the deliberate attitude an antidote to the tension that was rising in him. 'My name appears in his address book? Is it in yours, too? Am I some kind of local celebrity around here? How the hell should I know how my name is in that book – if it is!'

'It surely is, Frank. And it looks like his handwriting, too,' Culpeper assured him in a soft voice. 'You can't account for this, it seems.'

'The hell I can't! I never met Bannock; I never knew him; I don't think I even ever heard of him until they dragged him out of the Tyne. The newspaper accounts are headlines – that's all I know about it and him: the headlines. What the hell's going on here, Culpeper?' He stood up suddenly, sending the chair crashing backwards to the floor. 'I've had enough of this.'

Farnsby came up from his casual leaning against the wall, watchfully. Culpeper rose to his feet also, wary, but smiling. There was no humour in the smile. 'Bluster won't get you anywhere, Frank. Except in a cell. You've got to tell me things; things I want to hear. I want to know how come you knew Bannock, how come your name was in his little black book, and just what game was going on in which he and you were involved. There's no easy way out of this one, son.'

'Easy way?' Manley scoffed. 'There's only one way you'd want to see me go, Culpeper. You know, if you listen to the guys on the street, they'll tell you about the fuzz; they'll give you a thumbnail sketch of the guys they've bounced into over the years. And you know what your reputation is, Culpeper? Basically, a plod. There's some who'll tell you Culpeper's straight enough, all right, gives you a fair deal. Others don't rate you at all. But none of them know you the way I know you. What makes you tick inside.'

Culpeper felt the heat rising in his body. He clenched his fists. 'And what is it makes me tick?'

'A sour hate, a sickness in the head that has nothing to do with reason, or sense, or good police work. You got a sour gut, Culpeper, and it's been turning you all rotten for years. You got an obsession, and it's me: you won't rest until you put me inside on some charge or other. Trumped up will do, and that's what you're trying to do now. You want to tie me in some way to this Bannock killing, because you see it as a chance to get your own back after all these years. Why the hell you can't forget –'

'Forget?' Culpeper pushed his own chair aside and advanced towards Manley: fists clenched, jaw jutting belligerently. 'This will never be about forgetting –'

Farnsby stepped forward smoothly. He interposed his body between them, his back to Culpeper, staring at Manley. He barred Culpeper's way, cooling the atmosphere. 'All we're asking for is some information. Let's not get too excited here.'

'You tell *that* bastard to stop getting excited,' Manley grimaced, his black eyes burning with ill-concealed dislike. 'I don't know a thing about Bannock; I never even met him. The fact my name's in his book is your problem –'

'No. We don't have to explain that,' Culpeper said in a cold voice, slowly regaining control of himself. 'But you do. I've asked you for an explanation – you can give me none. Other names in that book are businessmen, personal friends, people in the circles in which Bannock moved legitimately. Your name stands out like a sore thumb. What's it doing there, Manley?'

'I don't bloody well know!'

And suddenly, Culpeper knew he was lying. Farnsby half turned his head, stepping back, and Culpeper realized that Farnsby knew it too. There was nothing either of them would be able to pin down: it was something in the swiftness of the reply; something in the tone or timbre of the voice. But something had happened; something had occurred to jar Manley suddenly. He was worried, and unconvincing.

'I want out of here, Culpeper,' Manley announced warningly.

Culpeper saw the pale sheen of sweat on the man's dark

forehead. 'Not today, Sonny Jim,' he said. 'Not until you come up with some real answers . . .'

He dragged his chair back to the table and sat down. After a moment, Manley followed suit. He seemed oddly shaken, but his mouth was set in a thin, determined line. 'Now then, suppose you reconsider your position, Frank,' Culpeper suggested soothingly, 'and we'll start at the beginning. Just when *did* you first meet Colin Bannock?'

2

'So,' Jane said, as she settled back on the settee with a glass of brandy in her hand, 'what did you learn from the book?'

She and Arnold had been to a concert at Durham University: it had not been an evening to remember as far as Arnold was concerned, since he was rather too lowbrow in his tastes to be inordinately excited by a string quartet playing pieces written by obscure eighteenth-century composers in a thinly-attended auditorium. But Jane had been given tickets by one of her university contacts – Professor Dennis, who Arnold suspected of having designs on Jane; and since the professor himself was unable to join her she had asked Arnold to go along. Now, they sat in the college junior common room, sipping superior brandy, and that at least was to Arnold's taste.

'*Deserted Medieval Villages*? Much of it dealt with background,' he replied, 'most of which I was familiar with. You know – the depopulation that occurred after the Norman invasion of 1066; the similar impact during the civil wars with Stephen and Matilda; and then the further depopulation – really, the often permanent village loss – caused by the development of monastic grange farming in the twelfth century.'

'None of that would apply to your search for Marchment,' Jane argued, 'because David Seton's dates are rather later.'

'That's so. But there's the Black Death to consider. Marginal settlements had already been shrinking before 1349, and certainly there are several well-documented cases of village destruction after the Black Death.'

'So do you think the plague could have caused the abandonment and destruction of Marchment?'

Arnold shook his head. 'I don't think so – at least, not directly. I had a word with a medieval historian at Newcastle about records: he suggested that the classical research sequence should be a check on the recorded population in 1086 – the Domesday Book – the village tax records of 1334, the records of high tax relief of 1352 under the Statute of Labourers, and then the poll tax records of 1377. More important, he suggested, was the question of relief from parish tax: there are records in 1428 of such cases. The disappearance of a village name from tax rolls after 1355 would suggest a case of plague depopulation. But that isn't the situation with Marchment.'

'Hold on a minute.' Jane stared at him fixedly. 'You mean you've discovered that Marchment did exist?'

'Oh, certainly – apart from the holding mentioned in *Terrae Templariae* we turned it up in Domesday also. And since it doesn't appear in any of the records I've mentioned, it would appear still to have existed in the fifteenth century. But sometime thereafter –'

'It disappeared?'

'That's about the size of it.' Arnold wrinkled his nose in thought. 'But after 1450, it would seem, the main force of depopulation was sheep.'

'The demand for wool, you mean?'

'Ahuh. The English cloth industry was expanding, and the post-plague population hadn't recovered enough to increase the demand for corn. Landowners turned to sheep, not least because this form of pastoral farming used a smaller labour force at a time when the bargaining power of labour was still high.'

'You're suggesting the Setons – who presumably still held Marchment in trust for the Templars – would have destroyed Marchment to turn a more profitable penny for themselves?'

'Or the Order.'

'But have you managed to trace the location of the village itself?'

Arnold ducked his head reluctantly. 'I . . . think so, but in general terms only. Not a precise location. My Newcastle contact has suggested several sites, just north and north-west of Dunstanburgh. I'm not sure about them. I've got hold of some old maps, and a couple of surveys, but I'll need to do some work on the ground.'

'When?'

Arnold shrugged. 'I was thinking of doing it this weekend. Driving up on Saturday – spending two days walking the terrain.'

'Without me? You're a pig!'

'I wasn't certain whether you'd wish to go along.'

'Humph!' She eyed him coldly. 'You could have told me about this sooner. You kept very quiet about this all through the concert. You never said a word.'

Arnold sighed. 'I was asleep.'

'That's even worse. You're an *unmusical* pig!'

They drove north together late on Friday evening. Arnold had tried to contact Sinclair several times during the week, with no success. He finally managed to speak to him on the phone on Friday morning and had attempted to persuade him to join the expedition. Sinclair had been evasive: he was rather busy, he suggested, and couldn't spare the time. His coolness surprised Arnold, since it was Sinclair who had been so enthusiastic in the first instance, and had fired Arnold to take up the quest. But there was something else on the man's mind, clearly: he had seemed only vaguely interested in an account of Arnold's searches.

Arnold had tried to explain to him that it was important to identify the link between the Setons and Marchment, if only to reinforce the entries in the texts, but Sinclair seemed to be barely listening to the suggestion. Arnold was left with the odd impression that Sinclair was no longer interested in the possibility of the existence of the Templar treasure; it was almost as though he was under some stress that left him brusque, and wandering in his attention.

He told Jane of his anxieties, but she seemed dismissive. Her view was that if Sinclair was no longer interested, that was his problem. She personally was looking forward to a tramp around the lanes and fields of Northumberland in their search for the lost village of Marchment.

Arnold had hoped to find accommodation near Dunstanburgh, but in the event they were forced to settle for a couple of rooms at the George Inn at Warkworth. Arnold knew the hotel and advised Jane it would be comfortable; it would simply mean they'd need to make an early start if they were to get in a full day's work on the Saturday, for they'd have a rather longer drive than he had hoped for.

The road north to Warkworth was quiet; it was one of those bright northern evenings when the sky never really grew dark and a dark blue glow suffused the horizon. There was little traffic, except for one persistent driver who hung back some two hundred yards behind them, and whose lights dazzled Arnold from time to time. At one stage he slowed, hoping the driver would pass, but he did not. When they reached Warkworth the nuisance was gone.

They ate well at the hotel after checking in, and made their way to the lounge bar afterwards, for a drink before they retired. It was surprisingly crowded. Arnold commented upon it to the thick set, shirt-sleeved man behind the bar.

'Oh, aye, trade's been busy these last days.'

'Tourists?'

'Of a kind.' The barman cocked an eye around the bar, and grimaced. 'The regulars have most of them shifted out for the moment, in fact. Too many outcomers, people who want to gossip, ask questions none of us around here can answer. It was the killing, you see.'

'Killing?'

'Aye, that councillor from Morpeth, the one they fished out of the Tyne.'

Arnold was puzzled. He stood silently as the barman

poured out the drinks he had ordered. 'What's the killing at Tynemouth got to do with Warkworth?'

'He had a cottage here, didn't he, that Bannock feller? Don't recall ever meeting him meself, even though he lived here. Maybe drank at home – kept hisself to hisself, for sure, bonny lad. But all the ghouls have come out – to gawp at the cottage, even though he wasn't killed there. Some folk will do all sorts for a thrill. Don't understand it, meself.' He began to polish the glass in his hand, vigorously. 'Takes all sorts. And it's trade.'

Arnold nodded. 'How much for the drinks?'

'Make it four quid.' He caught the flash of surprise in Arnold's eye. 'It's the demand, you see.' As Arnold handed over the money, the barman leaned forward confidentially, as though making up for the inflated prices. 'Mind you, it's not just all gawpers. See that guy over there? He's one of the coppers investigating the killing.'

Drinks in hand, Arnold turned and glanced in the direction indicated by the barman. The man seated by himself in the far corner was thick set, middle-aged; he raised his head as Arnold looked at him and their glances locked. Recognition flickered in the man's eyes and something cold gripped Arnold's stomach. He stood rigidly, foolishly, for a moment, until the man gave a slight smile and nodded, raising his glass slightly. Arnold inclined his head, turned and moved off through the throng – spilling a little of his whisky as he did so – to rejoin Jane.

He sat down beside her. 'You're not going to believe this.'

'What?'

'Our old friend Culpeper is here.'

'In this hotel?'

Arnold nodded. 'He's sitting by himself over there.' He hesitated. 'You know, I have a feeling –'

'Surprise, surprise.' Arnold's presentiment had been correct. John Culpeper stood looming over them, staring down with a genial expression on his face. From his manner, Arnold guessed the man was out to relax and had had a few pints. He nodded, uncertainly.

'Surprised to see you here, Landon, and Miss Wilson,' Culpeper said, nodding his head. 'What are you doing in this neck of the woods?'

Arnold shrugged and glanced at Jane. 'Nothing very exciting. We're looking for a deserted village.'

Culpeper laughed. 'That sounds right up your street – even if it'll be a quiet one!' He seemed delighted with the weak joke, and added, 'Mind if I sit down? I've had enough of being cold-shouldered by the locals and pestered by the tourists.'

He slid uninvited into the seat beside Arnold, forcing him to move along closer to Jane. Arnold heard Jane snort, as though she were about to protest, so he quickly said, 'This isn't exactly your local, Mr Culpeper.'

'Say that again. But . . .' Culpeper's tone cooled, as he seemed to consider his situation here in Warkworth, glancing around the bar. 'You know how it is. Duty. And it sometimes pays to hang around, out of hours, get the feel of a place . . .'

'Has this got something to do with the Bannock investigation?'

Culpeper turned his head slowly and stared at Arnold with a suspicious expression. Then his brow lightened. 'Well, I suppose it's obvious enough. I've already questioned the staff here: no doubt they'll have told everyone who I am. That's right. Bannock had a house here. I thought it would be useful to have another look around it. And after that, I thought, a beer . . .' His brow clouded again as he turned his thoughts inwards; Arnold gained the impression the policeman was angry and frustrated about something.

Culpeper's glance drifted back to Arnold. 'You must have known Bannock – did you?'

'Not really.'

'You chaired that *sudarium* meeting when he spoke.'

'That's right, but that was a professional situation. I came across him rarely before that.'

'How rarely?'

Arnold shook his head vaguely. 'Well, the occasional committee meeting. He was nothing to do with our department. And after the exhibition I did see him – at the meeting over the Ogle excavation, and then I had a drink with him one evening.'

Culpeper frowned, and was silent for a moment. His early *bonhomie* had swiftly evaporated and Arnold got the impression the man was sobering rapidly.

Culpeper drained his beer and rose to his feet. 'Can I get you two a drink?'

'We've barely had chance to start these,' Jane said tartly.

'I'll be back in a moment.' Culpeper lumbered towards the bar.

Jane hissed at Arnold. 'What do you mean, letting him sit down? I was quite enjoying the evening till now! He's hardly the companion I would want when I'm trying to relax!'

'What could I do to stop him?'

'You could have been rude! I shall be shortly, if he doesn't shove off.'

Culpeper returned a few minutes later to join the gloomy silence. He appeared not to notice the atmosphere. He was carrying a double whisky, which he sipped thoughtfully for a moment.

'Tell me . . .' he said suddenly, 'what you said a moment ago . . . the Ogle inquiry? Was that when some guy called Coulter got up and started shouting the odds about Councillor Flint?'

'That's right.'

'Bannock was there?'

Arnold nodded. 'He came in . . . wasn't really on the committee. Joined us out of interest, I suppose.'

'Hmm. Did he speak at the inquiry?'

Arnold considered for a moment. 'Yes, he did. Coulter came out with some statements that might be verging on the slanderous, and Bannock intervened: sort of warned Coulter about the seriousness of what he was saying.'

Culpeper stared at the amber liquid in his glass. Almost casually, he asked, 'Now why do you think he would do that?'

Arnold shrugged. 'He was a lawyer by profession. He was merely giving Coulter some sound advice.'

'Most lawyers give advice only when they're paid for it.'

Arnold had no comment to make in reply. He could feel Jane's annoyance rising; she was knocking her knee against his; urging him to do something about their unwelcome companion.

'You then said something about a drink,' Culpeper announced.

'We've already said no, thank you,' Jane muttered. 'Look here, Mr Culpeper –'

'No,' he interrupted. 'A drink, he said. With Bannock.'

Arnold shook his head in irritated understanding. He knocked Jane's knee firmly with his own, in response. 'Well, yes, Bannock and I had a drink together. It was . . . just the one occasion.'

'You weren't a drinking companion of his, then?'

'Of course not! He invited me – he wanted to talk to me about something.'

'And what would that be?'

'Mr Culpeper!' Jane had had enough. 'Arnold and I are going about our lawful business. We are relaxing this evening, before we do some possibly strenuous walking tomorrow and Sunday. We have our own leisure interests to pursue: they do not include conversations with policemen in pubs when all we're doing is minding our own business. We didn't ask you to join us –'

'So what was the occasion?' Culpeper interrupted, ignoring her outburst.

'*Culpeper!*' Jane almost squealed in indignation.

He looked at her. If he had been drinking steadily, the effects now seemed to have worn off. His eyes were cold and sober as he held her furious glance. His voice was low, and reasonable in tone, but it held a faint edge to it. 'Miss Wilson, I'm sorry if I'm spoiling your evening out with your friend, but I'm talking about a dead man here. A man Mr Landon had a drink with a few days before his death. Now, I'm in charge of the investigation, and that gives me certain powers. Weekdays, and weekends. One of them is to ask people to help me with my inquiries. At the station. Or, I can ask questions casually, friendly-like, in a pub. I don't mind doing it either way. I'd prefer to do it casually. What would Mr Landon prefer?'

Arnold put his hand over Jane's and squeezed it gently. 'Hold on. There's no need to get excited here. Culpeper . . . the conversation, the drink with Bannock was casual, unimportant. It's the only occasion we ever met socially.'

'So tell me what he wanted to talk to you about.'

'I've explained – it was nothing of consequence.' Arnold grimaced. 'You know the kinds of things that interest me – medieval matters, buildings, that sort of thing. Bannock was aware of that. Mainly through the *sudarium* find. He thought I might be interested in something he was involved in.'

'Such as?'

'He asked me whether I'd be interested in joining a certain organization.'

Culpeper's nostrils twitched suspiciously. 'Organization.'

Arnold sighed. 'You know . . . a sort of social, charitable thing; a kind of masonic order.'

'Freemasonry?'

'Not exactly.' Arnold hesitated, glancing at Jane. She was sitting quietly, but her mouth was set in a thin line. 'It's a sort of neo-Templar thing. They call it the Ancient Order of Sangréal. He asked me if I'd like to join. I declined. I'm not a joiner, you see. I'm interested in . . . esoteric matters but I've no desire to join any of these semi-secret societies that abound around the place.'

Culpeper's face was expressionless. He toyed with the glass in his hand. 'The Ancient Order of Sangréal . . . Was it just you and Bannock having this drink together, when he approached you?'

'No. There was a man called Con Burnley there. He's the librarian in the university.'

'Is he also a member of this . . . Order?'

Arnold nodded. 'As far as I can gather, Bannock was the Master of the Order, and Burnley is the Deputy Master. I imagine he'll now succeed Bannock.'

'I see . . .' Culpeper sipped at his whisky; there was a small gleam of veiled excitement in his eyes. 'So if I wanted to find out more about this . . . what kind of Order did you say . . . ?'

'Neo-Templar.'

'. . . This guy Burnley could tell me?'

'I imagine so.'

'Like who could be members of it?'

'He's an office holder,' Arnold replied shortly.

'Well, that's interesting,' Culpeper said. 'I suppose there's nothing else you can tell me about Bannock . . . the kind of man he was, that sort of thing . . .'

'I barely knew him.'

'So you said . . .' Culpeper abruptly finished his drink. He glanced at Jane and smiled genially. 'There, all that didn't really hurt too much, did it? I enjoyed our little chat, even if you didn't. But I do apologize most profusely, Miss Wilson, for intruding upon your evening. But then, for me, it's always a pleasure to see you both. Till the next time.'

His mood as he rose was almost jovial again.

'What the hell has got into him?' Jane hissed.

Arnold had no idea.

On Sunday they were in the hill country.

They had spent the whole of Saturday investigating possible sites north of Dunstanburgh, sweeping along the coast roads, checking old maps, visiting churches that dated back to Saxon and Norman times, but they had gleaned little. So, armed with camera and powerful binoculars, they had struck inland following drover trails that had been used for centuries before conversion in the 1850s to turnpike roads, and they had climbed over dry stone walls, grey against the vivid green of the sheep-pastured fields. As they toiled up the fells they passed only sheep, and the occasional soaring kite, hovering silently on quivering wings, but occasionally they glimpsed the flash of other binoculars, someone probably bird-watching on the hills. On a few occasions they caught sight of a solitary walker, in a field far below them, following a trail similar to theirs.

The heights they walked gave them a long perspective where they could seek telltale signs in the late evening sun-shadow, the evidence of buried stone foundations, sunken huts, hedge and ditch constructions. It had all been frustrating, nevertheless.

They had begun early on Sunday morning, striking further inland, closer to the Scottish border, aware that they were still following some of Sinclair's possible Templar escape routes through the Border country, tracing the courses of small rivers, identifying medieval hamlets, ruined crofts, ancient preceptories mentioned in the *Terrae Templariae*. Gradually they had whittled away at the possibilities, until, finally, they were left with three possible sites.

Jane had dismissed the first out of hand. 'It doesn't *feel* right.'

It was an unscientific decision, but one Arnold was inclined to agree with. He consulted the maps for the fiftieth time and shook his head. It was a matter of choice – either of the two final sites could be important: both were listed as deserted medieval villages in the index, but neither was identified by its original name.

'So what do you think?' Jane asked, tired at last, as they sat leaning against the crag of a limestone outcrop high on the green-grey moorland. The distant sea seemed to shimmer and dance, a vague blue line that merged with the sky under the hot afternoon sun.

'I don't know. We don't seem to be getting anywhere,' Arnold replied despondently. 'Maybe we ought to ask *him*.'

He nodded in the direction of the crags to their left: they could just make out the distant figure of a rucksacked walker, resting against a limestone wall and enjoying the view, as they were.

'Hmm.' Jane squinted up into the sun. 'It's odd, isn't it – when you're up in the hills like this you almost feel resentful when you see someone else. It's as though it's just us who're entitled to this view.'

'The view includes the Wharne site here,' Arnold said, stabbing his finger on the map. 'It was excavated in 1912:

there's certainly an old village there, but the survey marks it as mainly a Saxon site. And then there's the Deever site. There is a ruined parish church nearby, which apparently has a certain complexity of building sequences. We should be looking for a village with some church close to it – the *Terrae Templariae* mentions a foundation.'

'So, dump Wharne and go for Deever?' Jane asked. 'I'm getting leg-weary and mind-numbed.'

'I know how you feel. Let's try Deever.'

They made their way back to the car and drove along the valley, down from the fell, along the wooded gorge that led eastwards towards the coast; across small medieval pack-bridges and through tiny hamlets tucked away under craggy outcrops. The sun was dipping below the tall trees when they came to the field and the brown-painted Ministry of Works sign: Deever church.

The sun, lower in the sky, now sent long shadows across the field. Sheep scattered as they walked near the boundary hedge, and Arnold pointed out to Jane where the old village would have lain. The long shadows emphasized the folds in the ground; the indentation that would have been the old main street of the village, and the irregular mounds on either side which would have once been dwelling houses, dragged down to their foundations in disuse, and covered by the accumulation of centuries. Heather and gorse grew there now in profusion, ash trees spread magnificent branches above the quiet earth, and a bank of sycamores leaned across the waters of the small, winding stream that would have served the village long ago.

They walked on along the bend of the river: the sign indicated the demolished church. There was little left of it now: the stonework rose to a height of no more than ten feet in places, but much of the stone had been robbed to be used elsewhere.

Silently, the two walked around the ruins. Arnold could see where covering plaster had been removed, exposing straight joints and blocked windows and there was evidence of a Norman rebuilding of the church at the west end, with additional aisles and side chapels. It suggested an expansion of the parish at that time.

'It looks as though in the late fourteenth century the church was reduced: the aisles and chapels taken away. By Tudor times,' Arnold added, 'there'd have been nothing left but a truncated chancel.'

'It doesn't help us much,' Jane replied despondently.

'And yet . . . I don't know.' Arnold consulted the map. 'The location could well be correct, and the place has the right feel about it, you know? The isolation; the fact it is remote from the main medieval tracks, the notation that it was a Templar holding . . .'

He looked around him, shading his eyes against the dipping sun. Beyond the river the hill rose gradually. Arnold thought he could make out the faint markings on the ground that would denote an old trackway, some granite blocks that could have formed part of an ancient bridge, now long fallen and collapsed; and on the bank of the river itself, wheel-rutted depressions in the ground to denote a ford that had been used since time immemorial.

He looked back at the map. After a little while, Jane peered over his shoulder. 'What're you looking at?'

'This.'

Arnold traced with his index finger a line up and across the rising contour of the hill that faced them. Beyond, the hill dipped again to a roadway, clearly delineated on the map, leading to the small village named Ditchford.

'So?'

'There's a church there. It serves Ditchford . . . which is a Norman, open green village, planned and built in 1200, it seems. You can't see the church from here because of the rise in the ground, but look, away from the map, look at the hill. You see the contour, the fold in the ground? That's an old road.'

'So?' Jane shrugged. 'When this church was demolished, the villagers would have gone across the hill, a short cut to worship in Ditchford.'

'Maybe. But I have a feeling it's older than that. The ford

. . . they could have crossed lower down, but there was no road there . . . I don't know. Think about the timing of it all. The village of Ditchford is dated at 1200, but when was the church built? And rebuilt? You see, if you were to cart stone from this church to Ditchford, the natural route – the short route – would be along that track up there.'

'Are you really suggesting we might find remnants of this old church built into the fabric of the church at Ditchford?'

'Stone was a valuable commodity in medieval times,' Arnold asserted. 'They didn't waste good dressed granite.'

He led the way. They splashed through the ford, making use of ancient stepping stones that had lain undisturbed for centuries, resistant to the floods that came down from the fells. They followed the fold in the ground, the worn, greened-over track that led up and over the hill, noting the occasional paved stone that might have been Roman in origin, and they looked down on the small church that lay in the hollow above Ditchford village.

There was a sudden tightness in Arnold's chest. They walked down silently, until they reached the overgrown churchyard and manoeuvred between broken tombstones. Jane went ahead but Arnold idled, inspecting the older stones, many of which bore indecipherable names. After a few moments he stopped, as Jane neared the church entrance. He called her back. She returned, reluctantly.

'What is it?'

He pointed.

The stone was cracked and broken, leaning crazily, half buried in the long grass. Thick with grey lichen, it presented an impossible task to anyone who wished to read the inscription but as Jane stood puzzled, Arnold leaned forwards and rubbed at the stone, clearing away some of the lichen to make the outline of the carving more clear.

'A skull and crossbones,' Arnold said. 'And that's a sailing galley, with a cross in a floreate design.'

'So there's a *pirate* buried here?' she asked sarcastically.

'No. A Templar,' Arnold replied.

She was silent for a moment, and he realized that she

regretted the inanity of her response. She should have remembered that the skull and crossbones motif was a typically Templar one; a recognition of the inevitable corruption of the flesh. There would have been appropriate wording on the tombstone to buttress the device; the words were long eroded by time.

'Let's go inside,' Arnold said quietly.

They walked towards the great wooden doors of the church, iron-studded, protected by the storm porch. Inside, the chill struck at them, the unheated emptiness of a little used place of worship, serving the spiritual requirements of a decaying village high in the fells. The light was dim, the windows dirt-encrusted, so that the colours that once would have gleamed magnificently through to the richly carved pews were now muted and darkly seen.

Carefully and methodically, they moved along the aisles, inspecting the lattices and the walls, the chancel and the altar. The burial memorials in the floor slabs and on the walls were clustered, historically: they dated between the seventeenth and nineteenth centuries, but there were occasional carvings that were older – considerably older.

She stood above one smooth stone in the floor for several minutes. It held the vague image of a knight, hands clasped on a sword. She could make out the shape of the cross carved there, equal-armed, with the end of each arm wider than its base: the standard Templar device. But below it the name was still decipherable. She made out the letters with difficulty, but when she had recognized them her heart began to pound.

Seton.

She turned to call to Arnold but he had disappeared. She moved away from the slab and then caught sight of him, shadowed, half hidden by the buttress near the altar. He was standing quietly, motionless, staring upwards.

'What is it?'

He made no reply. His stillness intrigued her. She walked towards him, her shoes echoing hollowly on the cold stone flags. She looked upwards, following his glance.

Carved some six feet above their heads was a frieze – a series of figures in various postures. It was an old carving, part of the early medieval structure of the church. But there was a subtle difference in the colour of the stone.

'It's weathered badly,' Arnold explained. 'That would indicate it maybe faced elements it would escape in here. You see the jointing? See the cement at the edges? This frieze wasn't carved here in Ditchford – it was located into this wall some time after the original was constructed. A space was carved out for it; the frieze cemented in.'

'You think it was from the other church, beyond the hill?' Jane asked, almost in a whisper.

He made no reply for a moment, then nodded. 'It's likely. But I think it was located somewhere else, even before that.'

'I don't understand.'

Arnold pointed to the left of the frieze. At the base of the first figure shown there, she could make out some lettering.

'J – a – n,' she spelled out, peering at it on tiptoe. 'I suppose that will be for January.'

'I would imagine so,' Arnold said. 'And the second figure – you see it? An angel, left hand touching the right breast, right hand touching the right knee.'

'Feb . . . for February.'

'But the figure is a Templar motif,' Arnold said gravely. 'Do you remember where you've seen something similar?'

She frowned. 'The ruined collegiate church in the valley – the one Sinclair showed us.'

'That's right. Now, look at the third carving in the frieze.'

It was of a kneeling man, hands thrust forward and resting on his burly thighs. He was holding a cross: the arms were Templar. His hair was long and luxuriant, writhing in long tendrils about his head and shoulders and his mouth was open, as though calling to God. On either side of the kneeling figure were long, cornet-shaped devices, cornucopia from which rose a fluting that ran in long, sinuous lines to the top of the frieze and then along the edge; vine leaves trailing and twisting as a decorative lattice along the length of the frieze. There was something else carved in the centre of the lattice, some words, and a device, but they could not make it out clearly.

Jane read the word cut into the stone below the figure. 'March,' she said, and smiled as excitement suddenly caught at her throat. She grabbed at Arnold's arm, squeezing it tightly. 'There's a tomb back there; I just saw it – a Seton tomb. And here we have a kneeling Templar. David Seton – the Man of March!'

Arnold nodded, and smiled at her excitement, but there was a tingling in his own veins also. 'Look at the hair of the kneeling figure; does it not make you think of something else?'

For a moment she did not understand. And then she knew.

'*The Green Man,*' she said.

Her words seemed to hang, trembling, in the timeless air of the church.

3

Culpeper walked slowly back to his room, hands shaking with tension, the fury still hot in his chest. No one spoke to him in the outer office, aware of the situation. He entered the room and closed the door gently behind him and walked across to the window, staring blankly out across the rooftops of Morpeth. He heard the light tap on the door but did not turn his head. After a few moments he heard the door open.

'Can I come in, sir?'

He glanced back to see Farnsby, brow furrowed, staring at him. With a grunt, Culpeper nodded and turned to make his way to his desk. He sat down heavily. Farnsby hesitated for a moment, then came forward, taking out a pack of cigarettes from his pocket. 'Maybe one of these will help.'

'I haven't smoked for thirty years,' Culpeper snarled. 'I'm not going to let that bastard Baistow get me started now!'

'Was it rough?'

Culpeper could do without Farnsby's sympathy, particularly since the man had warned him previously that trouble could come of his action. He snorted, and shook his head. 'Nothing I can't handle.'

It hurt, nevertheless, to be bawled out by a man for whom he held little respect, and whose own conduct was in Culpeper's view, somewhat odd.

'We'd have had to release him in any case, sir. When you left on Friday morning, he still hadn't come up with anything we could use.'

'Frank Manley is lying through his teeth,' Culpeper ground out. 'I know he was tied in with Bannock in some way. He's come up with no explanation for the name in Bannock's address book – you heard what he said! It's up to *us* to show a link! And damn it, that's exactly what Baistow had the gall to say to me! Manley's a well-known villain, and yet *I* get hauled over the coals for giving him a rough time! It beggars belief.'

'We don't have anything on him, sir,' Farnsby argued. 'It was always taking a chance, keeping him in the cells until his solicitor arrived.'

'If I had my way he'd still be cooling his heels there. I know the bastard is linked to Bannock's death! How did Baistow find out we were holding him, anyway?'

Farnsby shrugged. 'When his solicitor came in we had to let him go. But the lawyer walked straight into Baistow and made a complaint. Manley swaggered out with a grin on his face.'

'It was as well I wasn't around to see it,' Culpeper grunted.

'Baistow was yelling for you on Friday, but we weren't sure where you'd gone. Or at least, that's what we said.'

'Hmm.' Culpeper shifted uneasily in his chair, aware he owed Farnsby something for his loyalty in the face of Baistow's wrath. 'Well, I thought it might be useful having another look around the Bannock cottage.'

'It was pretty clean, I would have thought. We went over it –'

'Yes, yes, I know. There was nothing there. But I had a mooch around the village, talked to a few people. Tried the pub, as well, but didn't get a great deal. Bannock used the place, but didn't talk to the locals much. One thing I did discover, though – his wife died some years ago –'

'Eight years.'

'– That's right, but there's been another woman in his life. Not recently, it seems, but a few years back there was someone who used to stay there with him. She's not been seen around for a long time. But one of the old gossips told me she was quite a bit younger than our deceased Mr Bannock.'

'Any chance of tracing her?'

Culpeper shrugged. 'Who knows? Still, there was something else . . .'

'Sir?'

The image of Deputy Chief Constable Baistow's face drifted into Culpeper's mind – empurpled with rage; it was thrusting forwards at Culpeper, leaving him in no doubt as to what would happen if he disobeyed instructions again. Culpeper wondered about links . . . 'Eh?'

'You said there was something else.'

'Ah, yes . . . I met Landon – you'll remember him – in the pub in Warkworth. He came up with an interesting piece of information. Something I think we should follow up.' He glanced at his watch, feeling better now that the tension of the Baistow interview was draining away, and with something positive to do. 'In fact, it's what I'm about to do now. I'm driving down to Newcastle, Farnsby, and I won't be back till this afternoon.'

'The way the deputy chief is breathing fire, sir, you'd better tell me where you can be contacted –'

'There's the car radio, for God's sake,' Culpeper exclaimed irritably, 'but if he needs to know, I'll be interviewing a guy called Burnley, who might cast some light on Bannock's extra-mural activities.'

The driver was able to drop Culpeper in Newcastle city centre at eleven in the morning: Culpeper arranged to be picked up again after lunch. He walked slowly along Northumberland Street, hardly aware of the people about him. He was still smarting from the dressing down he had received from Baistow: he felt it to be unjustified, for he was convinced that Manley was implicated deeply in the killing of Colin Bannock. He tried to wrestle with the thought, argue that this was part of his old obsession with the man, but there was still the unexplained presence of Manley's name in Bannock's address book.

It could not be coincidence – and Manley's arguing he had no idea why a stranger should have his name in the book simply didn't wash. Baistow had yelled at Culpeper, saying he was returning down a path he'd already trodden uselessly, and there wasn't enough evidence against Manley to hold him overnight in the cells. But facing Manley's solicitor was Baistow's problem, Culpeper thought slowly: it still didn't invalidate the argument.

Manley was involved.

Culpeper walked up through the quiet precincts of the university and made his way to the library. There were barely any students about and the library itself was almost empty. Culpeper asked at reception for Mr Burnley and without ceremony obtained access to the room at the end of the corridor. Culpeper tapped on the door, and when invited to step in, opened the door and saw a tall, balding man seated behind a desk, in his shirt-sleeves.

'My name's Culpeper – Detective Chief Inspector. Do you think I could have a word, sir?'

Burnley rose from his seat, stooping slightly and inclined his head in an odd, birdlike gesture. 'I've been half expecting you. Please take a seat.'

Culpeper walked forward and sat down in the tubular framed chair offered to him. He eyed the pile of papers and scattered files on Burnley's desk. 'I'm grateful for your time – you seem pretty busy.'

Burnley shrugged. His eyes were dark and intense as he stared at Culpeper, then his glance slipped to his desk. 'I took a few days off last week – walking is my hobby, and now the term's over, with no students around . . . there's time. But the work piles up – committee reports, that sort of thing.'

'The weather was good last week, for walking. Especially the weekend.'

'That's right. Nothing like fresh air in the lungs.'

Both men knew the formalities were over. 'You said you'd been expecting me,' Culpeper said abruptly.

Burnley's brows drew together, and he grimaced. There was a cynical, knowing twist to his mouth. 'I imagine this visit will be in connection with the death of Mr Bannock. It was inevitable I should be asked about him.'

'Why?'

Burnley gazed at Culpeper with eyes accustomed to prevarication. 'We were . . . associated, to some extent.'

'Socially?'

'No, I wouldn't say that. We were not close acquaintances, really. We didn't even like each other very much.'

The man was direct, at least, Culpeper thought. 'And not business?'

'Certainly not that.' There was a sudden edge to Burnley's tone, a sharpness that caught Culpeper's attention.

'So tell me.'

'You've probably heard we were associated . . . in a certain organization.' When Culpeper made no response, Burnley went on a little nervously, 'I imagine you will know something about it. That is to say, when a man dies, things come out . . . The Ancient Order of Sangréal, I mean. Mr Bannock is – was – the Master: I was Deputy Master. To that extent, we worked together.'

Culpeper shifted in his chair. 'A sort of Masonic society?'

Burnley nodded reluctantly. 'That's a broad enough description, I suppose. We have a long history, and a small, select membership. It's an essentially northern organization and it was headed by Mr Bannock: we do good works, maintain charities, have regular meetings, undertake research into our history, support educational foundations and, of course, support members or their families who have fallen on hard times. The usual kind of thing . . .' His voice tailed away. 'I've been remiss. Would you like a cup of coffee?'

Culpeper nodded. 'Thanks very much.'

Burnley left the room. He seemed edgy, nervous, but people often were when being questioned by a copper, Culpeper thought sourly to himself. It was one of the elements he had to discount: don't read too much into nervousness. He looked around him. The room was lined with books, some in elegant gold-blocked cases. He wondered whether the Ancient Order of Sangréal had peculiar rituals like other secret societies. He'd been approached to become a Mason once; it was rife in the police forces. He'd declined. Maybe that's why he'd never really got on.

Burnley came back in, closing the door gently behind him. He handed a plastic cup of coffee to Culpeper, apologizing for the service. 'Cuts in library expenditure,' he explained.

'So how often did you meet Bannock?' Culpeper asked.

'At formal meetings of course, regularly, once a month. That's over the last five years, really, since I became Deputy Master.'

'Apart from that?'

Burnley shook his head. 'Only for the transaction of business.'

'So you didn't get to know him really well?'

Burnley hesitated. 'I can't say I did. Ours was an . . . uneasy relationship.'

Culpeper sipped his coffee and let the silence grow around them. Burnley wanted to say something: let him think about it.

'Uneasy, you say?'

The words came out in a rush. 'He and I didn't exactly agree about things. My only connection with Mr Bannock was through the Order: I have no inkling how successful he might have been in his business as a lawyer, or in his work as a politician. They were worlds into which I have never strayed. I am a mere librarian, I've done my job well, and I've been promoted to a post I enjoy. Apart from that, my only interests – outside – lie in the Order.'

Culpeper raised his head. 'I'm not sure I know what you're suggesting.'

'Mr Bannock was different. He had . . . many interests.

And whereas my life is compartmentalized, discrete in its areas, his wasn't. It's what we clashed about.'

'I don't understand.'

'The Order is important to me. It has honoured me: I am committed to it. It contains many men of consequence, but I have been elevated to Deputy Master. I have been conscious of my responsibilities . . . the trust reposed in me. To achieve the position of Deputy Master was a high point in my life. But Mr Bannock was Master, even though his experience in the Order was slighter than mine, and he didn't see his position in the same light. It didn't mean the same to him. He had other credits he could point to: his activity on the council, his law practice, the circles in which he moved . . . He didn't see the Order in the way I did.'

Culpeper watched the man carefully. There was a feverish light in Burnley's eyes, as though he was reliving old quarrels.

'So what was the point at issue between you?'

'The Order. The different attitude he brought to it. He argued he was merely being pragmatic but . . . You see, Mr Culpeper, Mr Bannock didn't keep the different strands of his life separate! He misused his position as Master. In my view he corrupted it: he used it for personal reasons; there were hints of activities going on which had nothing to do with the Order. He introduced some people who I considered to be . . . undesirable. Their attitudes were wrong . . . they had *expectations*. There was the whiff of business dealings in the air. That's what we disagreed about. I told him of my displeasure: he didn't seem even to understand what I was talking about, let alone appreciate my point of view. And though I raised it with other members, they tended to take his side. They suggested I should bring myself into the twentieth century. But that's not what the Order is about, you see, it's about . . .'

He checked himself, aware suddenly that he was exposing his own feelings too obviously. Or maybe he felt he was giving too many secrets away. Culpeper felt the beat of a vein in his forehead, as a stab of excitement caught his chest.

'The people Mr Bannock introduced . . . they were important people?'

Burnley sighed. 'In the community, yes. But some of them, their attitudes . . .'

'I'd like to see a list of your members,' Culpeper said flatly.

Burnley's eyes were hooded suddenly. The cynical mouth was compressed into a thin, stubborn line. 'I'm not certain that would be acceptable to the Order. The rules and ordinances –'

'This is a murder inquiry, Mr Burnley,' Culpeper rasped. 'I could get a court order.'

Burnley hesitated. He sat silently for almost a minute, eyes downcast, as though contemplating the possibilities open to him. Then, slowly, he unlocked a drawer in his desk and took out a small printed document. 'This has a restricted circulation,' he said, almost whispering.

'I'll take good care of it,' Culpeper said ironically, and took the document from him. 'Tell me, Mr Burnley, when did you last see Mr Bannock?'

Burnley shrugged. 'It should have been on the day he died.'

Culpeper tensed. '*Should* have been?'

'The newspapers say he was killed on the 5th. Take a look at my diary . . .' He passed a desk diary to Culpeper, after opening it to the relevant page. 'As you can see, we'd arranged to meet in Newcastle, at eight-thirty.'

'And?'

'He never appeared.'

'Was his visit to Newcastle just to see you?'

Burnley shook his head. 'I don't believe so. He phoned me, said we needed to meet to discuss Order business. It concerned a problem we were having.'

'What kind of problem?'

Burnley wrinkled his brow. 'We have an ancient history. We have . . . many secrets. Our traditions are sacrosanct to members who believe in the Order and its history. But we have been bothered of late by a man who . . . probes, digs into our world, asks questions that are none of his business.

He was in fact invited to join us at one stage, but demonstrated his contempt for what we stand for. He has been . . . investigating us, trying to find out our secrets. They are harmless enough, of course, but his activities have caused us . . . problems. I believe it was he whom Mr Bannock was due to meet before our appointment. I don't know whether they did meet. All I do know is, Mr Bannock did not keep his appointment with me.'

Culpeper frowned. 'I see. And this man you mention . . .'

'His name is Sinclair.'

Culpeper slipped into a café and bought himself a coffee and a hamburger for lunch: he resisted the French fries, because his wife was constantly telling him he was putting on too much weight. As he ate he went slowly through the list of names provided by Burnley. He had been surprised by the ease with which he had obtained the list: he knew that many of these societies would scream blue murder rather than give up their membership lists, but Burnley clearly felt resistance would be useless. As he read through the list, however, Culpeper guessed at a different motivation. He began to appreciate just what might have been upsetting the Deputy Master of the Order in his relationship with the dead Master. Publication of the list could clear it of some of the so-called 'undesirables' in Burnley's view.

When Culpeper got back to his room in Morpeth he called Farnsby in.

'I've got a job for you to do.'

'Sir?'

'I want a list of the directors of the Midnorth Consultancy Group. I want a full list of the councillors presently in office, and those who've been in office over the last few years. Get me also the names of local managers and directors of the Quinton hypermarket chain.'

Farnsby looked puzzled. 'Is this tied in with the Bannock killing?'

'Just get me the names. Oh, and then have a word with O'Connor. Find out from him what names he dug out when he was looking at Coulter's business interests for Mr Baistow.'

'I'll do what I can.'

'And as quickly as you can. Then . . .' Culpeper hesitated, toying with the document in his hand, 'then you and I will check the names against the list I've got here.'

'List?'

Culpeper smiled thinly; there was no humour in the smile. 'Get the names first, then we'll look at the list.'

'As you say, sir.' Farnsby hesitated. 'I hadn't realized you were back just yet. There's someone in the building who's been wanting to talk to you.'

'Well, I'm back,' Culpeper said impatiently, 'but –'

'I think you might want to talk to her.' Farnsby's face was impassive. 'She won't explain anything to anyone else – says she just wants to see you.'

'Who the hell is it?'

'She gave her name as Anstey . . . Edda Anstey.'

There was a long silence in the room. Culpeper blew out his cheeks and stared at his hands, gripping the edge of the table. For a while, his mind was blank, and then the old images came back and the pain in his chest returned. It seemed there was no escaping Frank Manley.

'She wants to see me?' he said quietly. 'I think *I'd* like to see *her*.'

A few minutes later Edda Anstey was seated in front of him. She was nervous and ill at ease, her long black hair untidy. Her face was pale, but there was a determination in her eyes that was reflected in the set of her mouth. She was a good-looking woman, Culpeper concluded, whom life had been wearing away. Now, she was definitely on edge. He smiled cynically: who wouldn't be constantly on edge, tied in with a villainous bastard like Frank Manley?

'Well, then, Miss Anstey, I recall our meeting at the pub a while ago, with Frank, but on that occasion you didn't seem to want to say very much to me at all. However, I'm always happy to talk to members of the public. What can I do for you?'

There was a slight shake to her voice when she spoke. 'I want you to leave Frank alone. Get off his back!'

Culpeper stared at her. 'Now why should I do that?'

'He's got nothing to do with the killing of Colin Bannock!'

'You sound very positive about that. But,' Culpeper added, spreading his hands wide, and shrugging, 'all we've done so far is to drag him in for questioning. We let him go again.'

'But that won't be the end of it,' she flashed at him. 'I know all about you, Culpeper. You've had the knife in him for years, and you won't let go. You're trying to pin Bannock's killing on Frank, and you'll move hell and high water to do it. Leave him alone!'

'If he's got nothing to do with it, he'll be in the clear. But we do have a link –'

'You have nothing!'

'That's for you to say and me to disbelieve, Miss Anstey,' Culpeper replied coldly. 'We can link Manley with Bannock, all right, and when I've pulled a few threads together maybe we'll be having another little chat with Frank. Meanwhile, if all we're going to get out of this interview is some hysterical –'

'Leave Frank alone! It's nothing to do with him. It was just . . .'

Culpeper watched her carefully. She was trembling. 'Just *what*?' he asked suspiciously.

She raised her chin, glared at him. 'It's me, not Frank you should be talking to!'

There was a defiant ring in her voice. Culpeper, astonished, leaned back in his chair. 'What's that supposed to mean? What do you have to do with it all?'

'Whether you believe it or not, Frank's been trying to go straight since he and I got together. But the way you hassle him; the way he can't turn around without having you breathing down his neck – he's got to the stage where he's said he might just as well be back into the car scam, for all the trouble he's getting! But you're wrong about Bannock. That's nothing to do with Frank.'

'You're going to tell me what it *is* about, then,' he said quietly.

'You found Frank's name in Bannock's notebook. You don't know why it's there. I do.'

'How?'

'Because it was I who gave Frank's name to Colin Bannock.'

Culpeper was silent. Slowly he reached for a pencil on the desk and drew forward a notepad. He began to doodle on it thoughtfully: a series of whorls and circles, all interlinking but going nowhere, rounding back on themselves over and over again. 'How do you come to have known Bannock?' he asked at last.

Her tone was flat and unemotional. 'His wife died about eight years ago. I was working in the building society at that time: I was twenty-five. I'd been living with someone, but the relationship had ended; we'd split, and Bannock used to come into the office on business from time to time. We got talking. He asked me out. I was flattered, and there was no one else. I sort of drifted into the relationship. He needed a woman. I was . . . available. We . . . we spent some time together. I stayed at his place in Warkworth, often.'

Culpeper recalled the gossip in the town.

'All this was some time ago,' he suggested.

'That's right. It was all right while it lasted. He wasn't committed; neither was I, really. But then it all fell apart. I got pregnant.'

Culpeper stopped doodling and stared at her. 'Deliberately?'

She shook her head. 'Give me credit! I told you – neither of us was committed. He gave me a good time, looked after me, and we had regular sex. But I had no illusions. Pregnancy – that was a bad mistake. But it can happen.'

'So I believe,' Culpeper remarked drily.

'He didn't want to know after that. We didn't see each other for a while after I told him. He wanted me to have an abortion: I refused. I had nothing in the world – a child . . . I wanted it. And I knew he'd pay, in the long run. He could be a bastard, and he was as crooked as they come, but he had a funny sense of honour, as well. Then he came to see me; told me if I kept quiet, he'd make regular maintenance payments once the child was born. He was cold about it.'

'He wasn't prepared to acknowledge the child?'

'No way. But in any case, it made no difference.' She shrugged, almost indifferently. 'I aborted.'

'But you said –'

She shook her head. 'It was an accident.'

'So you let Bannock off the hook?'

'I didn't let him off any hook. I told you. It was an accident. I was almost eight months pregnant. I hadn't seen Bannock for months. I was edgy one evening; went out to get something to eat – a Chinese takeaway. It was raining, dark. I came around the corner and this car . . . it only gave me a glancing blow, but it knocked me over. It stopped about fifty yards away, and the driver came running back. He was scared as hell – then he saw the blood. He made a phone call, I understand – but he didn't hang around after making it.'

'He didn't wait to see how you were? He left the scene?'

She shook her head impatiently. 'He'd been drinking. He was scared of getting interviewed by the police. That's where Bannock came in.'

Culpeper stopped doodling and threw his pencil down. 'What do you mean, *Bannock* came in?'

'He was at the hospital within hours. He told me he'd act for me, as my solicitor. He guided me through my statement. It was a pack of lies.'

'What the hell are you saying here?'

She took a deep breath. 'I didn't call him to the hospital. He already knew about the accident. He had a shock when he saw it was me.' She shook her head in sudden desperation. 'Look, Colin Bannock was a bastard. He was into all sorts. He treated me all right when we were lovers, but afterwards, I was like all the rest. Someone to be used, manipulated for his own ends. He told me my hospital accounts would be covered, and I'd receive a regular payment, straight into my bank account, after I was released. But there was one condition. I kept my mouth shut about the details of the accident.

In particular, he told me I was to have no recollection of the man who had come out of that car, and who'd made the phone call.'

'You knew the man?'

'Not then. But I knew I'd recognize him again. And I did, later. I saw his picture in the paper. I recognized him.'

'And you said nothing?'

She grimaced. 'The money was paid every month. What else did I have to gain? Revenge, maybe? I couldn't afford it.'

Culpeper shook his head, puzzled. 'But what's all this got to do with Frank Manley?'

'I met Frank eight months ago. I know he's wild. But he's been good to me: so maybe I go for the wrong kind of man. But I think we can make it together. But you've been hassling him. All right, he's been in the scams, but though he was trying to get out, you were putting the screws on him. He was talking of going back in – so I made a phone call.'

Culpeper sighed. 'To Bannock?'

'That's right. I told him about the way the police were down on Frank. I told him I wanted something done about it. I didn't need to threaten Bannock: he was cooperative. I got the impression he didn't want any boats rocked just at this time, and if I told the right people what had happened to me, it wouldn't have suited Bannock's book. He told me he'd sort it out. And it seemed he had. Until you dragged Frank in last week for questioning over Bannock's murder. But Frank didn't even *know* Bannock. You've got to lay off him on this – it's nothing to do with him.'

'And *you* would have had no reason to kill Colin Bannock, would you?' Culpeper asked gently.

'Are you crazy? He's been making a regular payment to me all these years! What would I gain from his death? What would Frank gain?'

'Someone's gained . . . This accident . . . the man who knocked you down, caused your miscarriage, you said you've seen him since. You recognized him.'

'That's right,' she said firmly.

'His name?'

Her hesitation was only momentary. 'He's a local councillor,' she said. 'His name is Flint.'

5

1

It was several days before the photographs that Arnold had taken in the church at Ditchford were developed. He had no time to think about the weekend events in any case, since he was called upon to visit a site near Berwick where a gravel quarry had recently been opened. An ancient river channel had been uncovered during extraction of the overlying periglacial gravels and a request had come in for county support to establish an investigative team. There was the suggestion that the channel could contain large amounts of environmental data, including mammal bones, plant fossils and insect remains. There was also some evidence of stone tools.

He stayed near Berwick, at Spittal, and made his assessment of the site, then wrote up the report. In his view there was a considerable chance that they might find remains of large animals in the channel; grazing species as well as smaller mammals such as shrews and voles. It was an important site, well worth exploring. He knew that money was tight in the department, but when he got back to the office he presented his report to Brent-Ellis with confidence.

The director seemed anxious and preoccupied when Arnold saw him. He took the report and glanced at the summary sheet, humphed, and tossed it aside. It was clear he was not going to concentrate upon the proposal.

'You'll see I think we should give support to the site project, sir,' Arnold offered.

'Yes, yes, I can see that. If we've got the money . . .'

Brent-Ellis tugged at his moustache irritably. He looked at Arnold and his eyes widened as though recognizing him for the first time. 'Landon . . . you were at that Ogle excavation inquiry weren't you?'

'That's right.'

'You heard what that Coulter fellow had to say?'

'I did.'

'I'm sure it's him,' Brent-Ellis muttered. 'I'm sure that bastard started all this noise.'

'Noise, sir?'

Brent-Ellis stared at him in astonishment. 'Where have you been the last few days?'

'Berwick. Out of the office. The report, sir,' Arnold reminded him, gesturing towards the file on his desk.

'Report . . . Oh, yes. So you don't know . . . haven't heard. All hell's broken loose. Bad show. We had a directors' meeting yesterday. Every damn file has to be opened up, every contract given over the last five years . . . thank God we're not too involved. But the fuss . . . I'm sure it's that man Coulter. What do you think?'

'I don't really know what you're talking about.'

'Why the hell that man Bannock had to get himself killed is beyond me. The trouble he's caused . . . Powell Frinton is having a fit. And the councillors . . .' He glared at Arnold suspiciously. 'You've not heard anything, have you? About any of our chairmen?'

Arnold presumed he meant chairmen of committees involved with the work of the department. He shrugged helplessly. 'I haven't heard anything about *anything*, sir!'

Brent-Ellis grimaced, and nodded knowingly. He tapped his finger against his nose. 'Sensible chap. Play it canny. I'll take your advice. Keep the old noddle down. Below the parapet. Out of trouble that way: flying bullets and all that sort of thing. Sensible advice.'

Arnold hadn't realized he'd offered any advice. But Brent-Ellis had swung his chair to stare out of the window at distant golf courses, report and anxieties forgotten already. Arnold assumed he had been dismissed from the Presence.

It was left to the office gossip, Charlie Cleery, to tell him what had happened.

'It all hit the fan day before yesterday. Some heavy-footed coppers came cavorting in to talk to the DDMA. Don't know what they'll have got out of that attempt, but when they left he was shaking, white as a sheet and Old Iron-Knickers his secretary was apoplectic, having her dream boy treated like that! But the same thing was happening all over the departments, apparently. So Elsie told me upstairs, anyway.'

Cleery's rotund, malicious features were gleeful. 'Looks as though someone somewhere's been putting their fingers in the till. And no one is out of the firing line! Even Powell Frinton – that strait-laced stuffed shirt of a chief executive – even he's had his office files turned over. And the Contracts Department – they're being taken apart! Have to produce every tender, every contract that's been awarded for the last five years! I tell you, it's been chaos! I blame that Coulter guy, myself.'

'It's a corruption inquiry?'

'Looks like. Rumour has it Midnorth's being investigated – and they've done a fair bit of work for the council in the past. They must have had contracts when you was in the Planning Department, Arnold.'

The Midnorth Consultancy Group. That was why the police had been to see Brent-Ellis, as well. The department had been involved in the Ogle excavation inquiry, because of Professor Santana's submission – and Mel Coulter had stood up at the committee and denounced Councillor Flint, and Santana himself, for having some connection with the Midnorth Consultancy Group.

'Rumour has it that this was all sparked by the killing of that guy Bannock,' Cleery announced cheerfully. 'Gives us all something to talk about, though, don't it?'

And work in the office would have ground to a halt. Which would cheer up Cleery considerably, Arnold thought as he walked away. Cleery always preferred gossip to hard work.

*

When the photographs finally arrived, Arnold rang Sinclair to suggest they meet. He explained about the visit he and Jane had paid to Ditchford and what they'd found there, but Sinclair had few questions to ask, and when Arnold offered some times to meet, he seemed evasive.

'Fact is, I've got rather a lot on at the moment,' he said.

'I would be rather reluctant to pursue some of these things without you,' Arnold said. 'I mean, it was you who got me started on this. I wouldn't want you to think –'

'No, no, don't worry about it. Look, I really have to go in a moment. Perhaps we'll talk about all this again later.'

When Arnold met Jane on the Saturday morning for coffee she was as surprised as he had been. 'It's almost as though he was no longer interested,' she suggested.

Arnold shook his head. 'I don't think it's that. It's more that he seems preoccupied; has something else on his mind.'

'Well, he always was a bit weird,' Jane shrugged. 'Anyway, let's have a look at the photographs.'

The café was half empty and there was no one else seated at their table so Arnold was able to spread the photographs out for inspection. Pushing a coffee cup aside he arranged the photographs in order. There were twelve images in the frieze, each one nominated by a month of the year. 'Like zodiac signs, really,' Jane suggested.

'Except they have no connection with any zodiac I've ever seen. In fact, each carving has some esoteric motif involved in it: you see, here's another Templar cross carved within the circle, there's a Masonic set square –'

'And what's that . . . a hammer? An adze?' She peered closer. 'And is that not an axe?'

'Most of these symbols have been taken at some time or another into Masonic, or pseudo-Templar ritual,' Arnold asserted. 'But *this* is what I find intriguing.'

He pushed forward one of the photographs. It was a shot taken above and to the right of the carved figure for June. The figure itself was another head, vaguely reminiscent of the Celtic vegetation god, but above it Arnold had noticed some scrollwork encasing what appeared at first sight to be a box. Its location made it central to the frieze itself, effectively marking a balancing between the first six carvings and the remainder.

Now that he was able to inspect the photograph more closely, he could see the lettering underneath the square object.

'You see, it's not a box at all. It's more like a square, with a cross inside it, quartering the square.'

'And what do the words say? Can you make them out?'

Arnold peered closer. 'They've eroded with time, but it looks to me like a Latin tag. Three words. *Ex fenestra lux.*'

Jane wrinkled her nose in thought. 'I did Latin at school, and still have a fair working knowledge. But . . . I've not heard that one before. *Ex tenebris lux,* yes – light out of darkness. But *fenestra* means . . . what the hell is it now . . . ?'

'Window,' Arnold supplied.

'But that doesn't make much sense,' Jane suggested. 'You get light *through* a window, not *out* of it. Maybe their Latin wasn't up to scratch, you think?'

Arnold shrugged. 'I don't know. I can hardly believe that's the explanation. At that time, Latin was the common language, the international language. And what about these?'

He pointed to the top edge of the frieze. Along the length of the frieze ran a carved lip, a fluting that hung protectively over the series of carvings. On the underside of the lip had been cut a sequence of holes. They were plain, unadorned, but evenly spaced, a series of holes bored into the stone.

'They seem to serve little decorative purpose,' Arnold remarked.

'Termites?' Jane suggested flippantly.

'Be serious. And have you noticed how they run, dipping slightly as they reach the centre of the frieze?'

Jane nodded. She followed the line of holes to the point where they curved down, almost touching the words they had been discussing.

'There's another odd thing,' Arnold mused.

'What's that?'

'It's difficult to be sure, because the light and shade in a flat photograph like this can be deceptive, but have you noticed that the holes aren't even?'

'How do you mean?'

'I get the impression that they vary in depth. They're evenly spaced, but for some reason these –' Arnold pointed to four of the holes '– seem to be cut more deeply than the others.'

'Could be they were worn.' She peered more closely at the photograph. 'Or possibly the chisel slipped.'

'Maybe.' He frowned. 'On the other hand . . . when you look at esoterica it's as well to be very careful. It's easy to be dismissive, ignore something; it's important not to jump to conclusions. Very little is left to chance; the smallest things can be symbolic. I've never come across a series of drilled holes like that –'

'You're sure they're not later than the frieze itself? An addition?'

'It's another possibility,' Arnold said slowly. 'But I don't see –'

'Anyway, I'm going to have to leave you to it,' Jane interrupted, draining her coffee. 'I would have loved to discuss this further, but I've got an antiques book fair to attend in Harrogate. Are you sure you won't come? Pleasant day out.'

Arnold shook his head. 'You'll forgive me. Old books, I like, but a lot of the stuff you'll be poring over won't interest me. Half an hour and I'd want to be away.'

She laughed. 'OK. Keep in touch. Let me know if you crack the code in that frieze. Maybe Sinclair could help you – if you could get hold of the guy!'

She patted Arnold on the shoulder in a protective gesture and walked away. He smiled as he watched her go: he was fond of Jane, for all her shortness of fuse on occasions, her sharp tongue when she was displeased, and the way she could bridle if he said the wrong thing. She was direct, honest, plain spoken and was a good friend. And maybe she was right about Sinclair. Perhaps Arnold should try ringing him again.

Sinclair.

Something stirred turbidly in Arnold's mind.

A code, Jane had said. Sinclair . . .

It was Sinclair who had introduced him to this quest, set him on this trail. And the trail had begun in that dark Scottish valley, at the collegiate church, as Sinclair had described it.

Slowly Arnold finished his coffee. His mind was racing. He had a vision of the harassed Templars, fleeing the inquisition of Simon de Goncourt; leaving Kilclogan with their precious burdens, hiding in one of the sympathetic landholdings of Robert Bruce's followers. And when the initial hue and cry had died down, when things had settled and Bannockburn had been fought, establishing Bruce securely on the throne, they had had the confidence to start building the church in the valley. It would have soared in their imagination – creating a proper location and centre for the Order in Scotland, basking in the support of the king, confident . . . until the money ran out, or the pressures came back.

They had carved the symbols, the swords and crosses, the Green Man in the church, and they had carved the frieze. But the political situation had worsened: for a hundred years after interdict the Order had flourished in spite of their official suppression – until Sandilands became Master. The unfinished church had become an unsafe location and they had fled again – perhaps to Deever. The frieze was important and had been cut out, to be taken with them . . . but not the treasure. Secrecy was essential. Sandilands had betrayed them, and Templar lands were being sold. But David Seton led the true believers, and his family connection with Deevers and Ditchford led to the locating of the frieze in that later church.

A code.

Perhaps Jane was right; perhaps the Man of March had not only moved the frieze but encoded it. The evenly spaced holes, almost emerging from the quartered box . . . the words *ex fenestra lux*.

And then he realized he had been stupid. The truth was staring him in the face. His hand was shaking as he inspected the photographs again. And he knew he had to go back to the valley.

2

The chief constable came in with a thick file under his arm; Baistow came in behind him – soft-footed like a cat, treading warily. His face was impassive, but as he sat down in the silent room, Culpeper observed him closely: there was a nervous tic in his jaw that betrayed the tension he was under. Culpeper smiled grimly to himself – chickens were coming home to roost.

The chief constable cleared his throat. 'Sit down, gentlemen.'

There was a scraping of chairs and a shuffling of feet as the small group took their seats. The chief constable placed his elbows on the conference table and looked at each of them in turn: O'Connor, Farnsby, Culpeper, Hargreave and Inspector Stainton, who had undertaken liaison between the two investigations.

'All right,' the chief constable began, 'I called this case conference for two reasons. The first is to find out just where we've got to; secondly, I want to make sure that we put a stop to all the wild rumours that seem to be flying around, not just in the press, but here at HQ as well.'

His cold eyes slid around the group accusingly; they fixed on Culpeper for a fraction longer than anyone else, and Culpeper felt a cold knot harden in his stomach. Then the glance slid away and the chief constable went on.

'I need hardly stress that we are facing two important investigations here, at the same time. You'll be aware that O'Connor had been asked by DCC Baistow to undertake an investigation of a man called Coulter, who had made various damaging remarks concerning Councillor Flint. In the course of that investigation nothing significant was found . . . O'Connor?'

'That's right, sir.' O'Connor ducked his head and swallowed. 'I'm not saying Coulter's clean, and he certainly has a violent background, at least in the construction industry, but I've not been able to discover anything personally incriminating.'

'O'Connor's now been taken off that investigation,' the chief constable said evenly.

Culpeper leaned forward; his voice was cold but determined. 'I wonder whether I may ask *why* the investigation was started at all, sir? Why was Coulter being checked on?'

Baistow made no movement; he sat as though carved from stone. The chief constable glared at Culpeper. 'We needn't touch upon that at this stage – it's something I'll be discussing with you, Culpeper, outside this meeting. Suffice it to say that O'Connor abandoned that inquiry when . . . the other matters came to light. He has now been put in charge of the squad which has been visiting the council offices. What do you have to report, O'Connor?'

'Only that we've been to each department and explained the reasons for our inquiry. Each department head has agreed to cooperate –' He grinned suddenly, obviously enjoying what had happened '– they didn't have much choice, really.'

'Quite,' the chief constable said drily. 'And documentation?'

'I've arranged for appropriate officers to bring away sensitive material, and this we'll now start sifting through here at HQ, sir.'

'Stainton?'

The tall liaison man stiffened, and his head came up. He had a gravelly voice, and was known for his doggedness and persistence; a stickler for detail. 'I have a group of men dealing with possible links, sir, and I maintain close contact with both Culpeper and O'Connor, on their separate inquiries.'

'Fine.' The chief constable's cold eyes turned to Culpeper. There was a hint of distaste in his tone when he spoke. 'That leaves you. Perhaps you'd like to tell us where you've got to, what your initial conclusions are, and indeed, how you surmise these separate investigations tie in one with the other. And for my own personal benefit, I'd like you to start at the beginning again.'

Baistow looked at him: there was a deep gleam in his eyes, a warning that Culpeper resented. But he knew this was neither the time nor place to let rip with all his suspicions. On the other hand, it wouldn't stop him dropping some broad hints.

'When we began the investigation into the death of Mr Colin Bannock,' Culpeper started, 'we proceeded on the assumption that maybe it was a random killing – a robbery, a mugging on the Quayside. We quickly dropped that idea: the only thing that might have been taken was a diary, registering appointments – and we're not even certain Bannock carried one. However, when we looked through Bannock's office at Warkworth we came upon an address book, which included the names and addresses of prominent businessmen – as one would expect – and local councillors. Again, that's perfectly reasonable bearing in mind Bannock's life style and professional activity. At that stage, we had no reason to consider these entries as odd in any way.'

'Nor do we have any such reason yet,' the chief constable interposed warningly.

Culpeper felt the heat rise in his face; but he could bide his time, even if the chief constable wanted feet to be dragged.

'There was one name in the book which surprised me: Frank Manley.' He paused, and the silence in the room was cool. They were all aware by now of the fact that Culpeper had been chasing Manley for years: he knew there was still the thought that he had allowed an obsession to get the better of him.

'Manley is a villain, though one we've never managed to nail. But his name in the book was a surprise, because there was no reason I could think of as to why it would be there. Bannock had a law practice, but he did very little criminal work and Manley wasn't one of his clients. Accordingly, I dragged Manley in for questioning . . .' Baistow shifted uneasily in his chair, the first movement he had made since the chief constable had spoken. Culpeper glanced briefly at him, and then went on, 'He denied even knowing Bannock but could not account for the presence of his name in the address book. I held him in the cells to cool off . . . but then he was released after the intervention of his solicitor.'

'This dangerous villain is of course now at large,' the chief constable remarked sarcastically.

'I went to Warkworth to make further inquiries among the locals,' Culpeper went on, reddening, 'and came away with some more information which linked Bannock with one of these pseudo-Masonic secret societies here in the north.' He raised his head and looked the chief constable squarely in the eye. 'It's called the Ancient Order of Sangréal.'

The chief constable's face was impassive, but his eyes were watchful. 'Go on.'

'I ascertained that Bannock was in fact the Master of that organization; that on the night he died he had an appointment with a man called Sinclair; that he had a later appointment with his Deputy Master, one Burnley – but that he never turned up for that meeting.'

'And what about this Sinclair character?' the chief constable asked.

Culpeper, in full flight, hesitated, then glanced sideways. 'Farnsby?'

Vic Farnsby cleared his throat and leaned forward. 'I interviewed him, sir. He was rather difficult to contact: he'd been out and about quite a lot but we eventually caught him at home. Weird sort of person – ex-officer in the Scots Guards, but slightly eccentric. He told me he had received a phone call from Bannock and had agreed to meet him, but had not bothered to keep the appointment.'

'Why?'

'Bannock was unhappy with some kind of . . . investigation Sinclair was making into the Order of Sangréal. Like all of these orders, they're very touchy about outsiders probing into their activities. Sinclair says Bannock was abusive on the phone – but wanted to meet to discuss some kind of

. . . cooperation. Having thought it over, Sinclair decided not to keep the appointment.'

'Can we shake that?' the chief constable asked.

Farnsby shrugged. 'You mean the fact he says they never actually met that evening? We're checking. But Sinclair is a bachelor; lives alone so he's unable to prove to us what he was doing that night – he says he was at home, alone.'

'Right. Let's just hold on that one. Anything else?'

Farnsby hesitated, glanced uncertainly at Culpeper. 'I think perhaps –'

'Maybe I should go on,' Culpeper said firmly, taking over from Farnsby. 'I was still convinced – and remain convinced – that Frank Manley is at the centre of this killing in some way or another. When I got back to the office, however, I received a visit from Manley's girlfriend: a woman called Edda Anstey. She gave me an explanation for the entry of Manley's name in Bannock's address book.'

'Which was?'

'She had *asked* Bannock to help Manley –' conscious of the impassive figure of the deputy chief constable at the end of the conference table, Culpeper hesitated, then went on in a rush '– to stop police pressure being put on the man.'

The chief constable's eyes gleamed: Culpeper knew he was thinking it had been not so much police pressure as Culpeper pressure.

'And what reason did she give for suggesting Bannock would help her?'

Culpeper took a deep breath. 'She said that Bannock and she had been lovers. She had been in an accident – knocked down, a resulting miscarriage . . . and on Flint's behalf Bannock had paid her to keep quiet about the identity of the man who had knocked her down. At that stage, the inquiry was getting out of hand – the scope was widening; I thought it best to report –'

'To me,' the chief constable interrupted harshly. 'All right, Stainton, you'd better bring us up to date.'

Stainton sat a little more upright and consulted his notes. 'As a result of your discussion with me, sir, I accompanied

Culpeper to the office of Councillor Flint. We explained that we had certain inquiries to make, and Mr Flint seemed at ease to begin with, until we mentioned the statement made by Miss Anstey. Things got a little difficult at that stage, until we were able to persuade Mr Flint that straight answers might be best. He did make some admissions . . . but then decided he would say no more without a solicitor present.'

'What admissions?'

Stainton consulted his notes again. 'He admitted to knowing Bannock, to having dealings with him –'

'Who didn't, on the council?' the chief constable interrupted sarcastically.

'And that Bannock had acted for him from time to time in personal matters. He was certainly taken aback when Culpeper questioned him about the Ogle hearing and the placing of council contracts, and at that stage he decided to say no more. However, he denied knowing Miss Anstey; he denied paying sums of money to her after her accident; and he denied any knowledge of the accident itself.'

'So it would be her word against his, with Bannock dead?' the chief constable asked.

'We are getting access to Mr Flint's private accounts, that sort of thing, but the payments to Miss Anstey – though they certainly were made – appear to have been made under Bannock's name. So, we might have some difficulty proving that the payments were linked to the events Miss Anstey described.'

'So at this stage, we have little more than supposition.'

'Anstey's prepared to stand up in court,' Culpeper exclaimed.

'A reliable witness?' the chief constable snorted contemptuously. 'Especially when she's trying to protect her boyfriend? Whom you describe as a villain.' His eyes dwelled on Culpeper thoughtfully. 'But from that point on, you took it upon yourself to spread the inquiry more widely. You'd better explain, so we're all in the picture.'

'It was what had emerged about the Ancient Order of Sangréal,' Culpeper said stubbornly. 'The Deputy Master allowed me access to their list of members. I was immediately struck by something interesting. There were some very familiar names in that list.'

He glanced up, and caught the warning gleam in the chief constable's eyes. Culpeper was not to be held back now, however. Stubbornly, he went on, 'The list contained the names of prominent businessmen and men who were active both in the council and in departments of the local authority. Some of the names which particularly struck me – in view of the remarks made by Mel Coulter at the Ogle inquiry, and reported in the press, were people whom Coulter claimed were corrupt. They included executive directors of the Midnorth Consultancy Group, directors of the Quinton hypermarket chain, and Professor Santana, who submitted the proposal to the committee when Coulter spoke and hinted at corruption. The list also included Councillor Flint. All these people, moreover, were recent members, joining the organization in the last few years. And all were sponsored by the Master himself – Colin Bannock.'

'The list did not, of course, include the name of Frank Manley,' the chief constable said grimly.

'No, sir. But if I may revert to the statements made by Miss Anstey. Whether she'd make a credible witness in court or not is really beside the point. The fact is, her statement rang true for me – and it suggested that Flint was to some extent dependent upon Bannock. It began to make me think about the kind of man Bannock was – a wheeler-dealer, a power behind the throne. At that point I began to see a picture emerging.' He paused, holding the chief constable's gaze. 'These people were part of a close network; they had access to decision making on the one side, and were prominent business activists on the other. The Deputy Master of the Order hinted to me that Bannock's attitude towards what was acceptable behaviour in the Order was different from his; and if it is true, that Bannock used the Order – and his contacts with all these people he'd nominated – as a ring, to place council contracts to swing business –'

'We've no hard evidence of that so far,' the chief constable interrupted harshly.

'– But if we have such evidence, it means we'll have broken an important corruption activity here in the north-east – as well as solving a murder inquiry.'

'We haven't done either yet.'

'But people are running scared,' Culpeper said defiantly.

Stainton cleared his throat. 'There is a degree of nervousness around, sir,' he supported Culpeper. 'And though we've uncovered nothing specific yet, there is some evidence of special dealing in some of the contracts. The tendering procedures, for instance –'

'Spare me the details,' the chief constable growled. 'All I want is an assurance that you're going to find something that will prevent us ending up with egg on our faces. I have to carry the can, ultimately, on situations like this if we get it wrong. Culpeper, you've got us to stick our necks out, faster and further than I would have liked. But we've started down the track, and now we'll have to continue.' He paused, thinking. 'All right, so here we are. We have the list of members of this Sangréal Order. We don't have a *prima facie* case, but we do have suspicions now that there might have been some sort of collusion going on between members for the placing of lucrative contracts. Suspicion only . . . but I think I can justify continuing the investigation. As for the killing of Bannock . . .'

'In spite of what Edda Anstey said,' Culpeper intervened, 'I feel sure there's more to it all than her request for help. There must be a contact between Manley and Bannock. Frank Manley is central to it, sir, I'm sure.'

'But you have other people to look at carefully,' the chief constable grated.

Culpeper nodded. 'The man Sinclair is someone we have to look closely at.'

'There's the builder, too – Coulter,' Farnsby added. 'He's known to have uttered threats against Flint when he complained about corruption. But from all accounts, the man he was really after was whoever was behind the scenes.

Coulter's been convinced for some time that there was a corrupt activity in the building field, and that Flint was part of it. If he had discovered Bannock was involved . . .'

'And then there's Councillor Flint himself –'

'You'll go carefully there,' the chief constable warned Culpeper.

Stainton spoke up again. 'The man is running scared, sir. He's not a strong character – I've certainly been led to believe, after interviewing a number of people, that he was very much a puppet. Well liked on the council, but not decisive. Someone was pulling his strings. It could well have been Bannock. And if the corruption network involves him, and Bannock *did* cover up a drink-driving offence for him, it looks like we've maybe got a motive. If Bannock was pressing him too hard he could have snapped – killed Bannock, even if it was in a heated moment.' He paused, aware of the chief constable's cold disapproval. 'I'm not sure he's strong enough,' he added, mumbling, 'to plan such a killing in cold blood, but if Bannock was pushing him too hard . . .'

'Look at the possibility by all means,' the chief constable said. 'But go canny. And remember, if you see Flint as a suspect, partly because he's on a list of this damned Order, you'll have to look at the others . . . Santana, the Midnorth directors, the whole blasted shooting match.'

'And Coulter?' Culpeper reminded him with a touch of malice.

'And Coulter . . . who's *not* on the list. Well,' the chief constable added, looking around the conference table, 'I think you've all got more than enough to get on with. One last word. This is a damnably delicate operation we've got into now: keep your mouths shut, and your heads down. I want no screams from the press and I want no yells from suspects about the way they're being treated. Kid gloves, gentlemen, where the Councillor Flints of this world are concerned.'

He stood up abruptly, gathering up his papers. He fixed Culpeper with a gleaming eye. 'Culpeper, I'll see you in my room in five minutes.'

*

Hands locked behind his back, the chief constable stared out of the window, ignoring Culpeper who stood there to attention, waiting. The chief constable's broad back was rigid, unyielding, expressive of displeasure, and Culpeper steeled himself, knowing that he was to be carpeted, but resentful also. He had done his duty; it wasn't his problem if life wasn't as smooth as the chief constable might wish it to be.

Abruptly, the chief constable swung around and glared at Culpeper. 'I'm not pleased.'

'Sir?'

'There's been a lot of gossip around the office and it's come late to my ears. Some of it has emanated from you; some of it's about you. I gain the impression you're not happy these days, Culpeper.'

'I wouldn't say that, sir.'

'You've been saying other things,' snapped the chief constable. 'But we'll leave that for one moment. This Manley thing . . . what's it all about?'

'I think he's central to the whole investigation –'

'I didn't mean that,' the chief constable interrupted. 'It's common knowledge you've been trying to pin something on Manley for years. Villain he might be – reformed character he might be, if we listen to Miss Anstey – but why are you persisting in your chasing of him?'

'I know he's been mixed up in the car-nicking ring, sir, and –'

'I want to *know*, Culpeper,' the chief constable warned.

'I don't know what you mean, sir.'

'You know *exactly* what I mean. Forget the Bannock inquiry: I want to know why you've got your knife in Manley. It's important that I know – before I decide whether to suspend you or not.'

'Suspend me!'

The chief constable smiled wearily. 'Come on, Culpeper, why don't you take a look at yourself? You've become obsessed with this Manley character. You've let other work fall away; you harass him; you've been guilty of errors of judgement – all because of this obsession you have with him, the need you seem to feel to put him away. It's too *personal*, Culpeper – you know the moment we take things personally, objectivity flies out of the window and our vision gets clouded. Your judgement has gone: you're obsessed with putting Manley inside. Now I want to know why – or else I'll have no option but to remove you from these inquiries –'

'You can't do that, sir,' Culpeper interrupted desperately.

'I can – and I must, unless I get satisfactory answers. I want to *know*, damn you!'

Culpeper stood to attention, rigid, teeth gritted. He didn't want to talk about it; the years had gone by and it had festered in his mind, and talking about it could still hurt. She had been a lovely child, a beautiful young woman . . . Something slowly began to collapse inside him, resistance ebbing away, walls coming down at last. He was breathing with difficulty. 'I had a niece, sir.'

After a short silence, the chief constable nodded. 'So?'

'She was . . . very close. We were sort of brought up together; I was more like a big brother to her. Then I got married, and she used to come around regularly . . . Anyway, like lots of young kids, she got to go to parties, clubs, that sort of thing. That's where she met Frank Manley.'

'He started dating your niece?'

Culpeper nodded. His voice was thick. 'I warned her off him: he was older than her, more experienced, the wrong kind. I knew he wasn't suitable. He was smooth, but he was no good. She wouldn't listen though. I didn't see her after that, for six months. She took offence. And when we met again, she was different. I didn't know how different until I was a member of the squad that pulled her out of the Tyne one Christmas Eve.'

The chief constable's body was still. He stared at Culpeper fixedly. 'What had happened?'

'Drugs.'

'And this had something to do with Manley?'

'He killed her. He introduced her to drugs. He made her an addict. And he killed her.'

'You mean –'

'Oh, he didn't shove her into the water. It seems it was probably an accident. She was . . . high. Came out of the club. They said later she just jumped . . . thought she could fly. But it was days before they reported it. And Manley . . . he was responsible. It was as good as his pushing her in, wasn't it? I saw her face . . . bloated. He was responsible. But we couldn't pin anything on him directly. But I watched him. I've been watching him for years –'

'And now you stop watching him,' the chief constable said evenly. He hesitated, thinking for a while. 'It's a long time ago, Culpeper. You can't nurse a hate like that all these years –'

'Sir –'

'You can't nurse a hate like that – and keep this job. You understand?' There was a gleam of sympathy in the chief constable's eyes, but his voice was firm – his tone precise. 'This all ends here, now. In this office. You get off Frank Manley's back.'

Culpeper was silent; he could not bring himself to say the words. But his silence seemed to satisfy the chief constable, who nodded after a few moments and turned away. He sat down behind his desk and looked up at Culpeper, watching him carefully. 'And now we come to the other matter.'

Culpeper's mouth was dry with tension. 'Which matter, sir?'

'The instruction you had from DCC Baistow.' The chief constable shifted lightly in his chair, somewhat ill at ease suddenly. 'You . . . had a view about his ordering you to stop investigating Manley. The order has to come from me, does it, to meet with your approval?'

The sarcasm made Culpeper rise; it was a bait he could not resist. 'I knew there were other reasons for the order, sir.'

'Now what do you mean by that?'

'DCC Baistow didn't order me to stop checking on Manley because he thought I was being . . . obsessive. There were in my view other reasons.'

'Like lack of proof . . . the failure to build a case?' the chief constable sneered.

'No, sir! Like political pressure!'

The chief constable sat back and folded his arms. He lowered his head, like a bull about to charge. 'I see. So here's the nub of it; here's the reason for gossip in HQ. You think DCC Baistow's decision was based on political pressure. Would you care to expand on that?'

Culpeper's voice was shaky with suppressed anger. 'I guessed it at the time, and later events have confirmed it, surely! I was pressing Manley, so Edda Anstey contacted Bannock to do something about it, and Bannock – or his friend Flint – spoke to DCC Baistow. And that's when I was warned off! Then there was the Coulter thing.'

'What about it?'

'Coulter made allegations about Flint, and others. Next thing is, DCC Baistow asks O'Connor to investigate Coulter! *Why?* Because Flint asked him to dig some dirt on Coulter, to try to reduce his credibility in pointing the finger at Flint and his cronies who had their fingers in the till!'

'And why should DCC Baistow do such a thing?' the chief constable asked, almost gently.

'You know as well as I, sir.'

'Really?'

Culpeper stared straight ahead of him; his armpits were damp with nervous sweat. 'They were all in it together. Flint, Bannock, and Baistow. He's on the list. You've seen his name.'

'List?'

'He's a member of the Order of Sangréal. He was one of those nominated by Colin Bannock.'

The chief constable sighed. He was silent for a long time, staring at Culpeper. Then, slowly, he nodded. 'All right, now let me tell you a few things. First, you've been jumping to conclusions for years over Frank Manley: you've become obsessed with it. It's got to stop. Second, a similar obsession seems to be starting regarding DCC Baistow: you feel he's been persecuting you. That's got to stop, too. Then there's this Ancient Order of Sangréal . . . there's nothing in the rule book which stops a copper joining a masonic order or anything similar, and that applies to deputy chief constables as much as any copper on the beat. DCC Baistow has a private life: as long as it doesn't affect his work in the force, he's free to do as he pleases.'

'But the Order –'

'I've already spoken to him. I've told him –' the chief constable's voice dropped slightly. 'I've told him that he has been perhaps a little unwise . . . He gave me an assurance that he had not been approached by Bannock, and he took a decision on your file on the merits of the case. I'm inclined to believe him. As for the Coulter investigation . . . it was unconnected with the outburst at the Ogle inquiry. Various suspicions have been raised in recent months over Coulter's activities –' The chief constable appeared to be struggling somewhat now, seeking to persuade himself with doubtful reasons. 'Coulter's use of casual labour, some of the tendering procedures and site activities. It's this which DCC Baistow was following up on. He hadn't been asked to do so by Mr Flint. He's given me his word on that. And I'm inclined to believe him in this matter, as well.'

Culpeper was not. And he doubted whether the chief constable was telling the truth. There was something in the man's tone that suggested to Culpeper the deputy chief constable had been carpeted, warned, and was now perhaps under suspicion. But that was something the chief constable would never tell him.

'So there's an end to that also, isn't there?' the chief constable warned. 'I want no more open resentment; I want no more gossip. I've received an explanation from DCC Baistow, and for the time being I've accepted it.'

'And I stay on the Bannock inquiry?' Culpeper asked harshly.

The chief constable considered the matter for a while. Then he nodded. 'Yes, you stay. But only while you play it straight. You've plenty to get on with: I can't see a cast-iron case building against any of your suspects yet. You can have access to the file raised on Coulter – if Coulter *did* discover that Bannock was pulling Flint's strings, he'd be angry enough to kill. As for the others in the frame – build a case. But get rid of your obsessions first and tread warily. If I get a single suspicion that you're stepping out of line, I'll have your guts!'

3

The valley was quiet.

Arnold had driven across the fells with a tight feeling of excitement in his chest, barely aware of his surroundings, disregarding the sweeping shoulders of the Cheviots, careless of the vista into Scotland, his mind churning with the dark days of de Goncourt's mission, centuries ago. He could imagine the vicious triumph that must have surged into the inquisitor's chest when he believed he had at long last tracked down the fleeing heretics to their final lair. Arnold's thoughts swirled with the imagined sound of the hurrying soldier-monks themselves, forewarned of de Goncourt's descent, hastening to strip Kilclogan and flee south like the fox doubling back on its own tracks. And then there would have been the fury of de Goncourt, the railing against the clans, and the final, ignominious realization that the Templars had gone to earth, and de Goncourt's mission was a failure.

But the times, and the political situation had changed as the years passed. The power structures had shifted and James Sandilands had become the head of the Order, only to betray it for political and personal advantage. So a second flight had been necessary, and it had been the Seton family who had taken the responsibility – David Seton who had become the bearer of the Cross, and guardian of the new Templar Order.

But while Arnold's thoughts were in tumult with the noise of centuries, the valley was quiet, shaded, the pensive trees leaning in morose contemplation, nodding above the narrow track as it wound downwards from the hill, skirting the outcrops of limestone crags, past the carved pagan head, beyond the muted thunder of the waterfall and forward to the place where Sinclair had suggested they park, on the occasion of Arnold's first visit to the valley.

He parked there again now. He got out, picked up the rucksack from the passenger seat, locked the car and walked through the damp grass, brushing under the alder and birch, following the narrow track that Sinclair had pointed out to him and Jane. The old ruined buildings were silent witnesses to his passage, and the eroded cliff face towered above him as he pushed on through the deep undergrowth and along the half-obscured pathway.

Finally, he stepped out into the clearing at the foot of the cliff.

Arnold hesitated, a strange reluctance momentarily taking hold of him. It was as though he was suddenly unwilling to put his theory to the test; the need for some support touched him and he wished that Jane was here, so he could talk it through with her. There was a nagging realization in his mind that he needed her more than he had anticipated: for her sharpness, her wit, the way she could deflate him in a moment.

With a sense of unease, he moved away from the cliff face and on towards the chapel perched on the edge of the gorge, as though it could give him some kind of reasoned support for the theories that churned around in his mind. He did not enter it, for he remembered well the Gothic carvings, the Templar motifs, and the florid embellishments of the interior. He stood outside at some distance and stared at it, thinking back, trying to feel the presence of the long-dead soldier-monks; to consider the motivations behind the construction of this Gothic chapel; and to understand the passion and anger that must have grasped their hearts when they were forced to abandon the chapel, unfinished, in the valley.

They had gone to Deever, and in better times had built there, and incorporated their symbols, until the crisis of Sandilands arose. Then, when the Cross Bearer had made his decisions, they had left their signs, made the marks that would lead the cognoscenti to the important centre of their mystic world. But the external world had slowly changed, and memories had died and walls crumbled: now there was only the shell of Deever, the unexplained symbols in its sister church at Ditchford, and the long, ages-old silence of the valley.

Ex fenestra lux.

Arnold turned, and made his way back, away from the chapel, to return to the clearing below the cliff. *Out of the window shall come light . . .* Arnold stared up at the limestone cliff and fastened his gaze on the dressed stone window.

Behind that window, Sinclair had explained, lay a warren of tunnels carved out in antiquity, a legendary refuge for Robert Bruce at one stage. Or was that merely the excrescence of some other, half-forgotten legend? Perhaps the story of the fleeing Templars, determined to retain their Order against the depredations of James Sandilands.

There was a pile of broken rock in the long grass just below the carved window; Arnold looked up at it, and guessed he would easily be able to enter the gaping window by climbing on the rock fall. He swung the rucksack on to his back and climbed up; a quick heave and he was straddling the window itself, and a moment later he was dropping through the window, some four feet to the floor of the chamber beyond.

Dust rose around him in a cloud and he sneezed and coughed. He looked about him: he was in a chamber some eight feet high, carved from the living rock, but faced in parts with dressed stone, and the floor itself was paved with flagstones. The light that filtered through the window showed a fireplace built in one corner and a chimney that presumably ran up through the rock to some exit far above, blocked now, probably, by the debris of time. The chamber was bare and the flagstones thick with the accumulated dust of centuries, but nothing seemed to have grown there in the faint light, though lichen was thick on the damp walls.

Arnold unslung his rucksack and laid it down. He'd brought a flask of coffee with him and he poured himself a cup now, sipping it reflectively as he stared about him; leaning with his back against the lintel of the window. After a while, in the filtered light he thought he could make out incisions in the roof and he rummaged in the rucksack for the powerful torch he had brought. He flashed the beam around the chamber: there were some carvings high in the roof. He trained the beam on them and for a few seconds could not make them out. Finally, he traced the contours: tendrils again, a badly-worn head peering from among the vine leaves. So the Templars had used this chamber, at least. The tightness in Arnold's chest increased but he forced himself to stand there, calming his excitement, sipping the coffee, unwilling to move too quickly.

Haste could mean folly.

He finished the coffee and fumbled in the rucksack for the small compass; he took a reading, and then cast the torch beam around the chamber. There were two exits: dark arches that seemed to lead into the heart of the hill, framed in dressed stone, and carved at the apex with what seemed to be shields. Arnold inspected them closely: he could not make out the coat of arms, but they bore a resemblance to those he had seen at Ditchford church, at the tomb of David Seton, the Man of March. Arnold hesitated, then stepped forward into the left-hand passage, fumbling in his pocket for the piece of chalk he had there. If Sinclair was right, the warren of tunnels could be confusing, and Arnold had no intention of getting lost.

The roof of the tunnel was about a foot above his head and the tunnel itself was some five feet wide. He was able to move quite freely, and he wondered how they had first been constructed. The purpose might have been mining, and if so they would be centuries older than the time of the Templars. On the other hand, the purpose might have been troglodytic – the carving of homes in the hill, away from the danger of the predators that would have lurked in the primitive forests of the valley. He flashed the beam ahead of him: the tunnel was broadening.

Twenty feet further on, Arnold stopped: the tunnel was swinging left, and then it divided. Another entrance opened up on the right, with its tunnel lunging darkly northward, according to Arnold's compass; the main road continued forwards and after a moment's hesitation Arnold decided to follow it. He chalked his mark on the wall as a precaution and moved on in the silent solid darkness of the tunnel.

Two minutes later, he found himself up against a solid wall. Puzzled, he flashed his light around him. The stone was pitted and gouged but there were no distinctive marks and he was in a small chamber, bare and damp. Water trickled down the walls, glistening in the torchlight, and Arnold turned, frowning, and retraced his steps until he came to the chalkmark.

When he reached the northward tunnel he turned into it, but within fifty feet it too divided, offering him the option of an east-running tunnel or a northward continuation. He flickered the beam about him: the walls were crudely cut, burrowing deep into the hill, and Arnold paused, thinking.

Sinclair had talked of a warren; he had talked of Robert Bruce hiding here, and Arnold could guess how men might fear to enter these tunnels in search of a desperate man in flight. He shivered slightly, perspiration cold on his back in the fetid atmosphere: the claustrophobic pressures deep under the hill could prey on the mind, and he himself was beginning to suffer. The small, perhaps imagined sounds of darkness were around him and he had the skin-crawling feeling he was not alone – that he was surrounded by people of another era – and it was an uncomfortable feeling. Men had cut their ways in here, and left part of themselves in the cutting. And he guessed that there would be further divisions up ahead; further options to run into dead and dying ends . . . and somehow, the tunnels didn't feel right to Arnold.

He needed Jane with him; she would have told him he was being fanciful. Nevertheless, the feeling grew in him: he was on the wrong track. The Templars had *not* come this way: the bearer of the Cross had not entered these passageways. Arnold turned, played the torchlight on the roof and sides of the tunnel for a moment, then began to make his way back.

The light pierced the blackness and it was easy enough to pick out the broad chalkmarks at the convergences, and though the atmosphere was thick, the air was breathable; provided he did not stride out too carelessly, the dust was not affecting him now that he had wound a handkerchief around his mouth and nose. The tunnels were silent for the most part, a thick, heavy deadening silence, although as he drew closer to the chamber where he had started his search, he seemed to detect small, shuffling sounds – traces perhaps of disturbed rodents, denizens of the dark tunnels. Yet when he stopped, the sounds faded too, so they might have been the echoes of his own footsteps. Even so, his skin prickled occasionally when he picked up the sounds: they seemed to tell him he was not alone. It was not a comforting thought.

When he finally saw the faint light around the bend of the tunnel, relief flooded into his chest and he moved forwards more confidently, his spirits picking up, until he stepped back into the large chamber, lit by the carved window. He checked his watch. He had been walking for almost forty minutes.

Arnold leaned against the wall, calming his troubled nerves, unwinding the handkerchief from his mouth and taking in fresh air. Through the carved window he could see the trees swaying as a breeze rustled through the valley and somewhere in the undergrowth near the stream, a dog fox barked.

Arnold grimaced, then wound the handkerchief around his mouth again and directed the torch beam towards the second exit. He set off with chalk and torch to follow the same procedure, and within twenty yards reached the same situation as previously: a branching of the tunnel. Again Arnold hesitated, then plunged down the right-hand tunnel, marking his route with chalked arrows; but this was a lower roof, dropping rapidly, until he was crouching as he moved. He slowed, feeling his way with one hand on the roof: it was still getting lower so reluctantly he stopped, turned, and made his way back. Frustrated, he paused at the branching, and flashed his light forwards, across the roof and down the sides of the walls.

Then he stopped. The beam flickered as his hand trembled.

He steadied himself and the light was still as he raised it to fix on the incisions that had caught his attention. The beam concentrated on the marks cut in the stone: a tendril – it wound its way forwards for perhaps two feet and then he made out the carving at its end. A *fenestra*: deep cut, unmistakable, a depiction of the window through which he had entered the tunnels.

He chalked an arrow mark on the tunnel wall, his heart beating fast as he stepped forward into the branching, sloping entrance. He kept the beam trained on the wall but there were no further carvings until some forty feet on where there was a further branching: Arnold stopped and carefully inspected the walls, checking every inch. Finally, with a quick intake of breath he caught sight of the carving, high on the right-hand wall of the tunnel to the left.

The window – the mark of the Man of March.

David Seton had been this way; he had left the clues at Deevers, which his followers after his death had transposed to Ditchford, and deep here under the hill had lain the secret that the Templars had hidden from their enemies.

Carefully, Arnold made his way deeper into the tunnel. Twenty feet further on and there was another branching: once again, carved high against the roof, was the telltale signal: the window and the tendril, drawing Arnold forwards, into the left-hand swing of the passageway. He flashed the light about him: the tunnel was getting wider suddenly; the roof climbing as though he were entering a more natural area, a cave carved out of the rock by natural forces aeons earlier.

The structure of the walls was different, too: on the right, water glistened as limestone stalactites and stalagmites gleamed in deep greens and blues, but to the left the rock seemed pitted, crumbling. Arnold stood, flashing the torch beam about him, picking up the colours of the stone but not finding what he sought. The roof soared above him now like a silent cathedral and he almost fancied he could see religious figures carved in bas-relief in the stone. Closer inspection revealed it was his fancy – they were the structures of the rock face itself, and the seepage of lime through the stone, hardening into fantastic figures. But it was an awesome, mystical place, and Arnold knew he was on the right track: this was a place where the Templars would have felt as he did now; it was a route they would have taken.

At the far end of the cave he found what he was looking for. A further tunnel, carved by man and not by the elements. He stepped to the entrance: the sign was there, carved above the lintel, and the passageway was broad, perhaps ten feet wide. His footsteps echoed in the cavern at his back as he entered the passageway, an eerie sound that fluttered up like a dying sigh to the high roof of the cave. The passageway had been cut by man, but the stone here was softer, more friable, and pillars had been left to support the roof: thin, attenuated, roughly carved. He touched the friable, brittle stone: it crumbled under his hand and he guessed it would not take much to bring down the pillars – and perhaps the roof with them.

The tunnel stretched blackly ahead of him and there was a pounding in Arnold's skull: he had the feeling he was getting close, that somewhere ahead lay the conclusion of his theory and the solution to Sinclair's own searches.

The Man of March; the treasure of the Temple, here in a Templar tomb.

He moved carefully between the maze of supporting pillars, picking his way, shining the torch on every excrescence, every possible carving, but finding only the erosion of time, and the rough hacking of stone on stone. When he was forty feet into the tunnel it began to narrow again, swing left and the roof began to drop. He put his hand up, touching cold, dry stone that had been chilled by millennia of darkness and then he felt rather than saw the chamber open up in front of him, was aware of a lightening of the darkness. Almost instinctively, he switched off his torch and with one hand extended, groped forwards to turn the corner.

As he did so, he saw it.

It was a freak of nature. A narrow fissure in the rock that extended up to the surface, it permitted only a faint gleam of light to penetrate the utter darkness of the chamber. But it was enough to give the narrow chamber a glow in which dust drifted slowly – a bluish, ethereal light, insufficient to see by to any extent, but enough to give the chamber an atmosphere of wonder and mysticism. With his torch switched off, Arnold stood shaken; he caught his breath. As his eyes grew accustomed to the faint light he received an impression of openness and depth, of height and softness, of time and history. It was here; he knew it would be here. Everything he had ever known about the Templars convinced him that this would have been their tomb, their refuge and hiding place.

It was here that they would have placed what they valued. It was here the Cross Bearer would have come.

He stood there with the blackness of the tunnel behind him and felt the thoughts of long-dead men wash over him. The faint light in the chamber was almost hypnotic: it drew him into a past that was gone and dissipated the present. He could hear the voices of the soldier-monks and the chant of their tongues in prayer. He could pick up the faint whisper of their secrets, and the dry-leaved rustle of their minds as they plotted to confuse and defeat their enemies. He felt a lightness in his skull, a dizziness that affected his senses and he leaned against the wall, touching the cold stone, feeling its smoothness, dressed and trimmed by long-ago craftsmen. He let the faint blue light touch his mind, seep into his brain, take him back six hundred years to the relief they had felt when they finally entered this place.

And something told him they were still there.

His dizziness faded quickly, his senses suddenly sharpened, his nerve-ends alive. Deep in the tunnels, he had heard the soft shuffling of rats, the faint echoes of his own footsteps, the scratching of life in the darkness. It had tingled his veins then, prickled the hairs on the back of his neck, but suddenly it was different, sharper, swifter. He felt they were here, angry at his presence, determined to punish his temerity in entering their stronghold. But that could only be imagination – he began to turn, feeling for the switch of his torch, but he heard a wild swishing sound and it came out of the darkness at him, clumsily, blindly, like an owl flying sightlessly after its prey.

The blow took him on the shoulder and he staggered, falling sideways and rolling. The torch clattered to the ground as he lost his grip on it and there was a long moment of silence. Shaken, confused, Arnold lay there with his senses swirling and then he picked up the ragged, urgent sound of someone breathing above him. He scrabbled for the torch, while the faint blue light the Templars had known played about him, and wildly he thought of their vengeance, deep in the sepulchral chamber. But reason bit hard and he snapped on the torch. The beam wavered and then fixed on the pillared entrance to the chamber.

The man who stood there seemed to be tall and lean, his figure throwing a wavering shadow against the pillar to his right. He was temporarily blinded, raising his left hand to his eyes, but a moment later he was stepping back, withdrawing his face from the light. Then both hands were down, gripping the pickaxe handle, and it came swinging down again in a wild, vicious arc.

Arnold rolled frantically sideways, snapping off the torch as he did so. The pickaxe handle smashed against the ground where he had been a moment before and Arnold heard a moaning sound: part hurt as the shock of the blow was transmitted to his assailant's shoulders, part frustration as the man swung again, striking out almost blindly, still unaccustomed to the faint light after the flash of the torch. Arnold was equally blind, but panicked, scrabbling sideways to the wall of the chamber tomb. He and his assailant were in like state as far as vision was concerned, but Arnold had one advantage: he had seen the chamber, was aware of its dimensions. He found refuge against the far wall and crouched there, clutching his injured shoulder.

He could hear the frustrated breathing of the man at the entrance, waiting for his eyes to focus properly again. Arnold knew there was no time to be lost. He raised the torch with a shaking hand. Pointing it in the general direction of the entrance, he closed his own eyes, flashed the torch on for a few seconds and heard the snarl of the man with the weapon. He heard the scramble of footsteps and the swish of the axe handle again; once more he switched off the torch, rolled wildly away and then came up to his knees. He was aware of the vague, black figure of the man in the chamber, etched against the faint, smoky-blue glow from the fissure and he came up to his feet, charging unreasoningly forwards, thundering with his whole body into his assailant, and throwing him backwards against the wall.

Arnold broke away immediately, drawing back, groping for the entrance to the chamber, and was through it before his opponent could recover. Then he was into the passageway, scrambling along, one hand against the wall, not daring to use the torch because he knew it would light the way for the man behind him, as it had undoubtedly lighted his way earlier when he had followed Arnold into the tunnels.

The sounds he had heard before had not been rats, or echoes of the past: this man had seen him enter and had followed, with malice on his mind.

'Landon!'

The cry behind him was a mingling of rage and frustration, but Arnold paid no attention. He stumbled on, gasping, eager to place a distance between himself and the enraged man behind him but a moment later realized he had miscalculated, when light stabbed at the walls through the solid darkness. His assailant had his own torch, and was coming out of the chamber.

The light swung wildly along the roof, and Arnold tried to switch on his own torch but nothing happened. He lurched on, panicked, feeling his way with outstretched hands and in the darkness he struck one of the stalactitic roof pillars and almost fell, winded. He looked back and saw the bright beam flickering behind him, locating him, pinning him against the pillar. He froze for several seconds and the torch came nearer, until out of the darkness behind the torchlight he caught the flash of movement again, and the axe handle came swinging down.

It caught him a glancing blow on the ribcage and he felt a sharp pain as the bone splintered. He staggered and fell again, and he knew that he was helpless, unable to move as the harsh breathing above him tightened. He tried to roll away again and he struck the man's foot. He grabbed at the leg, and the axe handle crashed down inches from his face. He pulled himself upwards, grappling at the lean body of his assailant as the man's torch went out and they were fighting each other for a grip; Arnold's hands scrabbling for a face, fingers reaching for eyes, until he was thrown back violently against the wall again, cannoning sideways off another narrow pillar. There was a second's pause, the heavy grunting sound of the man's laboured breathing, and then Arnold heard the whistling of the axe handle again, swinging at him in a wide arc.

It never reached him.

There was a sharp crack, a solid thudding sound and a cry of agony from his assailant. There was a clattering noise as the pickaxe handle fell to the ground from nerveless fingers, but there were other sounds about them now. There was a long, low groaning – the creak of shifting stone; a rattling came out of the darkness and a growing distant rumble far above their heads. Arnold dragged himself along the wall, the useless torch still in his hands. He heard a cry from behind him, but it was overtaken by the moaning stresses in the roof as the stone began to collapse, first in a shower of small stones and then in a longer, thundering avalanche. As he ran blindly, Arnold realized what had happened. The pickaxe handle had swung out at him but it had struck one of the thin, attenuated pillars that had been left to support the roof. It had shattered the crumbling pillar, and the stresses of centuries had finally taken their toll: the massive weight of stone above them, fissured and faulted, had begun to settle, crumbling and crashing down into the narrow tunnel.

And if Arnold was unable to get back into the main cathedral chamber he would quickly find himself under the fall. He ran, slamming into walls and pillars, bouncing painfully off one and the other. The thunder behind him reached out with choking fingers, and he felt the roof moving above him, slivers of stone slicing past him, a thick, covering cloud of dust at his heels, rising, choking, threatening him as the collapsing roof rolled forwards, enveloping him dustily with violent intent.

A piece of rock struck him on the temple, and there was a sudden thump in his back as the roof finally came down. He was sent hurtling forwards on his knees, choking in the dust, unable to move his legs. His senses swam, and there was only the darkness and the suffocating dust and the thought of death. It was reaching out for him, touching his cheek, as behind him the thunder rolled, and slowed, and became more distant, to be succeeded by a soft, uneasy groaning and cracking as the ancient rock settled, and moved, and found its new location.

After that, there was only the silence.

4

'So what do you remember?'

Sunlight streamed in from the window of the narrow room. He was in a hospital bed and Jane was sitting there beside him. There were anxious lines around her mouth as she leaned forwards, inspecting him lying there. He grimaced and pain stabbed at his chest. The man standing beside him grunted.

'You got off surprisingly lightly. Concussion, and broken ribs.'

Shaken, Arnold looked at him. It was Detective Chief Inspector Culpeper, frowning as he looked down at Arnold.

'I don't remember very much. I seemed to be there a long time, in the darkness. But then there were voices, lights . . . pain. I must have been only half-conscious.'

'You were lucky,' Jane announced severely, but with a trace of relief in her voice as she contemplated him.

'When we entered the tunnels we found the chalked arrow

marks you'd left,' Culpeper said. 'And then there was all the dust and the fall. Once we'd located the fall, we were able to get to you, radio back for assistance. The ambulance crew dragged you out.'

'But how did anyone know I was there in the first place?' Arnold asked in a weak voice.

Culpeper shuffled and glanced sideways to the tall figure standing with his back to the window. 'That was due to Mr Sinclair,' he said.

The tall ex-Scots Guardsman came forward then, almost reluctantly, cadaverous in features, hands locked uneasily behind his back.

'*Sinclair?*' Arnold murmured, not understanding. 'How did you – ?'

'I'd been following you.'

'Following me? What on earth for? I'd invited you to join me –'

'And I told you I had other things to do. But in the end, they involved following you.'

'This doesn't make sense!'

'Sinclair wasn't really following *you* at first,' Culpeper intervened. 'He was keeping someone else under surveillance. The man who attacked you. Until he realized that the man he was keeping an eye on was actually tracking *you*.'

'I was being tracked? But who – ?'

'Con Burnley,' Sinclair said in a flat voice. 'The librarian at the university; the Deputy Master of the Order of Sangréal.'

Arnold's head was aching. He shifted uncomfortably in the bed. 'None of this is making sense to me.'

Sinclair came closer. 'When you insisted on having access to the *Terrae Templariae*, Burnley's interest – and anxieties – were aroused. He resisted you, didn't want to help you any more than he had helped me earlier, but was overruled by . . . I gather . . . professorial contacts you had. It must have been then he decided to follow you. He watched you at Deevers, and at Ditchford; he inspected the clues you yourself had found. And he followed you back to the valley, and the tunnels. To kill you.'

'But why on earth –?'

'You were getting close to Templar secrets,' Jane interposed.

'It was his obsession,' Sinclair explained. 'And you were interfering in it. His whole life outside the library was spent in following his obsession; he only existed for the twilight esotericism of the Order of Sangréal. He was fascinated, obsessed by it and he could not bear the thought of your digging out its secrets. He was jealous of its existence and of its membership. Don't you remember how you were warned away by Bannock? Burnley had got Bannock to warn *me* away, but you were dangerous – you were proving more effective in your search.'

'But we were researching the Templars, not Sangréal!'

'In Burnley's mind, one and the same. The Order of Sangréal was, for him, the natural survival of the ancient Templars; he had been frustrated in his own researches, and he felt you were getting close to the heart of it all – perhaps the Templar treasure. When you entered the tunnels he followed you. And down there, in the depths, he attacked you.'

'But why?'

'To stop you unearthing secrets that he wanted, alone, for his Order. He believed they were rightly in the ownership of the Order and he was obsessed by the idea of retaining the secrecy . . .'

Arnold stared at Sinclair, puzzled. He tried to sit up and pain stabbed at him again. 'But how do you know this?'

Sinclair's features were lugubrious. He shrugged. 'I guessed most of it, but we pieced it together, the chief inspector and I.' He glanced warily at Culpeper. 'Burnley made a mistake, you see. He tried to push police suspicions away from himself, and at the same time implicate me.'

'Suspicions? Implicate you in *what*?'

'The murder of Colin Bannock,' Sinclair replied tightly. 'He set the police on to me: told them I was probably the last person to see Colin Bannock alive. But I explained to them: I never went to my meeting with Bannock. I was annoyed, nevertheless – I couldn't understand why Burnley had acted like that. And also . . . I had the other feeling, that Burnley himself . . .'

Culpeper shuffled uneasily, as though there was an implied criticism in Sinclair's words. 'We interviewed Mr Sinclair. His . . . alibi was a bit thin. But, well, we didn't really have a go at Burnley.' He hesitated. 'We concentrated on . . . other leads. That was our . . . error.'

'Meanwhile, I was angered,' Sinclair went on. 'Burnley had set the police on to me, but I knew that his own relationship with Bannock had not been good. I knew he disliked the way Bannock used the Order – I'd detected hints of tension when I met them. Anyway, I decided to keep an eye on the man. That was why, when you rang me, I wasn't available to go with you on your hunting expeditions. Ironically enough, as it turned out I *did* go with you, after all.'

'I don't understand.'

Jane leaned forward. 'Do you remember when we were on the fells? We saw a walker up on the crags.'

'That was me,' Sinclair agreed. 'That first evening, I watched Burnley leave the library and then I discovered he was following you. I was shaken when I realized it: he was driving north, towards Warkworth, and I followed him. Next day, there you were, driving around, climbing the fells, and he was watching you, keeping his distance, but tracking your steps.'

Arnold remembered something else . . . a car, following him as far as Warkworth that evening.

'And as he followed *you*,' Sinclair went on, 'so I followed *him*. It was almost farcical. You were the only person who seemed to know where you were going, and *you* were searching blindly. But then . . .' He paused. 'I went to Ditchford after you. He had gone, back to Newcastle. I spent a long time there in the church. And I finally came to the conclusion you must have done. The end of it all lay in the tunnels behind the window. It was then that I went to the police.'

Arnold shook his head. 'But what on earth did all that have to do with the police?'

'The Templar treasure – nothing. But Burnley's behaviour

. . . It convinced me he might have something else to answer for. I went to the police. I spoke to Mr Culpeper.'

The policeman shifted uneasily.

'I had already been interviewed by them, as I told you, in connection with the murder of Colin Bannock. On that occasion they seemed to have no interest in what I had to say.'

Culpeper cleared his throat. 'It was early in the investigation,' he said defensively. 'And I . . . I had reasons to believe that someone else had been behind the killing. It sort of . . . clouded things for me.'

Sinclair observed him owlishly. 'You hardly seemed to hear me.'

'I didn't want to hear about Knights Templar in the middle of a murder investigation,' Culpeper snapped.

'Or murderous obsessionals?'

The words seemed to touch Culpeper on the raw. 'It wasn't exactly a clear accusation you were making, Sinclair! Wild talk about tramps over the fells, mystic carvings, a treasure hunt, for God's sake!'

'But I finally made out a case to you.'

'Case?' Culpeper snorted, then eyed Arnold a little sheepishly. 'When you mentioned Landon's name I was even less inclined to believe you at first, but then I thought back to the conversation I had with Landon myself – it was he put me on to Burnley – and then, well . . .'

'I told Mr Culpeper I never saw Bannock the night he died,' Sinclair explained. 'But Burnley told them Bannock had a meeting with me. How would he have known that? And why should the police believe him, and yet disbelieve me – simply because he had told them about my projected meeting? I pointed out to Mr Culpeper that there was no love lost between Burnley and Bannock. They might have been Master and Deputy Master in the Order of Sangréal, but that was a source of friction rather than friendship. For Burnley didn't like the way Bannock used the Order. He wasn't committed to the old faiths as Burnley was.'

'In fact,' Culpeper added heavily, 'it had come to my

attention – from other sources – that Bannock had been using the Order for his own political ends – building up a power base, establishing a network of close business acquaintances –'

'Corrupting the Order,' Sinclair supplied. 'That would have been anathema to Burnley.'

'We've discovered that there's a web of corrupt practices connected with Bannock's use of the Order,' Culpeper agreed. 'Mel Coulter wasn't far wrong: the Midnorth Consultancy Group, Santana, Councillor Flint and a bunch of others on the make –'

'It was when we talked about Burnley and the Order that I finally felt I got through to Mr Culpeper,' Sinclair added mischievously.

'I was reaching my conclusions before then!' Culpeper muttered, rising to the bait. 'I knew about the network and when I heard that Bannock and Burnley had been on edge with each other –'

'I told Mr Culpeper I was worried about the way Burnley had been stalking you, and it seemed to make his mind up.'

Irritated, Culpeper grunted. 'Not so. I had *already* decided it best to have another word with Burnley. But first, I wanted to get corroboration from you, Landon. But you didn't answer the phone. And Miss Wilson –'

'I didn't know where you'd gone,' Jane said helplessly.

'So Mr Culpeper questioned me about your search,' Sinclair added, 'the one I'd started you on, and I told him my guess was you'd gone to the tunnels in the valley.'

'We found Burnley's car parked near yours,' Culpeper intervened. 'And –'

'And when we came down to the foot of the cliff we heard the roaring sound from the tunnels. That was when Mr Culpeper called for back-up, and the ambulances . . .' Sinclair paused, wrinkling his nose and eyeing Culpeper with a wicked gleam. 'It was all very efficient. *Eventually.*'

'They dug me out?'

'With a great deal of difficulty, I understand. You remained semi-conscious.'

'And Burnley?' Arnold asked, looking at Culpeper.

The policeman shrugged. 'He was dead when they finally pulled him out.' He paused for a moment. 'We're pretty clear now about the killing of Bannock. Burnley had seen a report of Mel Coulter's outburst in that inquiry you attended, and he knew what Bannock had been doing, introducing his network into the Order of Sangréal. He knew the scandal could damage the Order; we think he met Bannock, they quarrelled over it, and Burnley struck him from behind, down at the Quayside. The scandal would still come out, but Burnley felt at least he would manage it, control the damage that might be done to the Order.'

'And even get me out of action by shifting the suspicions of the police in my direction,' Sinclair murmured.

Culpeper eyed him sourly: he resented being upstaged by Sinclair. He turned back to Arnold. 'Anyway, I only came around to see if you were OK. I'll need a statement from you in due course, but it can wait. I'll leave you with your . . . friends.' He glared at Sinclair for a long moment, as though there was something else he wanted to say, then he humphed and made his way out of the room.

Arnold was silent for a little while. He thought about the obsessive hate that had driven Burnley; the hate and the desire to keep the secrets of the Order. He had killed for them, and he had died for them.

'What about the tunnels?' Arnold asked, shifting his position in the bed as the sharp pain stabbed at his chest.

Sinclair lifted a shoulder dismissively. He seemed sorry that Culpeper had gone: there was no one else he could bait. 'When the roof collapsed it closed off a large section of the tunnel you had gone down. It would be a mammoth – if not impossible – task to dig down through that rock. Even assuming we could persuade some research foundation there was anything worthwhile to be found.'

'What *did* you find in there, Arnold?' Jane asked inquisitively.

Arnold closed his eyes. What had he found? Nothing physical, for certain. A flooding of folk memory perhaps, a feeling that he was close to the heart of a Templar tomb, a sense of the long-dead past . . .

'The Cross Bearer,' he said quietly. 'I think David Seton went that way six hundred years ago. I think . . . I felt he had been there, in that faint twilight. But I found . . . nothing. And perhaps there was nothing to be found.'

Yet he had the feeling that neither Jane nor Sinclair believed that. Or perhaps were reluctant to do so.

Jane sighed. She leaned forwards, adjusting Arnold's pillow slightly. 'Well, all I can say is, I'm getting more and more to the conclusion that you need someone to look after you.'

And to his surprise she kissed him lightly on the lips.

5

The mouse twitched its white whiskers in the darkness. She was albino: with her thick white coat she had spent her life in the cold blackness of the tunnels and had never seen the light of day. There was food and water down here in the darkness – and safety from predators, but her environment had changed recently with thunderous noises that had sent her trembling to her nest. Now, she was busy searching out new runs, fresh trackways, finding her bearings anew after the rock fall which had closed off the chamber where she had built her nest.

The rock fall itself was no problem: the mouse simply flattened her skull and slipped between the interstices of the crumbled stone, nosing her way through the settling dust, relieved that the thunder was over, and the violence had ended, but excited too at the new odours in the tunnel.

The voices, at least, had gone, but now there was something new under her nose: blood, and skin, and small pieces of flesh, all that was left of the dead thing they had dragged from this place. She skittered over the stone, searching out the remains of the violence that had occurred, hours after the lights and the voices of the men had disturbed her in the darkness.

Curiosity satisfied at last, the mouse turned back, slithering between the fallen rubble, seeking out again the faint blue light of the chamber behind whose walls she had her nest. The smooth stone of those walls had been carved ages before, but the tiny cracks at floor level allowed ingress to the mouse. She entered her home again, whiskers twitching, the nest lying in the echoing narrow chamber behind the wall. It was warm here, and comfortable, a good place to raise the white-furred, scrambling litter.

The nest was made of rotting cloth and decaying fibres, which had been strewn about the little chamber in profusion, torn and used and re-used over the centuries. The flesh had long since gone and the bones too had been scattered, clean picked in the darkness by worms and rodents, and spiders could sometimes be caught in the eye sockets.

She paid no attention to the hard bright stones that had been strewn about the tomb by her own ancestors, nor the wooden box which had rotted and collapsed, to expose the bones and jewels that had been secreted there six hundred years before.

The long, curiously-hafted sword buried with the Templar meant nothing to her, and the marrow had long since been drawn from the ancient bones of the Cross Bearer.